WARCHILD

RICHARD BOWES

D0003793

POPULAR LIBRARY

An Imprint of Warner Books, Inc.

A Warner Communications Company

POPULAR LIBRARY EDITION

Copyright © 1986 by Richard Bowes
All rights reserved

Popular Library® and Questar® are registered trademarks of
Warner Books, Inc.

Cover art by Richard Corben
Cover design by Don Puckey

Popular Library books are published by
Warner Books, Inc.
666 Fifth Avenue
New York, N.Y. 10103

 A Warner Communications Company

Printed in the United States of America

First Printing: April, 1986

10 9 8 7 6 5 4 3 2 1

THE RIDER—parasitic intellect, it held onto the base of Garvin's brain, forcing the Warchild to wage a mental battle that no man had ever won...

SCARECROW—benevolent guardian of Border District Four, he too was a telepath, a guardian of the Republic, and Garvin's closest ally in the vast expanse of Time...

RUMACK—bloodthirsty commander of the Hotlanders, he led his troops from the darkest worlds of the Time Lanes into the very center of the Republic's vulnerable heartland...

GARVIN—A teenage outcast from his own world, his telepathic talents were unlimited—and untrained. Abducted by Goblins, sold to a being who would inhabit his body, pushed from world to world, he is the last hope of the universe.

WARCHILD

FOR KAE & JOHN

CHAPTER ONE

IT BEGAN in a New York, a twentieth-century one. Buildings were tall, but there have been New Yorks where they were a lot taller. The Empire State Building stood but not the World Trade Center. Cars were makes like Buick, Ford, and DeSoto. Their design might have looked old-fashioned and square cut to some. A Coca-Cola sign hung over a deli. Right down the street on a billboard, something that looked like a coyote howled at the moon under the words "Lone Wolf Cigarettes."

There are ones who can step into a world and know its history after a quick glance around and a scan of people's minds. Those ones are explorers, or hardened exploiters, or fugitives from the Goblins, or the favored of the Gods. A man who qualified on all of those counts shuffled through the consciousness of those buying papers at a corner kiosk. REICH SUBS IN ARGENTINE WATERS, CABINET CRISIS TOPS OUT TONIGHT. Headlines told of trouble at home and abroad. The date was October 17, 1984. The year rang no bell in these minds. The book was never written. Research would show that Orwell had died in 1947 of cancer caused by radiation.

The number of military uniforms on the street was another clue as to the course this world had taken. An army major in dress gray overcoat hurried along with an attaché case, returned the salutes of three women in air force blue. A marine private in full dress chauffeured a Cadillac.

Some wore paramilitary outfits. A group of boys and girls in high school cadet khaki carried their books at their hips. A dozen others in leather jackets and boots watched them from across the street. Their minds could be entered without their being aware of it. They were telepathically naive, playing the teenage game of cadets and commies.

Then, out of nowhere, came a powerful series of images of classrooms and corridors. The scanner caught echoes in someone's mind of voices in an emptying school, smells of chalk and institutional cleaner. The mind was worrying about tests, excited about a girl. All that was thrown out carelessly, the sender unaware of what he was doing.

The one who scanned homed in on a high school building at First Avenue and Fifteenth Street. It was well after school had let out. Crowds of people were hurrying home to watch the television news. The last kids were dribbling away from the building as a side door opened and a nondescript kid stood in the doorway. From across the street, he was watched and scanned.

A clutch of girls walked down Fifteenth toward Second Avenue, their short skirts and bright panty hose a flash of color outside the brick walls and iron gates. The one on the end, Marie Tedechi, filled the boy's mind; the sight of her concentrated all his awareness. He saw her legs, her breasts, her long hair, her eyes. She was caught in midlaugh as she became aware of him. And then he was in her mind. He saw himself through her eyes, a goofy-looking kid with yellow hair sticking out over his ears, two big front teeth. The idea was formed in his mind, but Marie wasn't aware of that. She only knew the image had suddenly appeared. AN UNKEMPT LITTLE RABBIT INSIDE A REFRIGERATOR.

"The Westinghouse Wabbit! Garvin looks like the Westinghouse Wabbit," she said. Someone else automatically gave the tag line out of their childhoods: "I'm just taking a west in this Westinghouse." They couldn't help it; there was an explosion of giggles. The boy, Garvin, almost lost his balance on the stairs. There was more laughter. A couple of boys, brightly dressed, joined the girls. Garvin turned and walked quickly toward First Avenue. He felt pain. If there was any group he thought he might belong to, it would have been the Schizis. But there was something else. His mind had been inside Marie's. He was afraid that this meant he was insane.

He walked up First. The apartment buildings you may know as Stuyvesant Town and Peter Cooper Village were there. But the buildings were outfitted with ramps and emergency medical stations. Garvin passed without noticing them. He had lived in this neighborhood for most of his nearly fifteen years and knew the buildings as Ike Town. The Eisenhower Houses had been taken over and refinished by a horrified nation for the broken, seared survivors of the Battle of France. The kids said the place glowed at night.

This New York was still mainly a city of five-story walkups. Garvin, head down, hands thrust into the pockets of his jacket, was suddenly bumped into a doorway. Half a dozen kids surrounded him. Two of them held the outer door shut, two of them efficiently pinned his arms against the wall. Garvin was only aware of cropped hair with a short ridge running front to back. Mohawks. That's what kids called them. The traditional groupings in the school had been Colleeges, Schizis, cadets, commies. The Mohawks had come out of nowhere and were sinister.

Mohawks was a name they'd been given. No one really knew what they called themselves. They wore minimal clothing, shorts and sandals in the summer and thin khaki shirts and pants with slip-on sneakers now that it was getting chilly. It was said that any one of them could kick your head in, that they were a Jap front or something else subversive. Others said you didn't join them. They recruited you, just like the army.

A hand grabbed Garvin's hair and forced his head back. Eyes looked right into his. Two of the Mohawks stared at him. One of them was a dark kid that Garvin remembered from junior high. Then he was a fledgling Colleege in loafers, striped shirts, and bangs. The other, he realized, was a girl. Along with a Mohawk haircut, she had a slight ponytail. She had green eyes. She looked at him, concentrating on him. He could see her brow wrinkle. And then he felt his brain turn over.

WE WANT YOU, she told him. There was an image of him dressed like them.

Garvin tried to raise his hands. He was held too firmly for that, and his gesture turned into a mental one. AND YOU NEED . . . another mind was telling his. He blocked it. The girl looked at him, stunned. Then for a moment she gave him a glimpse of a disordered and unhappy life, a crying girl looking at herself in the mirror. At that moment the ex-Colleege planted in Garvin's mind a wavery image of the high school exit and indicated he should be there at four o'clock the next afternoon. The girl looked at Garvin and spoke. She hesitated on the words, her face troubled. "You need us. And we need you." Releasing him, they went out the door quickly and easily, as if they'd rehearsed many times. The girl's eyes went to his before she disappeared.

Garvin was shaking. He could feel them disappearing into the crowd. Leaving the hallway, he walked up to Twenty-fourth Street, past Angelina's candy store on the corner. Eddy the Red and some other kids huddled over an old jalopy. Garvin tried to be invisible as he passed. Little girls were skipping rope, women were looking out of windows. Few eyes followed him. Garvin kept his head down and tried to keep the world away. His building, when he reached it, had a front hall like the one he had been forced into. It was like the half dozen other buildings in the neighborhood he'd lived in during the years he could remember. The apartment was the third floor back. The name on the bell was Pyotski.

Pyotski was the man his mother had married after Garvin's father had left. Pyotski was a Ukrainian opera singer, a nice enough guy who drank but wasn't violent. He had just decided one day to run off with a Greek contralto and open a restaurant. There had been another husband, a bartender-director, and a few other ones that Garvin had trouble keeping straight in his memory.

Garvin's last name was Reilly, his mother Claire's maiden name. He got his first name from his father, Brian Garvin, an Irishman in New York under the immigration quota. According to Claire, his father was very persuasive. Garvin had plucked images from her mind, part nostalgic, part bitter. Even during their courtship and marriage, Brian Garvin had appeared and disappeared constantly. Not long after their son's birth, he had gone back to Europe or to South America.

He left behind a thousand dollars and Claire's memory of his charm and persuasiveness. When Garvin was younger, he had dreamed his father would come back. Lately he had given that up.

He could hear their voices as he turned the doorknob of the apartment. Along with stepfathers had come a string of honorary uncles, guys who either tried to ignore him or took out their paternal instincts on him. Some of these were all right and some were assholes. Garvin swung the door open and there was Cal.

The leather jacket and boots were perfect, just scuffed enough to look prole and slightly dangerous. A tiny red flag pin was stuck on the collar. He wore steel, foreign-looking reading glasses. Even the one-syllable first name was so right. Cal couldn't have looked more Red. His conversation was full of stories about hard-core friends in the Party and scholarly quotes in the original German. He spoke with a definite but untraceable foreign accent. Twenty-seven and pretending he wanted to be Garvin's big brother, Cal was the biggest asshole so far.

He looked up from the paper as Garvin came in, and Garvin caught another view of himself. It was bad. His clothes were nowhere; his hair neither long nor short, wild nor neat. Garvin saw himself standing there with his head down, a dumb kid with no direction, looking hopelessly young. Cal told himself to remind Claire to get the kid into some study groups, a cell, some team sports, anything to get him out of the house.

Claire was seven years older than Cal. She had just gotten home from work and was getting changed to go out. She stuck her head out of her bedroom. Garvin saw her seeing him. She didn't really look at him, just let it register that he had his head and all his arms and legs, that his eyes hadn't been put out. One moment she thought of him as being three years old, the next she wondered when he was going to move out. She wondered if he'd been smoking marijuana in the Village with the Schizis or drinking beer at the cadet clubhouses. She worried that he didn't have a girl and wasn't getting enough sleep.

"There's hamburger in the fridge," she said in a bright, chirpy voice which he hated. "And ice cream. We should be getting back kind of late." Garvin headed down the hall toward his room. He staggered, and Claire wondered if she should have him see the school doctor. "Are you feeling all right? Here, take some vitamins." He closed the door and she worried for just a flash that he might be headed for jail.

In the tiny room looking out on a narrow alley and a brick wall, Garvin fell flat on his bed facedown and bunched the pillows over his ears. But still it flooded over him. Cal reminded Claire somehow of Garvin's father. Or rather, he reminded her of being younger and meeting Garvin's father.

Cal had liked older women since he had been a ten-year-old sissy up on Fordham Road in the Bronx where he was born and raised. His name had been Etienne then. Garvin made a mental gesture that was like stepping back from the front of his own brain, of withdrawing his mind into a small back room.

He kept that up until they were gone. He could hardly speak, pretended to be asleep when they came in to say goodbye. When the apartment was empty, he relaxed a bit. The building, the street, the city breathed around him. Always, since he could remember, he had moments when he knew what someone was going to say, when he understood what they would have said without their being able to put it into words, when he saw something with what had to be another's eyes.

It had begun happening more often during the last summer, but never before like this. He could feel about him with his mind, catch the chorus of a hundred thousand other minds. It was ringing in his brain, and this time it never entirely died out. He got up and took some aspirin and stole a beer from the refrigerator.

He felt drained, exhausted. He followed idly the progress of Jake Pope, Top Cop, on TV, picking it up like a whisper from a thousand minds. He fell asleep while trying to explain to himself what had happened that day. Late that night he turned over in the dark, feeling as though something had gone through him. He was half aware of a tremor out of Ike Town where veterans shivered in memory of an atomic flash.

CHAPTER TWO

NEXT MORNING his mother called him, and in Garvin's mind was a welter of colors as Claire chose a scarf and examined her makeup. The Carettas, an old couple downstairs, were both thinking about their sore feet. Mr. Caretta was remembering the strong coffee he could no longer have. Mrs. Caretta was planning her day around the soap operas. For one instant they both felt young and alive and frightened. The secretary on the second floor back was thinking about a man in her office. The little kid in the fifth floor front had forgotten to do his homework and was pretending to have an upset stomach so he could stay home.

Memories he'd never had, ideas and faces he'd never known pressed in all around. Garvin took a deep breath and tried to step back inside himself. He held his breath and concentrated on that. He released it slowly in the chilly air of the back room. He drew his knees up to his chest and held on until the other minds receded.

"Garv, won't you get up without my having to yell at you!" Garvey, Garv, Gar—his was a name for which there was no nickname. He was someone for whom there was no place. He had known that and kept it a secret from everyone including himself for many years. He had always tried to blend in. He had never made it into any clique or faction at school, but until now he had been able to escape attention. "Garv, are you awake?"

I WILL BE RIGHT THERE. From Claire's mind he plucked an image of what she wanted to see: him in a chair with a clean shirt on and his hair combed, eating Wheaties.

Garvin wasn't easy until he was sure Claire didn't notice that the answer had appeared in her mind without his having spoken it. He slipped into the bathroom while she wasn't looking, called good-bye to her when she left for work, then collapsed, gasping when he was alone. Slowly, in the almost empty building, he got up, washed, and dressed. He had some half-formed idea of not going to school.

The rush of minds hit him again as he stood on the sidewalk. A man read the *Herald-Tribune* headline—HOUSE TO VOTE ON SPEAKER TODAY—and was very upset. Someone kept reminding herself to buy dog food. A skinny figure scuttled by, trying not to worry about ten thousand dollars' worth of heroin in a bag tied to his thigh. Garvin wavered for a few moments, then headed for school. At least there he knew what to expect. And it would be a challenge to see if he could get through a day pretending that he wasn't insane.

It became a tense and desperate game, but it kept Garvin going. Mrs. Mankoff, his homeroom teacher, was angry with him for being late. She was going to mark him down in her record book. Garvin caught that thought as she had it, turned her mind away from it. In another moment another student had a question and she forgot about him.

The tension didn't stop all day. In math class Mr. Rawly was going to ask Garvin a question. Garvin's mind was totally taken up with Chet Lennon's intense desire to fondle Sally Costello's breasts. Without even being conscious of doing it, Garvin filled Mr. Rawly's mind with an image of Chet staring at Sally. Chet got called. The answer to the question the teacher asked came floating out of the back of the class and into Garvin's head.

In the halls between classes, he staggered as the bombardment on his mind continued. A little kid with thick glasses was obsessed with anxiety over a chemistry problem he hadn't been able to solve. A girl was crazy with worry over a missed period. Two people were thinking about the same TV show. A male teacher wanted to tie male students to a pillar and cook a huge dinner for them. The lyrics to a popular song whistled through a mind and someone passing Garvin in the corridor thought that he was cute. He couldn't identify the source of that thought. From another floor of the school, the image of Sally Costello's breasts floated down to Garvin.

He couldn't eat lunch. In the cafeteria, the pizza parlor, the sandwich shop, the clash of tastes turned his stomach. Someone loathed the mustard that Garvin loved. Someone else was eating squid.

He sat in an almost empty study hall. The teacher at the front of the room was reading a newspaper, making some sort of coherent sense out of the stories. The sinking of neutral ships in South American waters had brought pressure on the President and cabinet. Congress felt that they hadn't responded firmly enough. The House of Representatives was electing a new Speaker, a man named Wright. The President and Vice-President were supposed to resign and let Wright become President. This they were refusing to do. Garvin held his breath and blocked this out.

He went from class to class like an automaton. History with Miss Ahearn, which he usually liked, was nothing more than a distant rumor to him. She had the map of South America down and was telling them that what was happening was a direct result of the Zurich Conference of 1945. Outwardly she was angry at the class for being so uninformed and uninterested. Secretly she was worried that her boy friend, a Red, and her brother, an ex-cadet and now a cop, were going to be on opposite sides in some very unpleasant times.

On the world map, the orange of Japan squared off against the red of Russia in the east. The thin strip of green that marked Anglo-American holdings in Europe was all that broke the solid black of the Reich. That was balanced by the pure green of the Western Hemisphere, marred only by the black of Argentina. Someone somewhere was afraid to go home because her father was going to be drunk and angry. Another person was in ecstasy over an early acceptance to Juilliard. Garvin tried to hold his mind together as the map spun in front of him.

When classes were over, he didn't go home. He couldn't even remember why he hung around. The level of intrusion from minds right around him had dropped, but the day had left him exhausted. From somewhere outside he caught a final burst of Chet Lennon. Sally Costello's breasts were more than just a fantasy; Chet had them in his hands.

Garvin went to a room where the wargamers met. The maps fascinated him. There was an answer if he could only figure out what the question was. In a book he had once seen was a series of maps of Europe set at ten-year intervals from Roman times to the present. Boundaries expanded and contracted. Empires burst forth and were gone. It was like seeing life in a drop of water through a microscope.

One of the group of gamers was playing a version of the Battle of France called World's End. The line from Churchill's speech was written across the board: "Thus our world ends and we must now win through in this awful new one." There were about twenty kids in the room, almost all male, a couple of artsy Schizis, one or two stylish Colleeges, a few Reds, and half a dozen cadets. But this was neutral ground and most were ones who didn't fit into any of the factions. The talk turned to the Mohawks. All other conversation stopped, and everyone started contributing what he or she knew or had heard.

"Johnny Myers's sister joined up and their father wouldn't even let her go out of the house. Then this Mohawk guy Johnny said was only a couple of years older than the sister came by the apartment, said a few words to the old man. Buzzo. She gets to stay out as long as she wants."

"This kid where I live, up on Thirty-fifth Street, name's Montoya, he was a basket case, walked around talking to himself. Kids used to throw lighted matches at him. The other week he's a Mohawk, walks down the center of the sidewalk, nobody touches him."

"One guy I knew didn't want to have anything to do with them, told them to get lost when they came after him. One day he comes home crying, won't talk to anyone about it, but he had the haircut and was wearing the pajamas."

"It's like a vampire cult."

"It's like the army."

"There's nothing in their eyes when they look at you. Scary!" All conversation stopped. There was a figure at the door. It was the girl Garvin had faced in the doorway of the housing project. She beckoned with one hand for him to come with her. Garvin realized that this was what he had been waiting for. He braced and felt a message. COME WITH US . . . PLEASE. With it there was a promise of warmth and understanding, an island in the raging sea of telepathic confusion which was drowning him. He saw an image of others in their khaki clothes kneeling in a circle. There was a single thought in all of their minds: Garvin joining them.

For a moment Garvin hesitated. Then, with everyone in the room staring, he got up slowly. Feeling the wonder and the fear in the other kids, he went to the door. He would become another legend. "He walked out like he was hypnotized or something." But Garvin didn't care. For a moment of contact, he had looked right into the girl. Her name was Stephanie Myers, and this assignment was very important to her. That wasn't just because it had been given to her by someone called Nick, but because she knew how frightened and confused Garvin was. YOU WILL FEEL WANTED.

I WILL LOOK LIKE A FREAK, he had answered her without speaking. He had done it automatically.

BUT YOU WILL NEVER FEEL LIKE A FREAK. Garvin felt the explosion of breath behind him as everyone in the room started breathing again. He didn't care. He knew enough to recognize warmth and kindness and to want to move toward it.

There were two more Mohawks in the hall outside. They fell in behind Garvin and Stephanie. At the Fifteenth Street exit, three more were waiting. One of them was the ex-Colleege Garvin recognized from the day before. DID HE GIVE ANY TROUBLE? he asked Stephanie. HE CAME WILLINGLY, was the reply. Their minds linked. Garvin felt it like a pocket, a nest in the confusion of the street.

Together they crossed First Avenue, walking between the cars in a traffic jam. They went south. Kids hanging around were very disturbed by them. Drivers caught behind a creeping cement mixer were enraged by the delay. An old woman thought of a nice present to give Father Clemente on his twenty-five years in the priesthood. Someone wondered if there was going to be a war. The Mohawks were like an escort. They linked together and Garvin was excluded, deflected from their minds. It seemed as if the warmth Garvin had been promised was a lie, and he thought of bolting and running. But where was he going to run to? The only thing that made any sense in his insanity was other crazy people.

YOU ARE NOT CRAZY. I THOUGHT THAT TOO. Again there was the image of Stephanie in her room, tearing her hair and crying.

WHY DO YOU DRESS LIKE THAT?

THERE IS NOTHING THEY CAN TAKE FROM US. CUT A SCHIZO'S HAIR AND HE LOOKS LIKE A CADET. TAKE A RED'S LEATHERS AWAY FROM HIM AND HE COULD BE A COLLEEGE. WHEN THE SCHOOL GETS MAD AT A FACTION, THEY MAKE THEM DRESS DOWN, OBEY GROOMING CODES. AND WE DO IT BECAUSE IT ATTRACTS ATTTENTION.

On the curb on Fourteenth Street a cop sat in his car and watched them. In his mind were the thoughts that this was the second group of Mohawks that he had seen that day, that the one in the middle not in costume seemed to be a prisoner, and that one more gang was one too many. He moved to open the car door, get out, and talk to them.

The Mohawks caught all of that as it came to the policeman. They moved to deflect his thoughts, to turn his attention to the traffic behind him. Stephanie changed the way he saw them. She summoned up in his mind images of a bunch of kids involved in some harmless silliness.

Then Garvin tried too. It was suddenly almost painfully clear to the cop that the kid in the middle was happy to be with the others, that he wasn't being coerced. The policeman in the car sank back feeling slightly foolish. But his partner in the doughnut shop where he had gone to buy coffee still watched them. And was still suspicious.

THANK YOU, Stephanie told Garvin. He looked at the Mohawks around him. They were a mixed crew, ranging in age from about thirteen to sixteen. Their sizes and colors varied. Some were graceful and some clumsy. But they moved as a unit, intact and proud, holding the middle of the sidewalk. Other pedestrians swerved away from them. Stephanie with ordinary hair and good clothes would have been plain. She was inclined to be chubby and her face looked as if it was used to glasses. He suddenly realized that she could tell what he was thinking. It didn't matter to her, though. She was happy to be bringing him in.

A busload of people swept past and Garvin was racked with dozens of different consciousnesses, sets of angers and wants and fears and secret joys. He almost staggered but stayed with the Mohawks as they turned off Fourteenth Street. Avenue C in that world was still part of an older Lower East Side, with peddlers just closing up their carts and cars bouncing over cobblestones, with children being called home in a dozen languages and the smell of cabbage cooking and strange foods frying.

Garvin was led down a flight of stairs. He felt as if he had entered an insulated room. Sensations from the street outside receded. Around him, sitting cross-legged on the floor, leaning against the walls, were a dozen kids like the ones who had escorted him. The room was a windowless cellar painted white.

Then he saw himself, hollow eyed and disheveled. He tried to block that image and felt another mind catch at his memories of the horrors of the night before. He tried to get free of that and felt the other consciousness reach out and soothe his own. IT IS ALL RIGHT. HERE WE UNDERSTAND. HERE YOU CAN REST. All attention in the room was away from Garvin and toward his left. Garvin turned and felt for the first time a telepath trained to be stronger than he was.

This was a figure in black shirt, pants, and boots, with the ridge of hair. But this one had a long ponytail tied behind his head. He was older than the others, maybe twenty, with black hair and tanned skin. YOU CAN CALL ME NICK, the other told him.

Garvin reached out to find more and felt himself blocked, turned aside from the other's mind. It was done very neatly, gently. I KNEW YOU WERE THERE, GARVIN. I FELT YOU A FEW TIMES SINCE THIS SUMMER. IT BECAME ALMOST CONSTANT THESE LAST FEW WEEKS. Garvin felt understanding of what he had gone through. His eyes burned and he trembled. From across the room Nick soothed him. IT IS ALL RIGHT. HERE YOU CAN REST.

Only later, when he had felt adepts calming frightened humans and animals, when he had done it himself, did Garvin understand what had happened in that cellar. At the time all he knew was that the Mohawks formed a shield around him with their minds, deflecting the outside world. Nick began to show Garvin the rudiments of blocking. YOU MUST HAVE SOMETHING INSIDE YOURSELF. IT CAN BE THE AWARENESS OF A SORE TOOTH. IT CAN BE A FAVORITE IMAGE OR MEMORY. THIS IS ONE THAT I USE. Garvin saw a hawk plunging at him out of the blue sky. Instinctively, he raised his arm. One of the youngest Mohawks giggled.

The hawk came at Garvin again and he kept his arms at his side, reached inside himself to the core of memories. He was watching snow falling as he sat at an apartment window. He must have been very young, four or five. The hawk in sunlight broke through the gray sky, sliced through the snow. It flew at the glass, flickered, and began to fade back. The snow closed in. Garvin had closed his eyes. He opened them to find Nick nodding. VERY GOOD.

They repeated that exercise until Garvin's head began to

hurt. IT WILL BECOME SECOND NATURE TO YOU, Nick told him. Around them the others formed an image, all of the minds melding together, producing something that lingered outside any one mind. It was an ornate room as seen reflected in an elaborately gold-framed mirror. Whoever was seeing the reflection was not in the room. It was comforting to Garvin to feel all the minds united like that. Some of them flickered in and out, unable to maintain their concentration. But the image never wavered or disappeared.

Then Nick brought out scissors and a clippers and cropped Garvin's hair back to the skull except for a ridge an inch tall and two inches wide. Garvin stripped off his clothes and knew that he wouldn't be seeing them again. He dressed in the khakis and sneakers. He felt the mirror opening, inviting him, and he joined his mind to the others.

The aching of the last few days had been going on for years without his being aware of it. Now it had stopped.

It was dark by the time he was ready to walk home. Other Mohawks were with him at first. A party of Colleeges, kids who pretended they went to private school, watched them from across the street. But what they were watching was the clothes and the hair. As they did that, Garvin could watch them.

He was cold in the night air; his feet felt close to the pavement. By holding that awareness of himself, he could keep the world at bay. Stephanie was the last one to peel off toward her own home. She had gone out of her way to walk Garvin almost to his own street. Their minds linked for a moment and then she was gone.

His telepathic capacity was constant now, but he had to steer himself very carefully. He turned the corner onto his own block. The newspapers on the stand outside Angelina's said the President would not resign, even at the urging of the Congress and cabinet. Reds had marched in Chicago in protest. The women, bundled up in coats to hang out the windows and talk, stopped their gossip and watched as Garvin walked by. Little kids playing on the sidewalk started to giggle behind him. "First Mohawk on the block," someone said and spat.

Garvin knew he wasn't a Mohawk. The group had no name that could be spoken. When they thought of themselves, what they thought of was the image of that mirror in that empty room. Garvin clutched that image close to him, concentrated to keep other minds outside his own. He knew he had strengths, but he didn't quite understand what they were. Kids his age and a little older were playing touch football. In the street in front of him, Eddy the Red and his friends stood around while someone gunned the engine of a car.

The city was divided, neighborhood by neighborhood, block by block between left and right, Red and fascist, commie and cadet. On some higher level it translated into politics and political office. On the street it meant the local gang, the ones who rules a specific turf. Manhattan below Forty-second Street on the East Side tended to be Red. Eddy ruled Twenty-fourth Street between First and Second. There were cells and clubhouses to which he had to answer. But if he wanted to show his authority and squash a weird upstart, no one would question him.

He walked over and stood in front of Garvin before Garvin was really aware of him. His friends flanked Eddy; other kids gathered around. Eddy stood six feet tall and barrel chested, cigarette hanging out of his mouth, belly just beginning to spread over his belt. "Jeeze, look at the hair," a girl said. Eddy smiled, "Last of the Mohicans."

There were maybe twenty strides between Garvin and the line of bodies in front of him. He knew enough not to break his pace as he tried to reach out to the waiting minds. He found curiosity mingled with uncertainty, boredom, and the anticipation of a little excitement. He couldn't tell whose thoughts were whose.

As Garvin's foot hit the pavement, he felt a mind that understood what had to be done. A brief show of force, a proper humiliation would send him crying home to his mother. That was Eddy.

Garvin's other foot hit the pavement. Every inch of him felt cold. He had lost touch with Eddy's mind. He took another stride. Everything seemed to be happening very slowly. He was seeing himself walking in the light from the street lamps.

He was almost close enough for Eddy to reach out and grab him. That, he realized, was what Eddy planned to do. Garvin took another step. Then Eddy was in focus. Garvin was in the other's mind. There were fragments and short bursts, half thoughts and brief flashes. There were fears. Garvin's foot came down again. They were going to take his uniform and burn it. Eddy was going to whip his ass right there on the street. There was a knot in Garvin's stomach. Then he was in the central terror of Eddy's mind.

Ten years before, when he was five, Eddy heard a noise from the cellar stairs, heard the door creak open, saw the black from the cellar leak out into the half-lighted hallway where he was playing. Outlined against the black were a mouth in a grimace and eyes rolling and white. There was a knife held in a bloody hand. His father, drunk, had just murdered his uncle and for a moment poised to kill his son, the only witness.

And as Garvin stepped deliberately right in front of Eddy, the door creaked open again; the dark came flooding out. Eddy fell back gasping, choking, tears in his eyes. Without breaking stride, Garvin pushed him aside and walked into his building. He left amazement and shock behind as Eddy fell to his knees on the pavement.

On the stairs Garvin himself swayed. The mental impulses of the whole neighborhood flowed into him. Then he took a deep breath, pushed back the hate and fear he could feel from the street. He formed in his mind the image of the mirror and planted his foot on the stairs. From that night he was on the hero's road and knew that nothing lay behind him.

He opened the door of his apartment. His mother and Cal had been in her bedroom and now were sitting in robes. Claire was prepared to be mad at him. Instead she just stared, seeing him for the first time in a long while. Cal had a lot of trouble seeing without his glasses. He squinted and did a long double take. "Dear God!" Garvin's mother said.

It took a moment for him to get his throat to work. "Is there anything to eat?" he asked, and realized he was starving.

CHAPTER THREE

IN A COUPLE of weeks Nick taught Garvin everything he knew. Sometimes Garvin learned with the other Mohawks: to forge himself into part of an invisible fortress, to move as part of a group that swept along streets like a cloud.

They formed a strike force to punish any students who tried to harm a solitary Mohawk. Some were weak and unfocused in their abilities. But in a group of half a dozen or more, they could always concentrate and find anyone's psychic weak spot. Separately, his new friends could be as irritating as family to Garvin. Together they were something that lifted him out of himself.

Sometimes Nick kept Garvin after the others. One evening after the group had held the image of the empty room with the mirror for almost a minute, Nick indicated that Garvin was to stay. The others left, going out onto the streets, into the subways. Nick stayed with them mentally for as long as he could, kneeling on a mat on the floor of their headquarters. Garvin sat opposite and cast about in the world outside. He knew almost as second nature how to block out minds he didn't want to scan. He could turn the great blasting life of the city into a kind of music.

That evening he reached out and found the mind of a concerned veteran going home to Ike Town. There had been some disturbances in the neighborhood, rock and bottle throwing in Union Square. President Hughes and Speaker of the House Wright were both going to address the nation on television that night. Garvin caught the man's thoughts. "Wright's doing what's got to be done for the country and party. Hughes, the no-good bastard, let himself get swayed by power and the Republicans. Got to stop him before he makes a peace treaty with the Reich. Submarines in the Caribbean and he does nothing."

Then the Vet was aware of a large white room with a figure kneeling on the floor. It was as haunting and real as a dream. The figure was one of those new Mohawks who should all be drafted. It disappeared almost as soon as he became aware of it. The man wanted to talk to someone about getting his disability pension increased.

In the cellar, Garvin rocked backward at a psychic slap from Nick. YOU WERE BROADCASTING MY IMAGE. THAT ONE SAW IT. WHO ELSE SAW IT? Garvin struggled free of Nick's probe. The older youth was serious. YOU ARE THE BEST I FOUND HERE. NOW STOP PLAYING GAMES LIKE A KID.

SORRY. Garvin indicated apology. He bowed his head then struck back at Nick suddenly. The other parried. A hawk headed for Garvin's eyes. Garvin turned it aside without thinking. He probed further, brushed aside resistance. He was inside Nick's mind. He caught images of Mohawks, some of them ones he knew. He felt the fierce love Nick had for each of the kids he was training.

Garvin caught a flash of other people dressed like Nick and found a name, COMPANIONS. Worlds lay around them like lighted windows in the night. Then Garvin broke deep into Nick's memory.

In a New York almost like the one he knew, people in rags lived in cold-water flats. Garvin saw Nick through other people's eyes: Nick as leader of a gang of kids, Nick beating someone older and stronger by knowing his thoughts, Nick outsmarting the police. Off and on, Nick knew other's minds, saw with their eyes. It came in handy. At fifteen he had a gang of pickpockets working the rush-hour subway.

After those images, Garvin caught others: Nick encountering a mind stronger than his, Nick caught and beaten senseless, Nick in a daze of pain and drugs standing naked on a slave-market platform, Nick humiliated, beaten, raped.

Garvin's breath stopped. Nick was in his mental defenses, was up and moving across the room with a look of cold murder in his eyes. Garvin knew the other was going to kill him with his hands. There was nothing else on Nick's mind.

As Nick grabbed him, Garvin got past the rage in the other mind at everyone who had ever hit or jailed or used him. Garvin stopped the hands that were going to snap his neck, the knee that was going to supply the push. Nick's eyes looked right into his and for long moments Garvin could feel the anger. Then the eyes fell and the rage broke.

Mental contact between them stopped. Garvin was the first to speak. "I'm sorry, Nick, I didn't mean to." Nick just shrugged and looked away. Garvin said, "If I had anything like that to share with you, I'd let you have it. But I don't have any adventures or anything. I've just lived at home."

Nick's voice was expressionless. "You've got nothing to apologize for. I knew you were strong. I just didn't understand how strong. It's my fault. I'm supposed to be protecting you. Instead, I tried to hurt."

"You had it bad where you came from?"

Nick kept his mind closed off from Garvin's. "I think we should shut this place down for the night." He looked at Garvin. "There's an automatic reaction I have that I don't really control." He showed an image of a loaded pistol. "Sometimes it gets away."

After Garvin left, Nick put on a thin leather jacket, locked the cellar room, and walked over to Tompkins Square Park. As he did, he cast about to make sure no one was watching and that no telepath was following him mentally. It was getting dark; people were preoccupied with the crisis. Nick never broke stride as he headed directly for a small brick gazebo.

Nick approached it at just the right angle, twisted himself slightly as he did. Only a telepath could see the air shimmer; only one who knew it was there would recognize a portal. Nick passed into the shimmer and disappeared from the world of Garvin's birth.

For a moment he tumbled in Time, felt a distant heartbeat, saw the worlds like distant windows in the dark. Nick reached out with his mind and caught another portal which he knew was there, tumbled through it, stepped out onto the grass of the neighboring world. Here there was no city and Manhattan was an island without native human life to name it.

In absolute terms this world was only half a minute later on the same November evening as the last. But it was a colder place and there was a chill drizzle. In the last light Nick turned up his collar and headed through the woods, probing ahead.

He had gone about a quarter of a mile when he caught a trace of a familiar mind. He moved on and that mind grasped his. Another mind joined it. He saw what those two minds saw, two people his age or a bit older, dressed as he was, with ridges of hair and long ponytails in back. They were sitting in a lighted shack that looked like a temporary guard post. NICK? They linked minds with him.

Nick halted. THE MOMENT IS HERE. TELL THE OLD ONE. He showed an image of Garvin, scared and trembling on the day he was initiated. Then he gave images of the mounting political tension in the world he had just left. When they indicated that they understood, Nick turned and headed back to his post.

The next morning Garvin saw Marie Tedechi again. He knew he could have her, could have whomever he wanted. He didn't quite know what to do with this knowledge. He was walking with Stephanie Myers and knew that she loved him. He liked Stephanie, was grateful to her for bringing him to the Mohawks, but he didn't want her the way he wanted Marie. The crowd hanging around the doors of the school was tense, and Garvin was too immersed in the limits of telepathy in social life to notice.

Up in a second-floor corridor a commie said something to a cadet, and the cadet knocked him down. The cadet himself was felled, along with his girl friend. Fighting spread to a couple of homerooms. A teacher who tried to break it up had his jaw smashed. By the time the police were called, cadets had gotten to the armory and broken out some dummy rifles, perfect for clubs.

The armory was just off the gym. They assaulted the commies who had gathered there and were driven back. The police arrived to break it up. An innocent bystander, a Schizo art student who was trying to take pictures, was shot in the face with a zip gun. There were fifteen arrests and two injured cops before the building was cleared and shut down for the day.

Radio and TV news was of a series of "gangland killings" in New Jersey. Vice-President Gilroy of Ohio was supposed to address a House investigative committee that afternoon. Garvin and Stephanie gathered up all the Mohawks at the school and led them off to their headquarters. On First Avenue an overturned car was burning. In the park on Second Avenue, the commies had been joined by adult supporters from Union Square. A car full of men in dark glasses and hats drove by and fired a volley into the crowd.

A girl was killed. Garvin could hear the screams and sirens, could feel the panic and anger. Some of the Mohawks wanted to remain. WE COULD MAKE A DIFFERENCE. WE COULD TIP THE BALANCE. Garvin understood what that meant to them, what it would once have meant to him to be in the clique the other cliques had to come to. He also knew there were more important things. Nick was signaling them all to come to him. The Mohawks projected a feeling of peace and harmlessness and passed by the police barricades.

There was excited talk on the radio in a store they passed. "Awful explosion, the Vice-President . . . just smoke and flames ... no one could get close ..." They quickened their pace. All around them people were frightened. There were images from television of fires in Seattle, hamstrung police horses in Boston. Nick had sent out his probes as far as they would go. Of the score-plus Mohawks, fifteen had shown up. They were there when the police appeared.

It was nothing much. Just a uniformed cop who stayed at the wheel of the car and a detective sergeant who came to the door and talked to Nick. He asked a few routine questions and secretly counted heads. The Mohawks knelt on the floor and projected good will as Nick explained that they were a harmless self-defense cult. He ran through the detective's mind. The man had been sent on rumors that there were arms stored in the cellar. Nick let him make a quick search. Mohawks tried not to giggle as the man looked in the closet and tapped the walls.

The policeman felt very tired and foolish. He warned Nick that the curfew was on and everyone had to be off the streets by dark. Then he felt as happy as if he'd just received a promotion. He didn't know why.

The Mohawks almost exploded as he drove off. Nick smiled but sought out Garvin's mind and asked, WHY IN A CITY GOING UP IN INSURRECTION DO THEY BOTHER WITH US? Garvin realized, shocked, that Nick was treating him as at least an equal. It gave him a tingle of excitement.

The Mohawks formed the image of the mirror in the empty room. Then slowly, one by one, starting with the weakest talents, Nick sent them on their way. It was done gently. One kid would feel a sudden urge to go home come over him. A moment later Nick would suggest to another who lived nearby that it would be a good idea to go with the first kid and watch out for him. As the last half dozen left, Nick told them to get to headquarters as soon after curfew lifted as they could. He would need them in the morning.

When Stephanie was the only one left with Nick and Garvin, another mind suddenly probed them. All stiffened at the same moment. Stephanie's eyes were wide with fright. Nick bit his lip. Garvin felt a mind move against his own. It was as brisk and competent as a cook breaking open an egg.

Concentrating on the white walls of the room, Garvin made that the only image in his mind. The other mind glanced off. Garvin felt for it. The other person was far away. Garvin probed, searching against the great, chaotic background of the city.

Whoever it was realized another mind was searching for it and began to block, to hide in the excitement and violence of the riots. The one who had probed moved away from Garvin rapidly. Somewhere around the Brooklyn Bridge contact between them was cut by the minds of National Guard Troops riding into Manhattan in trucks. Nick reassured Stephanie before she left. Garvin noticed scars on Nick's hands standing out white against a tan as he clenched his fists. THAT ONE READ ME AS EASILY AS I READ THE COP, he told Garvin.

Garvin probed in a circle around the headquarters. Nick spoke aloud so as not to distract him. "The Riders know I'm here. That's why we have to get you out. You're important, Garvin. Every Companion on this world has been looking for you. You traced that mind all the way to Brooklyn, past a million other minds, didn't you? I've never met anyone else who could do that, and I've been on thirty worlds, maybe more." At that moment Nick sounded very young. Garvin felt nervous and excited.

Outside, Avenue C was preparing to shut up early, peddlers were starting to push their carts home, food shops were getting ready to close, people were calling their children. And in the midst of the cars and pedestrians, the arguing, bobbing, excitement, and fear, there was something like a song that caught Garvin's mind. The song was a swirl of leaves in a gutter, the dust in the late afternoon sun, the moment when the whole city seemed to go quiet and the air rippled in front of you. Garvin was caught, hypnotized.

The door opened and was filled by a large figure holding a leather bag under his arm. Garvin's attention came back to the room. The figure was well over six feet tall and stoop shouldered. The man had gray hair and lines on his face that seemed to have been etched there. He was dressed in a long overcoat and thick boots. Garvin reached out for the figure's mind. There was nothing more than he would find in the mind of a well-trained Seeing Eye dog. The song continued. It came from the leather satchel.

OLD ONE. Wordlessly, Nick indicated Garvin. The song swirled around the boy, went past his defenses like the tide around a sand castle, paused, then told Nick, YOU HAVE DONE WELL. THIS IS A REMARKABLE ADEPT. UNTRAINED BUT POWERFUL ALMOST BEYOND MEASURE. Garvin felt Nick's pride at the praise.

Nick described the mind that had touched them earlier. The mind in the satchel reached out and scanned in widening circles all around him. At the same time it kept contact separately with both of them. The song Garvin had first experienced continued also. He tried to make contact with the satchel and found himself blocked. It was a remarkable display, half a dozen functions carried on at the same time.

The mind stopped its outward probe and settled back into the room, keeping watch on the streets around them. FORGIVE MY NOT INTRODUCING MYSELF I AM CALLED THE OLD ONE BY THOSE WHO WISH TO BE RESPECTFUL. THERE ARE ALSO THOSE WHO THINK OF ME AS THE TALKING SUITCASE, ONE ON WHOM THE GODS DECIDED TO CONFER IMMORTALITY IN THEIR OWN INIMITABLE WAY.

THIS—indicating the tall man who, having put down the satchel, was sitting on the floor—IS ROGER, WHO ACTS AS MY ARMS AND LEGS AND ON WHOM I DEPEND ABSOLUTELY. Nick brought Roger a glass of water, which the man accepted and drank without a word.

I HAD TO BE SURE. The Talking Suitcase almost seemed to be telling itself this. NOW THAT I AM, LET ME SHOW YOU THIS. The song of the satchel was around him again. Garvin saw New Yorks, ones almost like the one he knew, ones where there was nothing recognizable. Sometimes there were woods and streams, sometimes ashes blowing under yellow skies.

Worlds ran through the Talking Suitcase's mind like jewels. Garvin saw them in their thousands, rotating through the four seasons. He felt the pulse of Time. WILL YOU LEAVE THIS WORLD?

Kids ran off to sea or dreamed about the stars. This seemed like both. For only a moment did he weigh what he had against it. "What about my family?" The image that came into his mind was Claire.

YOU WILL BE PROTECTING HER MORE BY NOT STAYING AND DRAWING ATTENTION TO HER. THE RIDERS ARE COMING INTO ASCENDANCY HERE. IT WOULD BE A GREAT DEFEAT TO LOSE YOU TO THEM.

Garvin saw Nick nodding agreement and looking grim. He trusted Nick, and the older youth trusted the Talking Suitcase. I WILL GO.

GOOD. An image of the gazebo in the park appeared in Nick's and Garvin's minds.. Early morning sun shone on it. BE THERE TOMORROW AT SEVEN. THAT SHOULD BE JUST AFTER THE CURFEW LIFTS.

Roger stood, picked up the satchel, and turned to go. Nick went to the door with them. ARE THERE ANY RECRUITS READY FOR THE IMMORTAL COMPANIONS? the Talking Suitcase asked him. It blocked their minds from Garvin's.

A FEW. I . . . I THOUGHT, OLD ONE, YOU WOULD TAKE GARVIN NOW.

Roger opened the door and twilight flooded in. NO, the Talking Suitcase told Nick. A SPECIAL COURIER WILL TAKE GARVIN. GET THE RECRUITS OFF THIS WORLD TOMORROW. WE ARE WITHDRAWING FROM THIS PART OF TIME IMMEDIATELY. The song of the Old One was all the blue of dying sunlight, the traffic dashing home, the smell of tear gas and burning cars. It blended into the city and was lost.

Nick indicated that Garvin should start home right away. When he did, Nick went with him, walked about a dozen paces behind, their minds linked. Police cars and army trucks with loudspeakers warned people that curfew was going into effect. Passing Ike Town, Garvin thought of those desperate days of 1944 when twin atomic explosions in France and the Ukraine had made the Allied advances melt.

With thousands of allies burned and blinded, there was the famous meeting at Geneva of the dying Roosevelt and the dying Hitler. The American bluffed, lied, almost broke down under the strain. Hitler was described as being satanic, as vowing to burn the world rather than lose it. Bristol, England, blew up in September, and the British wavered.

Then came the indomitable Red Army, refusing to break in the face of German bombs. And there was the all-American eleventh-hour rescue, the miracle B-24 taking out the German atomic laboratories with the first American bomb. The war ended without winners.

THIS PLACE MADE OUT BETTER THAN MY WORLD, Nick told Garvin. THERE HITLER WAS THE STEED FOR A RIDER AND HE WON HANDS DOWN.

WHAT IS A RIDER?

A THING THAT LIVES INSIDE THE MIND OF A PERSON WHO IS USUALLY A REALLY POWERFUL TELEPATH. Garvin saw the image Nick had of a Rider, a Hitler inside whose burning eyes he could somehow see a pair of totally cold eyes. RIDERS GET CONTROL OF WORLDS, AND THEY LOOT THEM, TAKE EVERYTHING—ART, RESOURCES, PEOPLE, ESPECIALLY TELEPATHS.

YOU MEAN AS SLAVES? Garvin remembered the image of Nick on the block, seen through the eyes of a potential buyer. WHERE DO THEY TAKE THEM?

ALL ALONG THE TIME LANES, THERE ARE SLAVE MARKETS. PEOPLE GET SOLD FOR LABOR, FOR SEX. BUT TELEPATHS ARE THE MOST VALUABLE. WE USUALLY GET SHIPPED TO GOBLIN MARKET. THAT WAS GOING TO HAPPEN TO ME. . . .

Nick broke contact, but Garvin could feel his anger. They were at the corner of his block. "What's Goblin Market?" he asked aloud.

"Where we're all going to end up unless we're smart and

fast." The streetlights came on. Nick looked around. "It's always like this. Goblins and Riders can force us out of any world they want. Try to get a lot of sleep, Garvin, and take as little with you as you can tomorrow."

Claire was home worrying. Cal was still out. The television had pictures of tanks and troops, nothing much about the bomb that killed the Vice-President that afternoon. A brief speech by President Hughes was supposed to be reassuring. There was footage of the rioting in New York that afternoon but nothing to suggest that it was still going on. Garvin could tell by probing to the north and west that there were commie mobs still on the streets, defying the curfew. Police were moving to smash and disperse them. The lights went out and the TV went off at the same instant.

Garvin and his mother sat in the dark. She knew. Garvin realized that she was thinking of him as being much more like his father than he had been. Since he'd come home a Mohawk, she had been seeing him, not just remembering him as a child. She knew he was going to leave soon and had a fairly strong suspicion that she'd never see him again.

She had driven Garvin crazy at times. She was a feather-head who took her emotions from what was happening around her. Others' happiness made her happy. The rioting made her worried and tense. Garvin had never tried to probe her mind and didn't want to start now. He didn't begrudge her any of the happiness she had found. He would leave her with even less than his father had. She understood. For a moment they were silent in the dark room.

In the street mobs came swirling downtown, carrying torches in the dark, setting fire to trash, breaking shop windows, overturning cars. The commies were marching home. Some would keep the fight alive all night, avoiding police and National Guard, slipping from doorway to doorway till dawn.

Others, like Cal, just wanted to crawl away and hide. He had flinched in the face of a police charge that evening, and everyone had seen it. Garvin felt sorry for Cal and the Etienne he couldn't escape being by changing his name. There was nothing he could do, though, there in the dark. He excused himself and went to bed. For a while he thought about what had happened. Once or twice he probed out into the night and found New York wondering in the dark what the next day was going to bring.

After he fell asleep, late at night, a mind rippled through the neighborhood. There were sirens way uptown and an explosion somewhere out across the East River. A convoy passed, going the wrong way on Second Avenue. The night was tense, many slept only fitfully, many hardly at all. The streetlights came back on as power was restored. The probe rippled on, sorting through minds, looking for someone. It found Twenty-fourth Street and the apartment. It paused over Claire for just a moment before it found Garvin. The boy half woke up, and the mind withdrew.

That same night, on a world far enough away from the one Garvin knew, it was a quarter hour earlier in Time. Roger held an umbrella over himself and the satchel he carried. Headlights shone down an English country lane and a 1934 Bentley appeared. The Immortal in the satchel made contact with the mind of the passenger in the back seat of the car. GOOD EVENING, CAPTAIN TAGENT.

The car slowed to a stop and the back door opened. "The Talking Suitcase! Have your man bring you inside." A tall form sprawled in the back seat, its face hidden in shadows. Although a telepath, he spoke aloud. "Your message stressed importance and profit."

Roger carried the satchel into the back seat. After a moment's hesitation, the Talking Suitcase showed the Captain an image of a man cloaked and hooded as he stood in the summer sun selling a bedraggled slave to a tall woman with flickering green eyes and red hair.

"Unless I'm greatly mistaken, that's myself, and the woman is the Steed called Herself. The Rider who rules her owns a world far away. It would be high summer there now. I don't recall the incident you show me."

IT HAS YET TO OCCUR. IN TWO DAYS SHE WILL

BE SEEKING A STEED FOR A FELLOW RIDER WHOSE STEED IS DYING.

"I couldn't stride in Time that quickly. Not even Immortals or Goblins can."

THE ORACLE SHOWS YOU SELLING HER A SLAVE-STEED IN TWO DAYS. HERE HE IS. The Suitcase showed an image of Garvin the next morning in Tompkins Square Park.

"I have it on good authority that there is no Oracle."

I HAVE IT ON BETTER AUTHORITY THAT THERE IS.

"How much does it show me as receiving?"

FIVE THOUSAND CREDITS.

"Odd. I shouldn't think an Immortal would be so concerned about the well-being of a Rider that it is willing to give tips to a slave trader," said the Captain. But Roger was already out the door of the Bentley, carrying the satchel away.

Garvin got up at first light, washed, and dressed silently. It was cold enough for a jacket. He was ready to go when he felt Nick telling him, MOVE QUICKLY. His heart wrenched as he left the room that faced on the brick wall. He reached out with his mind and touched Claire and Cal and the rest of the people in the building. Then he was down the worn stairs and out on the street. Nick was at the Second Avenue end of the block. Only a few people were up and out. A volley of gunshots sounded way off on the West Side.

As they headed south, Nick scanned for the other Mohawks. Stephanie and two kids who were on their way to headquarters responded. Nick guided them toward a rendez-vous on the way to Tompkins Park. The streets were still almost empty. A police cruiser slowed down for a moment and then sped away. Suddenly a mind probed them. Garvin recognized it as the same one he had felt the previous afternoon.

It was getting closer. HURRY! Nick ordered. The two broke into a trot. At Fourteenth Street Stephanie closed up with them. As they headed east across First Avenue, two other Mohawks, a boy and a girl, joined up. They were running as they crossed Fourteenth, heading for the park. It was hard for Garvin to move and concentrate on the mind probing them.

An unmarked car which had been cruising along the other side of the street did a U-turn and came after them. Garvin probed, and a mind in the car deflected his. Suddenly many telepathic minds probed them all at once. Sirens sounded. One of the Mohawks screamed and fell headfirst on the street. They were in sight of the park. Nick stopped for the one who had fallen. "Run!" he shouted. "Garvin, get them to the portal."

An image of the brick gazebo hung in the air. Garvin stopped and looked back. Nick was crouched over the fallen Mohawk. Two cars had stopped; men with guns jumped out. One of them yelled as Nick grabbed his mind. Another stumbled and dropped his pistol. GARVIN, I AM ORDERING YOU. SAVE THE OTHERS! Nick told him.

Garvin felt Stephanie still running toward the park. There were hostile minds in front of her. Garvin started after Stephanie. Shots came from behind him. He reached for Nick's mind and found blinding pain. He let his anger blaze all around him. Enemy minds backed off.

He grabbed Stephanie and the other, urged them toward the gazebo. Someone was in there. A consciousness shimmered. Garvin reached for Stephanie. There was a volley and the other Mohawk went down. Garvin had Stephanie by the arm. Their minds were linked. He pulled her toward the shimmering portal. Then a mind at the edge of the park grabbed hers and wrenched it away from Garvin. It broke her defenses. Her eyes rolled back, her tongue went down her throat, her life flickered out as he reached for her.

Garvin turned with his back to the portal and reached for the mind that had killed Stephanie. From behind, a large hand grabbed him, a rag went over his face. His arms and legs stopped obeying him. The slave dealer dragged Garvin out of his world.

Unconscious, drugged, Garvin felt worlds slide past like

dreams. His captor carried him far faster than anyone in time could imagine. From November to July they went like a wind.

As they did, in many places in Time the Oracle carried images of Garvin. Beings like the Talking Suitcase and young men and women like Nick who called themselves the Immortals' Companions began to act. One group of Companions set out immediately for Herself's world.

CHAPTER FOUR

AS THE Talking Suitcase had shown, Garvin was bought and sold on Herself's world in July. Shortly afterward, in a London where it was early spring, a man who called himself the Guvnor sat at late breakfast in his rooms at the Savoy Hotel. He was tall, with the body of a soldier and the face of a rogue. Something seemed to occur to him suddenly. He rang for the waiter. "A lady will be here momentarily. Show her in."

The Guvnor would not be described as looking like a thoughtful man, but he seemed preoccupied, staring at the floor and stroking his mustache until the door opened and the woman appeared. She was dressed in black, with a large hat and veil. The cloak she wore seemed to bulge on the right side of her neck. She drew off the veil, revealing a lined face with infinitely ancient eyes. "Thorn," said the Guvnor, rising. She opened the cloak and showed a sleeping baby's head growing next to the old one. "And the Rose."

He motioned her to a chair. "An Immortal on this world? Hardly expected that."

The Thorn and Rose remained standing. THE DANGER

UNDERSCORES THE IMPORTANCE, she told him. I HAVE
AN OFFER FOR YOU, GUVNOR.

"No good has ever come of any dealing I've ever had with
the Immortals."

THERE IS A FEE OF A THOUSAND CREDITS.

"Hard for me to use as an enemy of the Goblins."

AND OUR HELP IN ESTABLISHING A MERCENARY
ARMY ON THE WORLD OF YOUR CHOICE.

"My life on this world suits me."

NOT FOR LONG. RIDERS AND THEIR CREATURES
ARE EVERYWHERE.

"Part of the Immortals' unblemished record of failure."

THE ORACLE INDICATES THAT THERE IS A CHANCE
TO CHANGE ALL OF THAT ON A PLACE ONLY A FEW
WORLDS FROM HERE. WHAT OTHER CHOICE DO YOU
HAVE, GUVNOR? DO YOU NOT FEEL TIME CLOSING
IN ON YOU AND YOUR WIND?

The Guvnor snorted. "The Oracle shows you so much and
you win so rarely. What is it this time?"

ONCE THIS IS SHOWN THERE IS NO TURNING
BACK. YOU ARE COMMITTED TO OUR PROJECT. The
Thorn turned her ancient eyes on him.

The Guvnor sighed and nodded. The Rose suddenly opened
her bright child's eyes, and the Guvnor, fascinated, saw the
Oracle's vision of Garvin hurtling through Time.

A few worlds away, in what Garvin would have thought
of as eastern Canada, the Thorn and Rose's operatives were
busy. They set in motion a chain of orders that ended with
an old scout named Uncle. He carried a message out of a
wilderness known as Hotlands into the forest of Frontier District Four in a nation that called itself the Republic. He was
headed for the Guardian's court of a telepath named Scarecrow.

When he arrived at the town where it was being held, he
avoided the Citizen guards, nontelepaths like himself. He
stayed beneath the notice of the trained telepaths, the Select
of the Republic.

From the back of the crowd, he watched Scarecrow conduct a case. THERE COMES BEFORE THE COURT LAMI OF PINE FARM, ACCUSED OF STEALING COMMUNAL PROPERTY, announced a young Select aide. Lami, in Citizen's denim, slouched forward head down. All eyes were on Scarecrow, the Guardian. He was tall and blond and a little uncomfortable looking in his long white robes. "Lami, what have you to say?" he asked in a flat voice.

Lami shook his head, said nothing. "Then we must see," Scarecrow said, and his blue eyes clouded over slightly as the Guardian deftly entered the Citizen's mind. Images, emotions were taken and transmitted to the people assembled. They saw through the man's own eyes the lumber he had stolen being carted away. They felt his thoughts as he did it. "Twenty years of the worst, hardest work the farm council can think up. They hated my father before me too." There were images of council members turning away without listening to him.

Scarecrow's mind withdrew from the Citizen. THE SENTENCE IS SIXTY HOURS OF EXTRA LABOR OVER THE NEXT MONTH. I ASK ALSO THAT THE COUNCIL OF PINE FARM REVIEW THIS CITIZEN'S WORK SCHEDULE. I WILL ASK THEM WHAT HAS BEEN DECIDED WHEN THE SENTENCE HAS BEEN SERVED. Scarecrow smiled a little crookedly. "All right?" he asked the accused, who nodded.

There was a brief pause while the court waited for the next case to be called. In that moment the old scout pushed forward. "Scarecrow!" he called. Guards and a young Select aide moved to stop him.

The Guardian looked his way. "Uncle!"

"Guardian's Intercession," said the scout. Scarecrow reached out and blocked the other Select from the mind of the old man. He alone saw an image of a frail figure with milky eyes. There was also a name: Grim Reaper. Scarecrow immediately called a ten-minute recess.

* * *

Two days later he drove himself in a small jeeplike rover to Axblade, a town near the border of his district. His long hair tied back, dressed in denims, he drove past the barns and corrals on the outskirts of the town. Scarecrow swerved slightly as his mind came into contact with the young Select captain commanding Axblade.

A corporal of rangers brought the guards to attention as Scarecrow drove through the palisade gates and parked the jeep at a crazy angle on the edge of the town green. He had sent word ahead to have a saddle horse ready, and one was led toward him as he arrived. A cluster group of children appeared and watched him. Their tutors tried to move them away. Scarecrow smiled. "This is nothing official. I'm just passing through, enjoying the spring." The voice was flat, but the smile was real. He scooped up a child; others gathered around him as the Select captain appeared. Scarecrow smiled and nodded at him, put the child down, and reached out to the horse. It was a big gray gelding. Scarecrow patted it, touched its mind before swinging up into the saddle.

The captain stood nearby. He had been out working in the sun and mud and wanted Scarecrow to see and remember that. Frontier service in moderation was looked at with favor back in New Liberty, the capital. A recommendation from the Guardian, even one who looked as if he had gone native and become a Citizen, was worthwhile. Scarecrow could see the other's career: a couple of years on the frontier, a season or two on coastal patrol, some time with Security, and a lifetime in the committees and councils of New Liberty.

As he turned the horse's head toward the west, Scarecrow knew that the captain was curious about what brought him to Axblade. Wordlessly, he expressed his regret at not being able to stay, hinted at official missions, and assured him that he was one of the best young officers assigned to District Four in recent years. That was meant to dazzle him and cover Scarecrow's escape.

It worked. As he trotted out of town, the captain glowed with pride. Scarecrow's position as Guardian was somewhere between that of commissar and resident holy fool. The children ran beside him until at the west gate of the town he waved and broke into a canter.

As Guardian, Scarecrow's actions could be called into question only by certain secret councils back at New Liberty. His duty was the protection of the forests and people of Frontier District Four. He was respected by the telepathic Select and worshipped by the Citizens. Yet he found himself sneaking through the district like a fugitive. He cast about to see if he was being followed before turning his horse south toward the border.

He felt a curiosity tinged with excitement. A question that had been at the back of his mind, unformulated, was about to be answered. Select called them ghosts, the thoughts that could hum in brains and haunt them. It was considered bad form to let yours intrude on another Select.

Scarecrow moved south briskly. Axblade was about five miles from the edge of the forest. The horse carried him through the new green woods as the Guardian probed gently around him. He brushed against a telepathic mind and quickly withdrew from contact. It was a border patrol, a dozen cavalry headed by a select cadet. The cadet's attention was focused to the south and Hotlands.

Scarecrow waited until they had passed by him toward the east. His horse trotted forward past a pillbox and a fire trench next to the road. The path twisted several times. Then the trees stopped and Scarecrow was looking out at two miles of open ground. Nothing stirred except for the disappearing rear rider of the border patrol. About a quarter of a mile to the west was an observation tower. It was staffed with Citizens, combination border police and fire wardens. Scarecrow deftly entered the minds of the ones on duty and turned them to other things. Each time one was about to concentrate on a horseman heading south over the dead ground, he or she would be distracted by something else.

The two miles of flat ground was the border of the Republic, providing a clear field of fire and a sanitary cordon. It was the first line of defense. The twisting forest paths and little towns like Axblade were the second line. In theory, nothing was supposed to cross the border. In practice there were trappers and traders who did. But not Guardians, who were never under any circumstances supposed to leave their districts.

As Scarecrow neared the scrub pine and rock outcroppings of Hotlands, he felt something subtly off in the rhythm of life. Around him the first hint of dusk; night life began to stir; light-loving birds and animals sought water and shelter. He saw albino oak trees, a two-headed lizard. He pulled his horse up near a prominent rock outcropping and cast around him. Insects and plants he filtered out. There were birds and a snake and a squirrel. It took him a moment to realize that the squirrel was wrong. "Uncle," he said aloud, and part of a tree moved, a buckskin clad figure revealed himself.

Uncle was a legend of the border regions, born at an observation station of a ranger wife and, some said, a Hotlander father. "You are right on time, Guardian." The man's voice was almost a whisper. "Grim Reaper was always strict about that."

Grim Reaper was another legend, one that tangled up with Uncle's. Both went back to Moriaph's Wars of thirty or forty years past. When Scarecrow had questioned Uncle two days before, the scout hadn't known much more than what he'd shown the Guardian. A Hotlander, a trained mental adept but not a shaman, had contacted Uncle, shown him an image of Scarecrow and then one of an old man with milky eyes. The name given to the old man was Grim Reaper.

"It looked like him, Guardian, or what he would look like by now," Uncle said as they turned their horses into Hotlands. "I can remember him when the tribes came out of the south last time. They smashed up things, burned every house and building they found. Until they came up against Grim Reaper. He stopped them at Fire Gates Citadel for weeks. Moriaph herself came from out west and relieved him."

Scarecrow touched the old scout's mind with his. Images appeared of Hotland shamans hanged and their encampments burned as Grim Reaper gave the war back to them. Then Scarecrow saw the scene he had encountered before in citizens' minds: Grim Reaper went mad. The tall, dark-haired Select stood on the parade grounds at the Fire Gates, tearing at his robes, his mind ringing in the minds of those around him. SELECT ARE LIKE SHEEP DOGS TRYING TO PROTECT A FLOCK. BUT THE WOLVES ARE NOT INTERESTED IN THE SHEEP. THEY HAVE COME FOR US.

That day he abandoned his district and disappeared. Officially, he had been found and returned to New Liberty for treatment. There were stories that he had been cured and was still serving the Republic in some minor post far to the north. No Select wanted to think too closely about it. No Citizen from District Four believed it at all. Too many lonely trappers had felt the touch of a familiar mind, too often many people in the same village would all sit up on the edge of sleep aware of their old Guardian. Rumor said he lived on in Hotlands as a great shaman.

As they traveled south, Scarecrow probed ahead of them. He caught animal minds, furtive and wary. Then there was something that wasn't quite a night animal. I AM MOLE, it told him.

Uncle felt it also. He nodded. "That's the one who showed me Grim Reaper." Scarecrow probed the other mind, felt himself blocked. The mind that did this was cruder than his own but not as crude as a shaman. He hesitated. The light was waning. He wondered if this could be a trap. I WILL SHOW YOU THIS, the other mind told him.

The Guardian felt and saw as Mole had. Out in Hotlands, in a primitive and squalid town the name of which meant nothing to the Guardian, a stunted albino was born. Mole was the nicest name he was called. As a child, he had learned to hide from the sun and come out at night. Children tormented him; adults kicked him. His mother died and he was put out of the house, lived in the woods in a small cave. As he learned to survive, he learned also how to keep enemies away, turning the fears that he found in their own minds against them.

Scarecrow moved into Hotlands, following the story as it was shown to him. Mole at about twelve emerged from his burrow one evening. Another mind found his, turned aside his frantic thrusts, and soothed his fright.

It was a trained Select consciousness. Scarecrow could recognize that. The mind was that of a very great shaman who called himself Grim Reaper. He brought Mole into his own place, washed and fed him, taught him to use his mental powers. As Scarecrow absorbed this, he saw in the last light a small, pale figure. At first sight of the Hotlander, Uncle stopped and motioned Scarecrow on.

Scarecrow rode just behind Mole. He had seen dead Hotlanders and he had seen prisoners, even had to interrogate some. But to follow one into an unknown woods at night made the back of his neck prickle. He cast around him in the night. Amid animals and birds just stirring and Uncle receding in the background, a mind found Scarecrow's. CONGRATULATIONS. YOUR CURIOSITY IS YOUR GREATEST STRENGTH. It was another Select.

Scarecrow knew that it was Grim Reaper. IT HAS HAD LITTLE EXERCISE LATELY. He projected images of council meetings, of Select in white robes and bored expressions, of minds linked and thought elsewhere.

There was a tinge of amusement in the other mind. NONETHELESS, SOMETHING DREW YOU OUT HERE. WAS IT NAGGING DOUBTS IN THE BACK OF THE BRAIN? I HAVE BEEN CURIOUS ABOUT YOU, MY SUCCESSOR. Scarecrow saw images of himself in white robes or in worn denims, moving in public ceremony or walking with his mate and child at his home in Weatherhill. Some of these images he recognized as secondhand, gleaned from the minds of Citizens who had seen him. Others were firsthand and alien, tinged with the same feeling he got from the mind of Mole. YOU SPIED ON ME, AND ON MY FAMILY. Scarecrow halted and began to probe back to Uncle.

YOU WILL FORGIVE ME. SO MUCH WORSE HAS BEEN DONE TO YOU AND YOURS ALREADY. SO MUCH WORSE IS CONTEMPLATED THAT YOU WILL FORGET THAT THIS EVER OFFENDED YOU. Scarecrow moved forward again and became aware of other minds like

Mole's in the dark around him. I HAD TO BE SURE. Grim Reaper was soothing, drawing Scarecrow on just as he had brought Mole out of his cave.

LET ME SHOW YOU WHAT MY APPRENTICES HAVE FOUND. Grim Reaper probed toward Scarecrow, who blocked at the outer edge of his own consciousness but absorbed what he was shown. There was a dusty square in a squalid village. Scarecrow saw a crowd of Hotlanders, barefoot children suffering from malnutrition, beggars with wasting diseases, warriors with missing arms and mutilated faces.

It was a crossroads town of mud huts around a stone keep two stories high. A man dressed in animal skins, his face tattooed, waved a stick with a human skull on top of it. This was a shaman from far to the south of the village where he spoke. He was preaching about the coming of a great war leader. The shaman reached a pitch of excitement, then summoned his powers.

The man's eyes went blank as Scarecrow watched through others' memories. His eyes rolled and each member of the crowd saw a crude image of a huge man with gigantic shoulders standing on a pile of human skulls. RUMACK WILL LEAD US TO A THOUSAND WORLDS OF PLUNDER. Rumack's eyes were yellow and fierce; his face was black with tattooing. He opened his mouth and roared as the shaman showed him to the crowd. THE ROAD TO THE STARS GOES THROUGH THE REPUBLIC! The shaman's powers were exhausted. He sank back and fell on his knees. But the crowd was excited, yelling for Rumack, whom they had never seen or heard of before.

In the light from a half-moon and the stars, Scarecrow was aware of a wall in front of him and of Mole standing aside. Part of the wall fell away: a door. Scarecrow hesitated. A second Hotlander moved to take the reins of his horse. Scarecrow probed back behind him again, looking for Uncle. Then a light shone and a figure beckoned him forward.

In contrast to the image of Rumack which he had just been shown, this figure was frail and white haired. GRIM REAPER? Scarecrow stepped toward the light.

SCARECROW. I KNEW YOU WERE ONE WHO AL-WAYS HAD QUESTIONS UNANSWERED. The old man allowed the younger Guardian into his Umbra. He let Scarecrow feel the pulse of Time. He showed him worlds like lighted windows in a dark night.

CHAPTER FIVE

GRIM REAPER spoke aloud in a voice cracked from disuse. "I have traveled through Time to some of those worlds, Scarecrow. I have been bought and sold at Goblin Market. I have bought and sold others. I will show you what I have seen. You may despise me when I'm done. You may hate some of what I am going to show you. All that I ask is that you believe me."

Scarecrow sat cross-legged on the clean floor of the ancient building. Grim Reaper sat on cushions and leaned on a saddle. Scarecrow opened his mind and the other's memories flooded in. There was a young woman with a slash of black hair like a cropped horse mane. She wore a black uniform. Her mind caught Grim Reaper's as he walked through District Four many years back.

SHE CALLED HERSELF A COMPANION OF THE IM-MORTALS. SHE TOLD ME SHE HAD COME TO SHOW ME TIME. Scarecrow felt the terror Grim Reaper had felt at being aware of the infinite worlds, of the heartbeat of Time. The Companion led him to neighboring worlds, empty of human life. Then she took him further away to inhabited worlds, to worlds where the people knew about Time, to worlds on what were called the Time Lanes which lived off the commerce of Time.

THAT WAS BEFORE THE LAST GREAT WAR. Scarecrow caught images of blood and smoke, burned villages, and hanged Hotland shamans in the war that had ended with Moriaph's Peace thirty years before. I FOUGHT NOT JUST FOR MY DISTRICT AND MY PEOPLE BUT FOR MY OWN PERSONAL SURVIVAL. I ALONE ON THIS WORLD KNEW OF THE EXISTENCE OF TIME. ONLY I KNEW THE HORRORS THAT WAIT OUT THERE.

Scarecrow felt Grim Reaper's nerves snap at the war's end. He stood with Grim Reaper at the Fire Gates and touched the minds of all assembled with images of sheep captured along with their sheep dogs. THERE HAVE BEEN HARD YEARS AND HARD TRAVEL SINCE, Grim Reaper told him. Scarecrow saw trade routes and human merchandise, hunting parties setting out to pillage and enslave. All of it was firsthand.

I WENT TO GOBLIN MARKET TWICE. ONCE AFTER I WAS CAPTURED AND WAS SOLD THERE. ONCE AFTER I WON MY FREEDOM AND RETURNED TO SELL OTHERS: TELEPATHS LIKE OURSELVES. Scarecrow saw pens of light, felt the suffering and greed as thousands of humans, telepath and nontelepath, were bought and sold. He saw the green skins and flat faces of the Goblins who ran the place.

THE IMMORTALS' COMPANIONS FOUND ME ONCE AGAIN. THEY HAD A MESSAGE FOR ME. MY YEARS IN TIME HAD PREPARED ME FOR WHAT THEY HAD TO SHOW. I MUST LET YOU SEE WITHOUT THAT PREPARATION TO CUSHION THE SHOCK. Scarecrow saw the forests of District Four burn. The towns lay in ruins. Over the charred, broken citadel of the Fire Gates, thousands of minds formed an image of the tattooed, screaming face Scarecrow had been shown earlier. RUMACK was the name on every mind.

The images were vivid but not firsthand, not substantial. One layer seemed to peal away and reveal another; the events wavered as he tried to concentrate on them. What he saw next was horrible. Lines of prisoners, Citizen and Select, bound and drugged and weeping, were herded away into Time.

THIS IS A TRICK, Scarecrow told Grim Reaper, breaking contact between their minds. "This isn't real," he whispered. "Someone made this up."

"The Oracle," Grim Reaper told him, "has shown these things to many who have come to it in the last few years."

He reached out and found Scarecrow's Umbra again. OUR WORLD IS RICH, SCARECROW. IN THE REPUBLIC ALONE THERE ARE OVER TWENTY THOUSAND HIGHLY DEVELOPED TELEPATHS AND MILLIONS OF CITIZENS TRAINED TO OBEY. WE ARE PRICELESS CARGO, SCARECROW.

There was much more. It was almost dawn when Scarecrow left Uncle at the edge of Hotlands and made his way back through the forests of the Republic to Axblade. There he got into his rover and drove back to the town of Weatherhill, where he lived. It was still early morning when he entered his observatory and had an orderly bring him his white robes.

Scarecrow looked out the window at Weatherhill. The observatory was an ancient citadel built on high ground back in the time of the Wizards' Wars. Here telephones and radio connected the Citizens of District Four with their Guardian. Here factors enabled Scarecrow to communicate telepathically with Select many miles away. Through his windows, Scarecrow could see down to the white wooden houses of the town, down through the square and across the common, down to the cavalry barracks and the palisades that marked the boundary of the town, out to the woods that surrounded it.

The ordinary business of a spring morning was suspended. A hunting party had delayed in setting out, farmers hadn't moved to the fields, cluster groups of children waited with their teachers outside the schoolhouse, troopers stood at parade rest before the barracks. There was an air of expectation; the Guardian's aides and orderlies, Select and Citizen, stood by, waiting for Scarecrow to be ready. Looking out, he saw

Amre, his mate, come out of her dispensary and stand, hands on hips, shaking her head at all the excitement. Her dark hair was tied back. She looked up the hill toward him, and Scarecrow could feel her amusement, her tolerance for the Guardian's eccentricities.

Two aides, both Select, stood in the observatory. One wore the white robes of ceremony, the other the tunic and pants of the army. One represented the purity of purpose of the telepathic rulers, the other the sureness and might of the state. Scarecrow paused for a moment. It was not quite eleven.

Out in District Four, all over its two-hundred-by-fifty miles, telepaths had moved into position, probed, and found their minds linked to others. They arranged themselves for the great Relay. They were junior cadets and senior officers, apprentices and veteran administrators, cluster groups of Select children on field trips with their tutors. Parties and single telepaths traveling along the Great East-West Road at the north border of District Four halted and dispersed into the woods.

Scarecrow nodded. The two aides looked at him, filled their minds with the image of their Guardian standing in the sunlight, trees and sky visible through the glass behind him. They broadcast this image, and others picked it up on the outskirts of the town and sent it further out into the district. The image of Scarecrow hovered in the air. Citizens sensed it. The forest seemed to be alive as thousands of telepaths stretched their minds and touched the consciousness of their neighbors. Birds rose in the trees; animals stopped, transfixed. The Select opened their minds to the Citizens around them, and for long moments the great Relay seemed to link every living thing within its reach.

Somewhere the mind of a Select child swooped erratically; elsewhere an old one lost its concentration for a moment. The telepaths were spread thin; the link was tenuous in places. Toward the border of District Three, a young geologist sensed a telepathic presence which tried to avoid her. A senior medical officer linked to her picked it up also. They tried to probe, but it was moving away from them. It brushed several other minds.

The image of Scarecrow hung in the air. With each mind it passed through it changed, lost its individuality, became less Scarecrow than an idealization of all Guardians, wise, serene, old in wisdom, smooth of face. His face became as one with the ancient wizards who had put the Republic together out of the chaos after the Holocaust a thousand years before. Scarecrow in his observatory shifted as he traveled through the minds of his district and became the symbol by which Select and Citizens recognized the idea of a Guardian.

The mind of each Select, trained since infancy, operated on three levels called the Umbra, the Curtain, and the Keep. The Umbra was where they dealt always with Citizens and usually with their own kind. Their training reduced communication to a set of symbols and images designed to evoke the proper ideas in the receiving mind.

Inside this outer layer was the Curtain. Here, even as he radiated well-being and serenity, Scarecrow kept his personal thoughts to himself. As a Select, he had learned from childhood the constant games of thrust and block that kept one part of his consciousness always alert, even when he slept. Within the Curtain were kept the secrets and business of District Four. Lately Scarecrow had been very careful about keeping this secure. Normally, a Select could allow another Select access to this area of mind. Now there were too many strange sights and troubling doubts rattling around in there.

Within the Curtain was the Keep, the innermost core of a Select's consciousness. Normally, no one was admitted there. The essence of a Select's being was there. A Keep was where the mind stood guard over the functions of the brain. Here, along with the most secret fears and dreams, was the vital center. Another mind getting in there could tear Scarecrow apart, could command his voice to speak, his limbs to move against his will. There an enemy could shut down the heart and lungs.

Above District Four, over the lumber camps and the clearings in the woods full of mills and truck farms, patrol planes could feel the probing of the great Relay. To the east in District Three and to the west in District Five, they were aware that the Relay was in effect. Word would reach Moriaph, warder of the border. It would get back to New Liberty. Scarecrow didn't care. He stood, radiating a feeling of calm, reaching out to touch his aides with it. Back into the forest it traveled, a Guardian's blessing to the people.

At half a dozen places Select, reaching out to share this with the Citizens around them, felt a fleeting touch of something alien. Some ignored it, some thought it was the presence of very young telepathic children misbehaving. Several would later report it. Scarecrow, in the secrecy of his Keep, held in readiness the excuse he could give if he were questioned about why he had activated the Relay. Security was lax. Hotland scouts were getting into the Republic.

Scarecrow projected a message, aware for a moment of the nearly one thousand telepaths and seventy thousand Citizens. Scarecrow asked them all to report anything unusual directly to him. He showed them what he meant: an image of a stranger, obviously out of place, wandering in the woods; unexplained lights in the dark; the feeling of an alien mind touching the fringes of consciousness. To show that, he gave a small taste of what he had felt out in Hotlands. The Relay stirred, surprised. The furtiveness, the touch of a mind trained to telepathy but not really domesticated was something even most of the Select hadn't encountered.

The Relay seemed to sway and lose coherence. Most Select could project and receive over a distance of half a mile. Beyond that the effect was extremely random, unreliable. At half a mile many of the telepaths in District Four were operating at a much wider range than they were used to. Their linkage with the minds nearest them began to slip.

Scarecrow summoned them again, spread a feeling of well-being and confidence. Then he took a step backward and signaled the two aides who watched him. They broke contact with the minds to which they were linked, and those minds did the same. The Relay disappeared. District Four resumed its routine.

Scarecrow wished he could have shown them all one thing that Grim Reaper had shown him. It had been given to him as a symbol of hope, and he didn't understand it. He thought about it as he dismissed his aides, removed his robe, and sank back on a couch to read and scan his daily reports.

Amre found him there shortly afterward. Scarecrow was asleep with his head back, defenseless. By reflex he scanned the mind that approached, recognized his mate, and mumbled a greeting.

As he did, Amre glimpsed the image that had been in his mind. It was a strange scene, an ancient city of glass and concrete which had not existed on their world for hundreds of years. In the foreground was a group of children. Their leader was a boy in his early teens. Seeing him, Amre felt the surge of hope that Grim Reaper had given to Scarecrow. The boy wore his hair like an apprentice forester, cropped with a short ridge running from front to back.

CHAPTER
SIX

SCARECROW WOKE up then. He still had a portable factor in his hands, his fingers resting on its keys. Pressing them, he could record sounds which would evoke his thoughts in any other telepath who activated it. "What strange sights do you expect to have reported, Guardian? Two-headed calves born? Drunken sentries seeing ghosts?"

Amre was teasing him, but her smile faded as she saw him hesitate, put aside his factor, and draw her down beside him. He sent an order that they not be disturbed, and activated a scrambler to hide his thoughts from outside the room. The life of deception didn't come easily to him. Amre knew he was hiding something.

She put that knowledge aside and sank down, laughed as their clothes came off in a tangle. Her understanding had nothing to do with telepathy. The only Select she could read was Scarecrow. She had known when they first met that he was attracted to her, even though he never looked at her directly. He used the Select trick of staring at her through the eyes of a third party. But Amre knew.

Scarecrow picked up from her mind memories of their first time together. It was summer of his first year in the district.

A Hotland raiding party came out of the south, led by a young shaman anxious to make his name. They were stopped and destroyed before they reached a village, but not before they had left the seeds of plague. It spread like forest fire and put a large part of District Four under quarantine.

As assistant Guardian, Scarecrow led a medical crew through quarantine lines. Amre, a novice medical orderly, was among them. In the next few weeks he forgot her in the exhaustion and horror. There were the silent, isolated cabins to be approached because minds mad with delirium still flickered inside. There were bloated corpses to be disposed of, fever fears of Citizens to soothe. Then one morning Scarecrow was sick.

It was said among Citizens that at times of danger Select became very scarce. Certainly at that time and place there wasn't another to be spared to care for a delirious assistant Guardian. The mind of a mad Select is like an unexploded bomb. Lashing out against a nightmare, he could kill every untrained mind around him. Scarecrow lay in fever, all the careful structure of his mind reduced to chaos. A woman with dark hair and cool hands appeared in his dreams. Amre flowed through Umbra, Curtain, and Keep.

Amre understood him as she never had another Select. It was she who saw his fears, took each one, and disarmed it. She talked to him and laughed to him, called him back again and again when he was ready to crush her mind with his.

When it was over, when his fever was gone and other Select were around, she was in love. She had found the person behind the Select. Scarecrow had been open before her in a way no Citizen had ever been. There were the usual jokes when they mated about what happened when Citizen and Select got together. They waited out the jokes and pursued their lives, she as orderly, then as medical officer, he as assistant and then as Guardian.

The Citizens approved. Scarecrow was Guardian in their minds years before the appointment took place. There were three children born to them. The oldest and youngest, a boy and a girl, were tested and found to be sensitive. They were

Selected by the Republic and taken to be trained. The parents, of course, had no further word of them. The middle child, Miche, seven, they loved very much. But the other children, now fourteen and five, somewhere in the Republic, haunted them both.

Two minds linked with each other that same night in woods near the Great East-West Road north of Weatherhill. One mind had been waiting in the dark. It was old and highly trained, an Immortal like the Talking Suitcase. The other had just appeared through a portal that lay close to a huge oak tree. This mind was untrained and crude compared to the other. It probed and found the one who waited. THORN?

YES. GUVNOR?

AT YOUR SERVICE. AND THE ROSE?

SHE SLEEPS FOR THE MOMENT. THE WIND? At the mention of the name, the branches of the oak rustled in the night. The mind of the Immortal called the Thorn retracted for a moment with involuntary revulsion. The one called the Guvnor didn't seem to notice. The Thorn continued. THEY WILL PASS HERE SOON. IT IS CALLED A SELECT CLUSTER GROUP. The Guvnor saw an image of a group of children, about thirty of them, all around twelve years old. Half a dozen adults were with them, their tutors. YOUR WIND MUST BE PREPARED TO EAT ITS FILL.

IT IS MORE THAN READY. THEY WERE ALL GOING TO DIE ANYWAY, I TAKE IT.

THE ORACLE SHOWED THEM DOOMED TO GOB-LIN MARKET. THERE WAS NO OTHER PROBABILITY.

WHAT ABOUT THE BODIES? The Guvnor asked.

The Thorn indicated a small owl held hypnotized on a branch of a nearby tree. IT IS WHAT THEY CALL A BURNER. IT HAS A SMALL EXPLOSIVE CHARGE AT-TACHED TO IT. THEIR ENEMIES HARASS THEM WITH THESE SOMETIMES.

"You seem to have covered everything." The Guvnor reached up into the trees with his mind. The Wind rustled the leaves. The Thorn cast her mind down the road, probed carefully far into the night. Then the Thorn seemed to shake herself in the dark. Like a small candle coming to light, another mind probed. Childlike, half awake, the Rose reached out and touched the Thorn and the Guvnor. She reached up and the Wind moved gently in the branches. The Immortals are all haunted, thought the Guvnor.

I HAVE CONTACT WITH THEM. HAVE YOUR WIND READY, GUVNOR.

The Guvnor felt the transport approaching. It was Select Cluster Twenty out of New Liberty, fifteen boys and fifteen girls, the jewels of the Republic. Selected at the age of two weeks, brought together in a cluster group at six months, they were each of them capable of killing a dozen Citizens with a careless blow. In white tunics, long hair tied back, they sat in small groups or alone. Some used mind tracks, others sounds; music hummed in the air. One of the tutors groaned inwardly at the thought of all thirty of them entering puberty together. A group of the children played block and thrust, giggling aloud. The word CALM was repeated slowly, silently. Colors changed into taste and taste into shapes.

They all felt it at once: a mind childlike and clear, trained but unlike any Select. HERE I SIT/IN THE DARK/ I HAVE A SECRET/ CAN YOU GUESS IT? It seemed like a childhood rhyme that couldn't quite be remembered, a color once seen but now just beyond recall. They all felt drawn by it. The tutor-driver pulled the giant transport off the main road and onto a spur to get closer.

Was it a joke or a test? When they were under the oak, the transport motor stopped and the child mind was replaced by another one just as strange to them but infinitely older. It swept every mind with an image of a boy. There was a name that they all heard. GARVIN. For a moment it was all any of them, child or tutor, could think of. They had been caught by the Rose and stung by the Thorn.

One of the tutors became aware that the driver was slumped at the wheel, his body a shell. One of the children lay empty eyed and then another. Something was rushing around and around the transport. Minds were being unraveled from bodies. The head tutor rose to his feet and probed. The Wind moved clockwise in tighter and tighter circles. The head tutor's mind filled with the image and name of Garvin, and he fell dead face first on the floor. Outside, the Thorn stepped behind a tree and guided the owl. It flew straight up the exhaust pipe and exploded. The inside of the transport turned fire-red and thirty-six lifeless bodies were consumed.

The Wind sailed out through the portal and back into the Republic. It went through the fire and out into Time again and again. Inside the Wind all the newly absorbed minds reflected the face and name of Garvin. The Wind returned to the treetops. The Rose, bright eyed, watched the flames.

The Guvnor felt something coming toward the portal from out in Time. He acted instinctively, moving to break the fall of the one who appeared. It was Garvin. The Guvnor lowered him to the ground. He probed the boy's mind and stepped back quickly. Garvin was in shock.

The Thorn indicated a bundle of clothes. GET HIM DRESSED IN THESE BEFORE THE FLAMES ATTRACT ATTENTION.

"I'm a good man in a tight corner," said the Guvnor. "But I've never had any strategic sense. I can't understand, for instance, why an Immortal is so concerned for the welfare of a Rider and Steed."

FOR THE SAME REASON THAT AN IMMORTAL WOULD DEAL WITH ONE WHO HAS A TAME WIND, A CREATURE OF THE GOBLINS.

"Perhaps the back of my head's too narrow."

I HOPE AT LEAST YOU UNDERSTAND WHAT A RICH PASTURE THIS COULD BE FOR YOUR WIND. The Thorn bent down and began pulling off the elaborate eighteenth-century costume that Garvin wore.

Amre was awake when an orderly brought word of the transport disaster to Scarecrow. "Is this the call you've been expecting, Scarecrow?" He knew she understood more than he had intended. He also knew he needed her help. He nodded when she said, "I can drive."

He was searching the messenger's mind for details. There were the remains of a Select cluster group in the ruins. There was also a survivor, a hunter apprentice on the grass a short distance away. The ranger sergeant on the scene didn't think anyone could have lived through the explosion. But as he approached, he had felt telepathic activity. This was an unusual event such as the Guardian had told them to report. Scarecrow staggered out the door and into his Rover.

Amre drove skillfully down the twisting dirt track onto a logging road, then onto the great highway. Scarecrow sat beside her, trying not to read in her mind the list of reasons why a Citizen should never trust a Select. There was the old joke again: How do you hide a horse from a Select? You leave it out in a field and never think of it. Select needed Citizens to feed and clothe them but never noticed them outside of that. Scarecrow saw in Amre's mind the image of Garvin from his dreams and knew he had put her in great danger.

His hands clenched the door of the rover as they came within sight of brushfires that still burned. Amre brought the rover up alongside the fire trucks and ranger transports. Scarecrow scanned for the strange mind and found it. There was trauma and unconsciousness; the boy had been severely knocked around. He was a telepath, as Scarecrow had been told. He had little trouble getting past the other's defenses.

The name was Garvin. He had fallen to the Republic through Time. He had rushed past more worlds than Scarecrow could imagine. Something inside the boy's mind brushed him away. 'back off,' it told him.

RIDER! Scarecrow recognized it from what Grim Reaper had told him.

'my steed has come to grief. repair him and i will be on my way.'

YOU ARE NOT GIVING ORDERS, RIDER. Scarecrow broke contact then. Amre was already out of the rover and over beside the boy, examining him. HE IS A HUNTER APPRENTICE WHO RAN AWAY FROM HIS FAMILY, Scarecrow told the ranger sergeant.

Scarecrow reached out and touched the minds of the fire fighters who had scorched their faces fighting their way through the flame. He thanked the ones who were trying to make sense of the tangle of charred bodies. He wondered how much more of this all of them were going to see. At the same time he kept a watch on the mind of the boy and the Rider who controlled him.

Amre crouched next to the local medical orderly. "There are lacerations and bruises, none of them really serious. We believe he is in shock, Guardian. Is that the case?" Scarecrow nodded. He could feel in Amre's mind the question she didn't ask aloud. Who is he?

HE IS A HUNTER APPRENTICE WHO RAN AWAY ABOUT A WEEK AGO. HE MUST HAVE BEEN NEARBY WHEN THE EXPLOSION OCCURRED. THAT MANY SELECT MINDS GOING ALL AT ONCE WOULD HAVE CREATED SOMETHING LIKE A WAVE OF HORROR. The medical orderly nodded, feeling privileged to share the Guardian's confidences. But Amre had seen Scarecrow walk into trees when he wasn't paying attention. She recognized the face that lay before her now from Scarecrow's vision. WE WILL TAKE HIM BACK TO WEATHERHILL FOR FURTHER EXAMINATION. I WILL TREAT THE SHOCK MYSELF.

Amre looked down. Garvin was the right age to be their eldest son. He had Scarecrow's hair color and her eyes, or nearly enough. She got him onto a stretcher and oversaw its being fitted into the back of the rover. Scarecrow had counted on this.

He was going to need Amre's help to heal this skinny, bruised, terrified stranger. In return, the boy was supposed to save them. He felt Amre's doubts overwhelmed by her concern and love. The night had disappeared; first light was showing. Amre sat in back with the patient. Scarecrow drove as carefully as he could and kept watch over them.

CHAPTER
SEVEN

THERE WERE days and nights in which Garvin drifted between waking and sleeping. Hands sat him up and fed him. He tried to speak but something would stop him. He tried to open his eyes and found that he couldn't. A cool hand passed over his face. Another mind came into contact with his. Garvin felt himself blocking it. He realized that he didn't want to, that more than anything he wanted to sit up and ask questions. Even as that thought occurred to him, it slipped away. He had trouble holding on to any kind of thought. Once, at a time between light and dark, a woman's voice sang very softly. She sang the oldest songs, the ones we all know.

Garvin grasped at that, the voice, the dying light, the song. It all came back in a moment. New York at Christmas and going to the Santa at Macy's, Claire leaving work early to wait for him after school on his first day, the picture of his father going on the subway alone for the first time, kids playing in the street, cars and candy stores. He was breathing in short gasps. Something in his head was trying to make him stop remembering, but it all came out: Mohawks and

Nick and Roger and the Old One. There was that awful morning and Stephanie going out like a spark.

Garvin was sobbing. It was as painful as vomiting. He was aware of two forces. One in his mind was working to choke off his thoughts and paralyze him. There was also a room which he was in where there were people telling him aloud and in thoughts that it was all right and everything was going to be fine. The thing inside was trying to control him again, to have him scan the others in the room. He would not do it. That place was safety. He felt his breathing stop.

Amre washed Garvin's face with a towel. She knew. She looked up at Scarecrow, who leaned against the wall. He had tried for the thousandth time to get through to the boy. He was blocked once again. Brushing his mate's mind, he found her thinking about the Retreat, the prison hospital where deviant Select were kept. He had served a brief apprenticeship there, as most young Select did. One night a hundred mad and damaged minds turned the trees and bushes of the island madhouse into the heads of men and horses aflame and laughing.

"You think that if you say nothing and show me nothing I won't be charged," she said.

"And I am right," he told her. "A crime committed by a Citizen at the behest of a Select is a crime committed by that Select."

"Look at what I saw, Scarecrow." He touched her mind lightly and found a telepathic fragment which he had caught too. It was an alien world of concrete and bricks, of color and noise. "I know of nothing like that," Amre said. "Not in Hotlands or High Peru or Tibet."

"It is an adventure track distorted by fever. . . ." He began to tell her. Then he caught her memory of him turning over in his sleep a few days before they had found Garvin. There was the same world; there was the face of the one they had later found in the woods. "You care for him now under the orders of your Guardian." He turned away and looked out the window where it was night.

Amre persisted. She was going to know the truth. "His hands and feet are uncallused. He is no hunter apprentice."

"There was a long hospital stay."

"I find no evidence of that, Guardian."

Scarecrow bit his lip and showed her the fate that awaited if he was caught and she knew too much. Miche would be taken away, and Amre would be assigned as special medical officer up north in the ice fields.

"Scarecrow, if you are taken away, I might as well be in the ice fields as anywhere. I couldn't remain here. I would volunteer for hazardous duty just to show you it isn't just Select who can make stupid gestures." She stood behind him and put her arms around him. "To save that boy, we have to act together. Your secret, whatever it is, makes that impossible. Who is he, Scarecrow, and what have you seen that is driving you?"

With a kind of relief, he opened his mind and showed her Nobody and Hotlands. He showed her Rumack and his shamans and the promise he had been given of help from Time.

Suddenly he felt the boy's mind in his. It passed right through Umbra and Curtain as if they weren't there. Scarecrow was shaken. For an instant he felt the Rider, an ancient consciousness twisted around the boy's limbic system. Garvin's mind was in his Keep.

RIDER, WHAT DO YOU WANT?

RETURN TO THE PORTAL WHERE I WAS FOUND. It was Garvin's mind but the Rider's will. DO THAT AND I WILL DO MY BEST TO FORGET THAT I HAVE BEEN KIDNAPPED.

On the pallet Garvin's eyes hung half open. His hands were tense at his sides. He was in a trance. Scarecrow tried to move toward Garvin and found himself sliding helplessly along the wall.

Amre was on the floor beside Garvin. She placed a hand on his shoulder and called softly. His eyes rolled open; a trickle of drool appeared at the side of his mouth. For a moment the eyes focused on her and there was the hint of a smile. His mind stopped battering Scarecrow's. The boy looked at them both, nodded, and went back to sleep.

THE DANGER IS TOO GREAT FOR ME TO KEEP HIM HERE.

"I have dealt with the deliriums of Select before, Scarecrow." In her mind he saw the awareness that always existed of the danger to Citizen from telepath. Their main protection was their own anonymity. Amre's concern for her patient was taking over and carrying them on. "We will sleep in shifts."

OTHER SELECT WILL PICK UP HIS THOUGHTS.

"Move a scrambler up here from the observatory."

THERE ARE MY AIDES. THERE ARE THE GARRISON OFFICERS.

"Give orders that will keep as many of them away from here as possible." As she spoke, it all became logical. Scarecrow knew he had endangered her. He also knew that if they couldn't save Garvin, all was lost anyway. In the next few nights the Rider gained control of Garvin many times. Always the boy came around and realized what was happening before it was too late. Finally everyone, Select and Citizen, Garvin and Rider, collapsed, exhausted.

Next morning, early, Garvin woke just as it was getting light. He looked around and realized that he was lying on a pallet on a wooden floor in a white room. There were bandages on his right leg and arm, but the wounds did no more than itch. He was hungry and needed to use the bathroom. Standing, he realized it was some time since he had gotten up. There was an enormous sadness that he couldn't quite remember. He wrapped a blanket around himself against the chill and walked to a window.

He was on the second floor of a large wooden house. Turning, he could see a tall gray stone tower to which the house was attached. There was an open field right outside and a town of wood and stone spread below that. Beyond, rising and falling with the ground, was the forest. The sun hit dark pine and new leaves. There was a bugle call and half a dozen mounted figures trotted across the green and down through the town. A woman in an apron passed from one building to another. Something that sounded almost like a car engine began. Near the edge of the woods, a boy a little younger than Garvin dug his bare heels into the ribs of an old horse, driving cows ahead of him. Smoke rose from the chimney of the building the woman had entered, carrying with it the smell of frying ham.

Garvin remembered his hunger and his need for a bathroom. As he turned from the window, his memory gave him Stephanie and Nick and home. An enormous sob escaped as if it had been trapped. Leaning against the wall, he wept. Something stirred within his mind. He stopped crying, not wanting the Rider to seize his grief and pain. He ground his teeth and never cried again.

The bathroom was right off the room he was in. It was big and plain, with a sink and tub and toilet which he used. There was a mirror into which he tried to look, but his eyes wouldn't rise. He felt his legs give way. The Rider was asserting its control. Garvin dropped the blanket and stood shivering in the chill just as he had been taught as a Mohawk. He kept his balance and struggled to look in the mirror: His neck ached, pain shot through his head, but finally his eyes met his own eyes.

It seems like nothing, but it was a victory. That was the moment when Garvin began to be Warchild. The muscles in his neck strained, his teeth ground, his eyelids felt heavy. He looked deep into his own eyes as if to see what was inside him.

Then he noticed that his hair was growing in, obscuring his Mohawk. On a shelf were soap and towels and a razor. His fingers turned to rubber when he tried to reach for the razor. The thing inside was afraid of the sharp edge. That was enough for Garvin to thrust a clumsy hand out and jam his thumb against the blade. Blood welled up and his Rider flinched.

Garvin washed away the blood, aware of his Rider's fear. He had found a way of fighting it. He walked to the bedroom. On a chair was a pair of shorts and a long, sleeveless denim shirt. The kid he had seen riding had worn the same. He put them on. The shirt went on over the shorts and reached half-way to his knees. They weren't new and they were a little big, but they would do. He felt almost the way he had as a Mohawk.

He went out a door and down the stairs, wood creaking under his bare feet. He went through an open door. Standing inside was a tall woman in white shirt and pants, with her dark hair tied back. She looked tired but smiled when she saw him. "Gavi," she said and some other words which he couldn't quite understand. He knew the voice. It was the one which had sung to him during the nights, the one which had called him back from the stranglehold of his coma.

She spoke again, her words soft and slurred. He could catch only one: Amre, her name. He didn't want to skim her mind because of his uncertainty about the thing inside him. She brought food, fresh bread and butter, oatmeal in milk lumpy with cream. He ate quickly, the Rider approving of nourishment. Garvin wanted that time in the kitchen with the light coming in the windows to go on forever.

Then another mind was brushing his. Without his willing it, his own mind was lashing out. He caught himself before he tried to crush the other.

THANK YOU, GARVIN. YOUR STRENGTH IS GREATER THAN ANYTHING I HAVE EVER FELT. AND YOUR RIDER IS COLDER AND CRUELER THAN ANYTHING I HAVE EVER IMAGINED.

A man in a long white robe appeared in front of Garvin. I AM SCARECROW, GUARDIAN OF THE DISTRICT. THIS IS AMRE, MY MATE. I WAS TOLD TO SHOW YOU THIS. Garvin saw Roger and the satchel. THIS IS YOUR HOME FOR AS LONG AS YOU NEED TO MAKE IT YOURS. WE WILL HAVE TO DISGUISE YOU IF YOU WISH TO STAY AMONG US. YOU MUST PLAY THE PART OF ONE OF OUR OWN CITIZEN CHILDREN. I WILL EXPLAIN TO THE OTHERS THAT YOU ARE STILL TRAUMATIZED AND UNABLE TO SPEAK. YOU MUST NOT USE YOUR TELEPATHY NEAR OTHER SELECT.

TO DO THAT WOULD CAUSE MY RUIN. WILL YOU ACCEPT?

Garvin wanted to nod his head, to answer that, yes, he would stay until he could get his bearings. His head wouldn't move, his larynx wouldn't form words. From deep inside him came his Rider's order: 'have this backwoods wizard transport me to a portal.' Garvin's mind was linked to Scarecrow's. He knew the man had felt the thing inside him, the Rider.

Scarecrow smiled but continued to watch him carefully. WILL YOU ACCEPT? he asked again as if the Rider had been nothing but a rude interruption from a third party. The effort required to make his head nod yes caused Garvin pain. But he did it. He would have trusted these people even if there had been a choice. As it was, there was none. They offered him time and a place to understand what had happened.

A little girl with long dark hair and blue eyes appeared at the outside door and looked in. She wore a shirt like his own. She said something and Amre answered her. Scarecrow spoke aloud to her. Garvin caught "Gavi," his name. Scarecrow told him, THIS IS MICHETTE, MY DAUGHTER, WHOM WE CALL MICHE. SHE WILL BE IN CLUSTER WITH YOU. I HAVE TOLD HER TO BRING YOU THERE NOW.

The child took his hand and led him out the door, smiling up at him. Outside it was cool in the shadows but warm in the sun. Garvin stubbed his toe and winced. Miche giggled and tugged his hand. Scarecrow was walking right behind them. This was all like a puzzle or game. He thought of Nick and the Mohawks, and that seemed to make him stronger.

On the other side of the town green, outside a one-story building under a huge oak, was a group of children ranging from around six to fourteen. They were all dressed as Garvin was. A couple of the oldest ones even had their hair cut Mohawk style. There were two adults, a man and a woman in their twenties, standing with the group. Garvin felt Scarecrow's mind reaching out and touching each one of them. THIS IS GAVI, WHO WILL JOIN YOU FOR A WHILE.

HE HAS HAD AN ACCIDENT AND HAS FORGOTTEN
MUCH. HE WILL LEARN IT AGAIN. IF WE ARE PA-
TIENT AND KIND, WE WILL LEARN MUCH FROM HIM
WHILE HE IS WITH US.

Then he turned to Garvin and spoke slowly and clearly.
"Garvin, this is Cluster Group Two of Weatherhill. These are
the teachers Cela and Win." The man and the woman smiled,
and on a signal each of the children said his or her name
aloud. Most of them Garvin couldn't catch. It happened too
quickly and their English was too soft and slurred. There was
a girl nearly his own age with a Mohawk who was Maji and
a boy half a head taller than he who scowled as he said
"Darrel."

Miche took Garvin's hand and led him into the group. He
stood with the younger children and faced Scarecrow. He saw
the tall man in his white robes look around and smile. At the
edge of the Guardian's consciousness, Garvin caught the man's
appreciation of the beauty of the morning. There was uncertainty about how many more like it there would be.

Then Garvin felt the hope that was always with Scarecrow.
He felt his mind touched directly by the telepath, felt all the
minds, children's and teachers', caught up by their Guardian.
Scarecrow took them and swept them over the town where
hundreds of people went about their morning tasks. He caught
horses in the barracks stables and cows in pastures.

Up in the sky against a few white clouds was a V of geese.
The tip of the formation was passing by the stone tower of
his observatory like an arrow out of Hotlands. Scarecrow
focused his attention on the lead bird of the chevron. He
probed delicately, catching it all, the strange, flat radar sight,
the sound of geese honking behind, the feel of the breeze
they balanced on. Scarecrow shared with everyone the beating
wings and thumping of hearts, the smell of water ahead, the
sense of the flock behind. For just a moment he caught what
drove them north, the urge beyond hunger and longing, im-
printed at conception, the great migration instinct.

Out of habit he scanned the rest of the flight. The bird at
the end of the left leg of the V brought him up short. The

children understood what he had found. The bird was a monster. It was huge; a second pair of wings, small, bare, pumped along uselessly. This gander was faltering, falling behind the flight. How far south could it have flown? Scarecrow could sense the children urging him to kill it.

Their teachers were shushing them, but Scarecrow knew it had to be done. Hotlanders had cared for that gander and released it as the flocks came north. He broke mental contact with the cluster group and grabbed at the bird's central nervous system. He stopped its brain as if he were flicking a switch. It fell stone dead. The loss caused a ripple in the flock, but they didn't lose a stroke on their journey to Hudson Bay. The gander came down in the grass and a small charge went off. An anti-infiltration team was already running up from garrison barracks.

Scarecrow suggested that the teachers take the children back to the classroom. For a moment he remembered what he had felt the Rider inside Garvin call him: 'a backwoods wizard.' He felt like a man whose every gesture was bound to turn out badly, whose life and everything that he loved was about to be lost.

Most of the cluster group was watching the soldiers put out the fire, making sure that the "burner" was now disarmed. But Garvin looked at Scarecrow. For a moment the boy had managed to break free of the Rider's control. He was full of wonder at the morning and admiration for Scarecrow. The teacher Win put his arm on Garvin's shoulder and ushered him into the schoolhouse.

CHAPTER
EIGHT

IN THE SCHOOLROOM the older children watched him covertly, looked out the sides of their eyes at this stranger who was so pale and thin and didn't seem used to going barefoot. They were sizing him up. The younger children looked at him, openly curious. Garvin sat with them at first. They were in a circle; each one had put on a set of headphones and closed his or her eyes. Garvin did the same. He was curious as to what was going to happen and how far his Rider would let him go. The teacher, Cela, moved behind him and adjusted his earphones. He sat with his eyes closed.

The next moment he saw the Practical Pig teaching his two stupid brothers the table of twos. The wolf was in the woods behind them, zipping from tree to tree, from rock to rock. The pigs were small and pink. The wolf was gray and bent. They were dressed like children; he looked alien. Garvin was fascinated and could tell that his Rider was also. It didn't take long to understand the game. A correct answer kept the wolf at bay; a mistake brought him closer. There were five children aged six and seven, and there was Garvin. Only their answers could save the pigs.

The Practical Pig turned and wrote on a blackboard strung

between two trees, $2+1$? The little girl across from Garvin answered, "Three."

The wolf's head stuck out from behind a tree as it hesitated. Practical Pig wrote, $2+2$? The boy next to the little girl answered, "Four."

The wolf shook with rage as he faded back behind a rock. The next boy, getting excited, ran ahead of the question, saying, "five," before the pig had written, $2+7$?

The scene echoed in Garvin's mind like telepathy. It was as if the machine was communicating with him on a very simple and primitive level. It was to telepathy what television was to life. The wolf came bounding forward.

Miche was next. She waited and answered, "twelve," to the question $2+10$? The wolf receded. It was Garvin's turn. They waited. They all knew he was there. $2+8$? wrote the Practical Pig. Garvin couldn't speak. His mind was paralyzed, held by the Rider. He sensed amazement from far within himself. The Rider wondered how so primitive a culture could produce such a jewel. Garvin's time ran out. The wolf came closer.

The little girl next to Garvin was so distracted by what had happened that she missed the answer to $2+12$? The pigs looked up in horror to see the wolf leaping into their midst. They fled, knocking over the blackboard, with the wolf right behind.

Garvin felt his eyes open. The images faded but were still there in his mind. Five stricken children remained in a circle around the factor. Garvin's hands came up and took off the headset. He got to his feet. His Rider wanted to know more and was moving Garvin over to a circle of slightly older children. Garvin's feet moved without his willing them to. The Rider still held him. Cela said something to Garvin which he couldn't understand. He felt the Rider block his vocal cords.

There was a circle of eleven- and twelve-year-olds. Garvin sat in their midst and put on a headset. At the back of his brain was the greed and curiosity of his Rider. He understood that to the Rider it seemed that a collection of yokels had stumbled on something, however little they might understand it. They used them as children's games, but they were unique and possibly invaluable.

Garvin concentrated on the track. It was the story of someone called Van Winkle, a long time ago, after the Holocaust. That was indicated in a sort of shorthand, a series of images of plague and fire, famine and a frightened, screaming, skeletal face. Somehow in the midst of all this not everyone died. Certain people even managed to behave decisively. They executed plans, evacuated to prepared positions in remote areas.

One of these was Van Winkle, a young man with long white beard and hair, who appeared between the year of no sun and the year of deadly rain. He was telepathic, as was the crew of the large sailing ship he commanded. He called himself Van Winkle because he had slept for many years and awakened to find the world changed. He built a stronghold, an island fortress, and set out to conquer. People who had been enemies were transformed into loyal vassals. Garvin was fascinated, but the story was of no interest to his Rider. What the one inside him was concentrating on was the subliminal shocks and sounds that produced the images in each mind.

Garvin found himself standing up and removing his headset. His Rider had seen enough. It was as if Garvin were a nontelepath being controlled by another mind. Win asked him if he was all right, and he nodded his head. He wanted to shout. He wanted to kill the Rider. For a moment he stood there swaying back and forth. He was powerless. It reminded him of the way he had been before the Mohawks found him.

His eyes scanned the room. Almost all the children had on headsets, their eyes were closed. But one looked right at him, the girl Maji. She was tanned and her short hair and taller crest were blond. She wore a little wooden whistle around her neck. It hung just inside her shirt. She smiled at him and Garvin felt warm. He found himself forcing his mouth into a smile.

There was a coldness in his stomach; he felt himself turn away, jerked around like a dog on a leash. His helplessness turned to anger and he remembered the fear his Rider had felt when he had cut his finger that morning.

Garvin forced himself to walk, stiff legged and spastic, fighting the Rider every inch of the way out the door. Someone snickered behind him; Garvin didn't turn to see who. Outside on the green, a young trooper tried to bring a half-trained horse under control. The soldier sawed at the reins; the animal fought to free its head from the man's control. Garvin walked straight at them. The horse reared up; a shod foot passed a few inches in front of Garvin's eyes.

Garvin felt fear but recognized a colder fear inside of him. His Rider tried to force him to step back. But Garvin moved closer. The animal bucked, moving to the side. The trooper began to panic. A mounted corporal galloped up to help him. The teachers tried to pull Garvin away. Amre ran over from the infirmary. The soldiers were angry, yelling. They fell silent when Amre appeared, looking to her as she looked at Garvin. It took every bit of concentration that he had, but he formed the word in his mind. His larynx moved. His tongue worked. "Amre," he said aloud. He said it again. She patted his shoulder, understanding the victory.

Garvin staggered back to the room where he had awakened that morning and lay down. The rest of that day he struggled with his Rider. It was a battle in which keeping his eyes open when the Rider wanted them shut was triumph, in which lapses into unconsciousness were humiliating defeats. The boy began to get some idea of the strengths and weaknesses of his Rider and even its location. The Rider sat deep in his brain, somewhere between memory and reflex.

It was strong and rarely seemed to rest. It was a consciousness, an inner mind without an outer one, without a brain or a body. But it had thoughts and ideas, memories and secrets. It could be read like any mind. Garvin had done that accidentally when he became aware of its interest in the instructional tracks. The Rider knew that and wanted Garvin semiconscious. Garvin realized there were moments when the Rider was vulnerable to him.

Every time he thought of the Rider and probed inside immediately, he could catch bits and pieces of alien thoughts among his own. If, on the other hand, his mind wandered, recalling his old life or thinking of Maji, he would suddenly realize he had lost control of his body, couldn't open or close his own hand.

He tried to get into the habit of thinking RIDER at those moments. The more he was aware of his Rider, the more in control he was. He knew the Rider was aware of everything about him. It had been in control of him for a period between the time in Tompkins Park when he had passed out and the moment he awoke in Scarecrow and Amre's house. His memory of that was blocked and he had to unlock it.

He already knew that if he got into another mind and wanted to find a certain piece of information, he injected that thought into the mind. If he wanted its name, he thought NAME inside the other mind. The information would automatically come to the fore, even if it was a mind highly trained in evasion and defense.

He tried it many times that afternoon. It was hard because he had no idea what he was looking for. There was no image, no hard, concrete detail that he could latch on to. He thought of what he could remember of the time before he regained consciousness. He forced himself to think again of Tompkins Square Park, the screams, the darting minds, the presence looming up in front of him which he had thought at first was the Talking Suitcase. Then in the middle of familiar memories he remembered something else, the image of a woman with red-gold hair and a dark green dress that caught the color of her eyes.

He held on to that, not knowing who she was or where he had seen her but knowing that he knew more about her. He was exhausted and hungry. Amre's voice from downstairs called him to supper. There was a sort of truce: he got up and the Rider didn't try to stop him. Garvin washed and went down, walked beside Amre to a building across the green. He caught the smell of food and the sound of voices. He hadn't realized how lonely he had been all afternoon. Inside, he found the kids he had met that morning. They watched him as he sat down with the youngest in the group, Miche, another little girl, Sari, and two little boys their age, Loren and Berry.

Sitting apart from Cluster Group Two were half a dozen youths in their middle teens, the remains of Cluster Group One of Weatherhill. They were dressed in hunter's buckskins or cavalry fatigues. There were tiny kids off in a corner, the beginnings of Cluster Group Three. In another few years Cluster Group One would disappear and a new Cluster Group One would begin forming. Garvin snatched this out of the air. Then food began coming around. There was hot bread and butter, pea soup thick with ham and onions, beefsteak and roast potatoes and greens, apple pie and milk. On the other side of the room adults were eating, artisans and mechanics, washers and hospital attendants. The air was thick with the smell of food and the sound of voices. A couple of garrison troopers broke into loud laughter.

Garvin was aware of Maji sitting at the next table, of Darrel looking at him and saying something to the boy next to him. He knew Amre sat across the aisle talking to the chief nurse and watching out of the corner of her eye. He was also aware of calculations going on inside him of the garrison's size, of the technological capacities of this nation. As soon as he realized that, Garvin thought of the woman with the red hair and cast the question, WHERE DID I SEE HER?

The answer that he got, the image that suddenly filled his mind, surprised Garvin too much for him to hold it in. There was a moment's dead pause in the noise of the place. Only Amre looked at Garvin, saw the expression of wonder and pain on his face. But everyone was touched for a second by what Garvin saw, and everyone thought it was something of their own. It was a great formal garden with figures in knee breeches and wigs. Fauns lurked in the shrubbery.

Outside the hall Scarecrow walked with an aide. They both saw the image and felt the pain that went with it. The aide was about to cast his mind to find the source. Scarecrow smiled and indicated that he had done it.

*   *   *

A few days later Cluster Two gathered kindling wood a couple of miles outside of town. The teachers weren't with them. Maji, Darrel, and some of the older children were in charge. They were up a slope littered with branches fallen that winter, using axes to chop up the larger pieces. The younger children hauled the wood down to the pony cart waiting on a path below. Maji had turned the work into a game, seeing who could gather kindling fastest. The woods rang with laughter and the sound of axes.

Garvin went up the hill and came down with his arms loaded. Although beginning to blend in with the others, he still wasn't as agile. He slipped on pine needles, tripped over roots, couldn't give his full attention to anything he was doing. There was a constant duel between him and his Rider. The Rider assessed this world and its people. Garvin caught the name Goblin Market and saw pale green figures with yellow eyes.

He stopped where he was. Miche and some of the other children were loading his arms with wood. Garvin forgot everything, wasn't aware of the kids telling him he had as much as he could carry. He didn't notice Darrel coming down the slope behind him. The heel of a bare foot found the small of his back and sent him sprawling. He slid on leaves and moss; his head just missed a root; his knees and hands were skinned. Garvin saw it happen through the eyes of the little kids. Darrel stood slapping the flat end of his ax against his palm. "Sleepwalking, boy. You're no woodsman. You don't even know how to carry wood, boy."

It wouldn't have taken a second to tear the life out of the other. But Garvin wasn't aware of Darrel. His fall had frightened the Rider, which had lost some of its control over his mind. The question he had kept ready—WHO IS THE GREEN-EYED WOMAN?—was asked.

The answer stunned him. He left the wood lying where he had dropped it, walked down the hill past the cart and away by himself. He couldn't hear Darrel laughing, see the concern of the little kids, hear Maji blowing her whistle and yelling at Darrel.

There was dirt in his eyes but he didn't care. When he was far enough away, he sat with his back against a tree and examined what he had seen. First there was the garden. He had caught glimpses of it as he had been led, stunned and confused. There were fauns behind manicured hedges and unicorns peeping around the sides of picturesque ruins. A gentle wind stirred the tops of an avenue of trees. A distant horn sounded a long and lonely note.

There was the woman with the flaming hair and green dress. She walked down the avenue of trees toward him. As she got closer, he saw her white skin and her lips parted in a smile. Half a dozen people in blue jackets and gray knee pants walked beside and behind Garvin. They were telepaths, and although none was as strong as he, together they kept him off balance and unable to concentrate on any one of them. He was also drugged. They were holding him up. The woman stopped in front of Garvin. He raised his eyes and looked into hers.

The ones around him thought of the woman as Herself. Her mind probed his. The beautiful face was almost a mask. The features, despite the smile, showed nothing. The mind that probed was nothing but an instrument, a tool for opening minds. In the eyes of the mask he could see an intelligence. Behind the mind that probed, he could feel something that wasn't quite a mind. For the first time Garvin saw and felt a Steed, a person under the control of a Rider.

As he sat remembering, Garvin became aware of a voice nearby saying, "Gavi." He opened his eyes and saw Maji. She bent over and asked if he was all right. He couldn't catch the English spoken in a soft slur. Brushing her mind very lightly with his, he understood: she was sorry for him, curious, and impatient that he let Darrel treat him the way he had.

"What town are you from?" she was asking. "What's your cluster like? She pulled some leaves out of his hair and wanted to know, "Have you been apprenticed yet?" He saw himself as she saw him, scraped and disheveled, staring at her blank faced. He realized how stupid he looked and started to laugh. She smiled and gave him a hand up. For part of the way back, she let him hold her arm. Garvin hoped his face didn't look as masklike as Herself's.

CHAPTER NINE

SCARECROW STOOD on the parade ground at the Fire Gates, the stronghold of District Four. The commandant of the fortress, a ranger general, was at attention next to him. Aides and orderlies stood behind them. To their left an honor guard of rangers came to attention. On their right a squad of border cavalry pointed ceremonial lances to the sky.

From the west came a distant hum that turned into a roar. Half a dozen gunships flew in formation over the trees and the open ground and bluffs which guarded the Fire Gates to the west and south. To the north and east the waters of a river, diverted centuries ago by the wizard White Robert, secured the fortress, its garrison and town.

The two drawbridges which brought roads over the river were open in salute. The bluffs were lined with artillery and blockhouses. Their crews watched the gunships fly in. This place was famous. Way out in Hotlands the Fire Gates were known. Many a young war leader had sworn to carve his sign on the cliff sides of the fortresses. In District Three there was the Eyes of Hell, a mountain drilled and shaped into a half-mile-high tower. In District Five, on the plains, Joyous Freedom was built behind moats and swamps. All of them had stood for centuries, all of them were now in danger. Scarecrow put that knowledge out of his mind for the moment as he felt himself being scanned from the gunships.

They came in without breaking formation and touched down on the parade ground. Crewmen were out, letting down ladders as the machines hit the ground. Staff officers in jump suits were out, watching, scanning, making sure all was well and everyone was impressed. Figures in white robes picked their way down the ladders. One with a yellow sunburst on the huge front of his robes was familiar to Scarecrow. Their outer minds brushed together. Gepeto was a Deep Select, a telepath capable of opening the minds of other Select. He and Scarecrow had been cluster mates many years before.

A tiny figure came down the ladder, assisted for the last several steps. Her gray hair was almost white; her eyes couldn't make out Scarecrow as he walked forward. But her mind probed as sharply as ever.

SCARECROW! WHAT IS THIS I FIND ABOUT YOU SHOWING THAT UGLY FACE OF YOURS TO EVERYONE IN DISTRICT FOUR. WAS IT SOME SORT OF MASS PUNISHMENT?

Scarecrow felt himself grasped by the force of Moriaph, Warden of the Border Reaches.

Her staff formed behind the Warden. Some of them, Scarecrow knew, were very pleased that she had opened the visit so. They wanted to see a sound slap delivered to this Guardian, one appointed at Moriaph's insistence, one who made such a fetish of unconventionality. Gepeto, who bore Scarecrow little good will, displayed no elation. Only Moriaph could rebuke a border Guardian, and he knew that wasn't going to happen. The old woman grasped Scarecrow by the arm.

Enemies said that Moriaph, years before in her time of great triumphs, had been permitted to look within the unbreakable secrets of the Republic. It was said that she had a child who was Selected and that she alone of all the mothers in the land knew who that child was.

THEY TELL ME YOU ARE DOING WATCHMAN'S

WORK, SCARECROW, RESCUING CATS FROM TREES AND GIVING RUNAWAY CHILDREN A HOME.

Scarecrow managed to chuckle and hold his grin.

Together they inspected the troops as though this were an ordinary tour and not a special visit requested by him last week and announced the day before. She stopped before an old ranger sergeant. Moriaph spoke aloud, her voice hoarse and throaty: "I remember you at Satan's Grove. You were a standard bearer then and you won your wings."

"Aye, Warden." The old soldier looked down at the silver wings on a flat shield, highest decoration of the Republic. "The ones of us left remember you too, coming into the front lines when we thought that we were all finished."

"How long gone is that, sergeant?"

"Forty years come fall, Warden. There are still some of us left."

"It isn't easy to kill us old war dogs, sergeant. These ones"—indicating her staff—"know whatever they may think they know because they flew over a couple of skirmishes, experienced some old adventure tracks." She pointed at Scarecrow. "How's this one; is he measuring up?"

"None better, Warden, not even . . . No sir, none better." The old man had been about to say Grim Reaper until he remembered that Guardian's disgrace.

Later, with formalities and a meal with local dignitaries over, Moriaph sat in the spring evening with Scarecrow. A scrambler was on, distorting their thoughts outside of a range of a few feet. Her staff had been reluctant to leave her, but Moriaph had ordered them away.

THE BEST OF THEM HAVE BEEN TRAINED UP TO THE POINT WHERE THEY ARE ONLY USELESS, she told him, and then without seeming to change subjects she asked, WHY WAS THERE AN ALERT AND A GREAT RELAY HERE TWO WEEKS AGO? She showed Scarecrow the reports she had received from neighboring districts, reminded him of the lost work the disruption represented.

I FELT IT NECESSARY. He showed her the unexplained alien presences detected in half a dozen parts of the district.

YOU SUSPECT INFILTRATION? NO OTHER GUARD-
IAN HAS REPORTED ANYTHING.

Scarecrow showed her what Grim Reaper had shown him,
the shamans at work out in Hotlands, the images of Rumack.

She nodded. THERE HAVE BEEN VAGUE RUMORS.
BUT THERE IS ALWAYS SOMETHING OF THE SORT
BREWING, AND THIS SEEMS TO BE GOING ON WELL
SOUTH OF THE LAKES. Her eyes narrowed. WHAT
SCOUTS BROUGHT YOU THESE, SCARECROW? THEY
FEEL FOREIGN.

Scarecrow drew a deep breath. NO ONE BROUGHT
THEM. I WENT TO THE SOURCE. He showed her Uncle
and the way they had traveled outside the borders.

She looked at him, her eyes focused, her brows turned to
wrinkles. She glared. The Hawk of the North they called her
to the south, the Killer from the Sky. NO GUARDIAN IS
TO LEAVE HIS DISTRICT, NO SELECT IS TO GO INTO
HOTLANDS WITHOUT MY PERMISSION, AND THAT
PERMISSION IS NEVER GIVEN. YOU MAY CONSIDER
YOURSELF REBUKED, GUARDIAN, AND I WILL NOT
HEAR OF YOU DOING IT AGAIN. Then, without changing
her expression, she spoke aloud. "Still, if I were thirty years
younger, I'd have done just that. Now, who was your in-
formant?"

Scarecrow showed her the image. ONE WHO WAS ONCE
CALLED GRIM REAPER.

This time Moriaph blinked and showed him a series of
images. He recognized Grim Reaper before he fled. He stood
proud and strong, disdaining danger. Those images were old
and clouded by all Moriaph had seen and known since, but
they were firsthand.

There were other images showing Grim Reaper's flight and
recapture: the figure with filthy hair and face, in tattered white
robes, being lured out of Hotlands like a runaway dog and
tied up to prevent him from tearing his own face. Half a
dozen Deep Select escorted him to the Retreat. These later
images were flat, something Moriaph had been shown by
someone who hadn't seen them for himself.

THIS IS GRIM REAPER, SCARECROW. THAT ONE WITH WHOM YOU COMMUNICATED IS A SHAMAN OF SOME KIND. DO YOU UNDERSTAND? When she was sure Scarecrow understood, she asked aloud, "And what did that renegade old fool have to show you?"

After Scarecrow had shown her as much as he thought wise, not telling her about Time or portals or Garvin, she nodded.

SHOW NO ONE ELSE WHAT YOU HAVE SHOWN ME. UNTIL THERE IS SOME SIGN OF THIS HAPPENING, YOUR STORY WILL BE A MARK AGAINST US. Scarecrow saw images of staff officers, of committee members back in New Liberty. They all wore tight little smiles of pleased anticipation.

Moriaph said, "It would be all they needed to undo us both, a general who has grown too old, a Select superstitious as any Citizen. They keep me here as a symbol to reassure people, Scarecrow. These smiling shits from New Liberty are convinced that there's never going to be another war, that there's no need for people like me. They think they can eliminate the border Guardians too and turn these woods into a place to take their vacations. I will pass on what you showed me to those Guardians I think are able to use it." Scarecrow understood that Moriaph saw here the chance of one final campaign to warm her old age.

Next morning before the entourage departed, Gepeto took Scarecrow aside. He had gone much to fat in the years since cluster. He fingered the yellow sunburst on his robes as his mind and Scarecrow's touched Umbras, kept to the politest of formalities. Then Gepeto smiled. MANY STRANGE DOINGS HERE, GUARDIAN?

NO STRANGER THAN ONE SHOULD EXPECT, DEEP SELECT, WHEN ONE IS IN BORDER COUNTRY AND CLOSE TO HOTLANDS.

Gepeto stopped smiling and entered Scarecrow's Curtain defenses. The fingers tightened on the sunburst like a threat to tear open Scarecrow's mind. Instead, all Gepeto did was to deposit a single image: Garvin walking with Cluster Group

Two. STRANGE AND NOT FROM HOTLANDS, GUARD-IAN. It was shown too quickly for Scarecrow to know who had seen Garvin, who had guessed at his being an interloper, who had reported it. The Deep Select bowed and made his way to the gunships. Images of the Retreat floated in the air.

That was on Scarecrow's mind a few nights later in his observatory at Weatherhill. Scarecrow watched as Garvin did simple exercises for mental concentration. They were given to small children in Select clusters. The boy drummed his fingers lightly on a table, concentrated on the feel of the surface of the table. He thought of his Umbra, the outer layer of mental defenses, as he did. He listened to the soft drumming and called into existence the Curtain layer of defense. At the same time he looked just to the side of a light on the wall behind Scarecrow's head. He concentrated on the Keep at the center of his consciousness.

Scarecrow probed lightly at Garvin's mind, and the defenses held. Then he told the boy NOW and attacked repeatedly in short probes. Garvin tried to defend and at the same time to switch the sensations and the awareness attached to each of them. He made the light remind him of the Umbra, the sound of the drumming the Keep, the tabletop his Curtain. His defenses held. Scarecrow probed constantly, looking for an opening. He showed Garvin the image of a boy sitting there, staring at the light and drumming one hand. The defenses wobbled but held.

Garvin shifted once again: the drumming was the Umbra, the touch the Keep, the light the Curtain. Scarecrow went after him again. The image he showed the boy was of a juggler dropping several pieces of fruit and three or four plates on the floor. A raw egg came down on the juggler's head. Garvin laughed; the defenses wavered. Then Scarecrow was past the Umbra and into Garvin's mind.

There he was again in the vivid but unreal world. Traffic lights made a red and yellow pattern as far uptown as the eye could travel on a rainy spring night. A roaring subway express with hundreds of people inside it sailed through a lighted station.

Before Scarecrow could get through that, Garvin blocked him. There was nothing subtle about it. The Guardian's mind was overpowered and swept outside by the boy's. Garvin was still laughing. "If you make me laugh, how can I concentrate?"

"Garvin," the Select spoke slowly. "They will show you much worse things than that to startle you."

"It's what that's like, juggling. I'm never going to be able to do that the way you do."

Scarecrow knew that was true. But with the power of Garvin's telepathy it might not matter. The Guardian gave the sign for Garvin to begin the exercise again. Something passed behind Garvin's eyes. All animation left his face. TELL ME ABOUT SOMETHING, SCARECROW. TELL ME HOW YOU GOT YOUR NAME.

Very softly, watching the boy's face, Scarecrow reached out and touched the other mind. Garvin was partially distracted, turned inward as he struggled with the Rider. Still he held on to the story that Scarecrow was showing him. TO UNDERSTAND YOU MUST UNDERSTAND SELECT AND HOW WE ARE TRAINED, he began. Garvin was looking away but still paying attention.

Scarecrow showed him the thirty children assembled at a few weeks of age from all over the Republic. They were raised in nurseries first by Citizens overseen by Select and then by Select tutors. The children wore white tunics and long hair. They attended classes and went out into the Republic on field trips. As they formed friendships, quarreled, played together or sat apart, their minds began to form a web.

It was in some ways like the childhood Garvin remembered, with allegiances made and feuds formed, fast friendships and furious battles. He saw two seven-year-olds tumble over one another wrestling. Then one reached out with her mind, and the other blocked it. The gesture was as automatic as raising the arm to guard the eyes. There were things Garvin recognized immediately: favored teachers and feared ones, foods everyone liked and others they all hated. There were also things as strange as waking up in the night and being caught in the undertow of a dream that flowed from mind to mind.

Scarecrow could feel Garvin holding on to those images. The other's face was strained, every muscle was tensed as Garvin felt his brain succumb to his Rider. Scarecrow saw Garvin slump in his chair, his head loll back. Still, there was contact between their two minds.

The Guardian showed him Old May, an ancient Select who had been allowed to retire to a small cottage in the woods. The sun shone bright in the front yard as she showed the cluster group her animals. Birds would stand nearby as foxes appeared to dump grouse on her doorway and pad off. Otters came out of the streams to sit on her lap. YOU NEVER PICK UP THE OTTER, the old woman told them. YOU DO THAT AND IT WILL THINK YOU ARE GOING TO EAT IT. AN OTTER WILL PUT ITS TEETH INTO YOUR HAND FASTER THAN YOU CAN THINK TO STOP HIM.

Scarecrow stopped and waited. Garvin's mind came to him seemingly from far away. MY RIDER DOES NOT WANT THIS STORY. IT WISHES TO KNOW . . . There was a pause as long as a couple of heartbeats. Garvin stirred in his chair and said, "Go on, keep showing me the story, Scarecrow. You're what I'm holding on to."

So Scarecrow showed Garvin how he had learned from Old May's patience with animals to be patient toward everything. He showed himself sitting under a tree at a huge farm collective where his cluster group had spent a summer. Through a hole burrowed under a fence, he watched a rabbit get into the trunk gardens. A hawk circled in the air far above the chicken yards. Then he put the smell of fox in the rabbit's mind and touched the hawk's sense of balance. Citizen children watching from a short distance saw the rabbit scramble off in terror, heard the shrieks of the hawk as it plummeted. The hawk regained the use of its wings and flew off. The children cheered.

He showed Garvin an old farmer giving him the nickname

Scarecrow. Select changed their names when they came of age. For a Select to take a name given by a Citizen wasn't unprecedented, but it was a sign. The tutors noticed it and subtly young Scarecrow was steered into the service of a Guardian on the Atlantic coast. As he showed Garvin all this, he watched the boy very carefully. There was spittel around Garvin's mouth. Scarecrow felt the other mind become more distant. Finally contact between them broke.

Garvin seemed about to fall out of his chair. Scarecrow got up to catch him. The other spoke. "I want to know about tracks and factors." The voice was slow, slurred. "I want you to show me how many of them there are, where they are manufactured . . . specifications . . . designs . . ." Garvin was bleeding where he had bitten his lower lip, He shook himself and his eyes came into focus. His mind reached out for Scarecrow's again. DO NOT TELL IT ANYTHING LIKE THAT WHEN IT ASKS. SHOW ME MORE ABOUT YOUR BEING A KID.

Scarecrow did, watching Garvin all the time, keeping his mind in touch with the periphery of the other's. At times what he recognized as Garvin seemed to go into eclipse and the body in the chair opposite slumped at an impossible angle. It seemed horrible to the Guardian that anyone should go through this torture. He wondered what help this half-grown boy fighting to control his own mind and body could give this world.

At that moment he felt Garvin reach out his mind and at the same time straighten up in his chair. NEVER LET ME OUT OF THIS WORLD, SCARECROW, IF YOU THINK THE RIDER IS IN CONTROL. KILL ME IF YOU HAVE TO. Garvin's eyes were in focus then. He took a handkerchief out of the pocket of his shirt and wiped the blood off his mouth.

Scarecrow went into the next room and brought back a cup of water. Garvin sat cross-legged in the chair, his fingers twined into his toes. "That's going to go on until I break him," the boy said. He drank the water. Scarecrow caught from the other mind a knowledge of what had been promised to Scarecrow. Garvin knew that Scarecrow expected a hero of some kind. "I love this place," he told the Guardian. Scarecrow caught images of himself and Amre and Miche and the cluster group. "You've been good to me."

CHAPTER TEN

THE CHILDREN were working to free the third little pig, the one who had built his house of straw. His house had been blown down and he had been captured while they were trying to master their $+3s$. But the pigs' bad fortune had begun a couple of weeks before when Garvin had first sat down with them. He sat with the children again because he felt a certain obligation and knew the children wanted it. He saw their serious faces and tightly closed eyes. Then he closed his eyes and watched the other little pigs creep up on the cage where the wolf had their brother.

The wolf was sound asleep and snoring. Occasionally one of his eyes would almost open. When that happened, the question appeared on a tree. $4 + 3$? Garvin knew it was Loren's turn. With the lightest of scans he was able to feel the boy licking his lips and preparing to answer. "Seven," said Loren, and the wolf's eyes closed again.

The pigs were at the cage. On the bars was $4 + 7$? Sari, who sat between Garvin and Loren, had her eyes crunched shut. "Eleven," she said. The pig who had made his house of wood bent down, and the Practical Pig stood on him. His trotter did not quite reach the latch. On the door appeared

$4+10$? Garvin's throat worked. He was very much in control that morning. "Fourteen," he said.

There was a little stir when he did it. A couple of the children clapped their hands. The Practical Pig gave a little hop in the air and freed the latch with the tip of his nose. Garvin nodded as they all laughed aloud, and felt that he had begun discharging his debts.

Later, Cluster Group Two was all outside gathered around an old hunter woman who was showing them how to skin a rabbit. The oldest children, Darrel and Maji, who were going for their apprenticeships, stood at the front and watched carefully. Garvin stood next to them and forced himself to watch. "Best friend you can have," said the woman in a soft twang. "Use it right and it's an extension of your hand." Then the blade turned and flashed sunlight in his eyes. Garvin's hand went for the cutting edge. He nicked his finger. The woman looked at him and said, "Now you know how sharp it is, sonny."

He could feel Darrel's contempt and Maji's concern, but Garvin didn't care at the moment. He turned and walked away fast, went out beyond the town perimeter clutching in his mind the image that he had caught. He lay with his back against a tree and recalled what he had grasped in the brief flash of his Rider's panic. He was back in the garden of the woman with the red hair and green eyes.

They had taken him into a drawing room, half a dozen minds batting at his own, the woman's mind weaving a pattern that made him follow. They brought him through French doors into a room full of ornate furniture. His sneakers sank into the thick rug. There was blue and white wallpaper with peacocks, and there were telepathic servants in wigs and knee breeches. Two of them opened a pair of arched doors. There was a corridor and another door much simpler and more functional across it. That also was open. Inside was the metal and glass of a hospital or a laboratory. There were several green figures with yellow eyes.

Garvin remembered them. He gained control of the pieces one after another. His Rider fought him for possession of every moment of that awful day. Garvin passed out once or twice. His breath stopped in his chest. He banged his hands on the ground in pain as nauseating headaches tore at him. But he remembered it all.

Green hands took his clothes and moved him around like a puppet. Once or twice he had almost managed to get control of himself. Each time he was about to, the woman distracted him. Or rather, her Rider used her mind, her memories, her beauty to keep him from sweeping the other minds aside. Once he managed to broadcast, DO NOT TOUCH ME. The green hands stopped their prodding and poking and taking samples of blood and semen and saliva and urine and marrow. For one moment everyone—the telepathic guards who stood inside the door, the green ones—turned and looked to the woman.

And she smiled and told them, HE IS A FRIGHTENED BOY WHO WILL SOON BEGIN TO KNOW PERFECT SECURITY. HIS POWERS ARE VERY GREAT AND HE IS INCLINED TO BE FRISKY. Then she looked into his eyes. He stared at her as the green hands got busy with him again. She showed him herself at eighteen, standing naked in front of a mirror. He watched her smile, aware of strange clouds passing behind her eyes.

In the Republic under the tree, every humiliation and pain he had known came back to haunt him. His body was paralyzed, but Garvin growled deep in his throat. He felt it and formed an Umbra. He listened to the sound and formed a Curtain. He smelled the damp new life of the woods and formed a Keep. He threw the image of the beautiful lady inward at his Rider and was blocked. He tried images of the green faces and got nothing but pain. He tried details of the room itself.

Doors were the trigger. There was a second set of doors, double swinging ones. He had been pushed on a wheeled table and had raised his head to see his feet passing into a lighted area. Other minds had forced his head down. But not before he had seen another table.

Garvin's Rider tried to bang him unconscious against the

tree, but Garvin remembered. There was a body covered with a sheet. All that was visible was a head and shoulders covered with bandages. The little patches of skin were gray, the cheeks pulled in, the eyelids darker than the rest. Garvin couldn't tell the age or sex. They placed him in the center of a bright light. Machines were being pushed up all around him. He was plugged in; wires were attached to his chest and head, his hands and feet. Something was put over his eyes and in his ears. His breath became shallow; his sense of smell, taste, and touch dimmed.

The memories that came next cost Garvin some very bad moments under that wide oak. He writhed on the ground, covered with fever sweat. He foamed at the mouth. Once or twice he blacked out. Through it all he held his memory of the operating room and what had been done to him. For a moment he saw himself through another's eyes. He looked down at himself, small and helpless amid the equipment and the moving, white-clad figures. For an awful moment he thought of an old movie in which a mad doctor transferred brains between two bodies. He realized that the glimpse from above which he had caught was that of the person on the other table who was dying.

Garvin's heart beat and then the other heart beat. His heart beat and the other one beat. His heart beat and the other one missed. The dying one was floating above the room. Garvin felt the other life trying to tug free. He felt the infinite weariness of the other, the relief to be free at last of a life that didn't belong to it, of a will that wasn't its own. The dying one was a Steed whose only desire was to be allowed to die.

The green doctors móved faster as Herself's Rider kept Garvin calm. The dying body sank back into itself. The departing life saw the room from further and further away. At that moment of remembering, Garvin's pain became most intense. It was then that he caught what his Rider above all did not want him to remember. As life flickered out of the old Steed, something small and afraid of death hurtled between the two minds. Dials moved and respirators registered and something that couldn't be measured crossed the three feet that separated the two skulls. Garvin felt his Rider, and realized it as clearly as it could be realized, a small bundle of will and memories, of ruthlessness and fear.

Herself's Rider had sent him an image of a warrior proud and bloody leaping in one great move from a dying horse to a fresh one. The new horse was young and eager and plunged forward into battle. But Garvin knew what he had just felt and wasn't fooled. He managed to twist around as his Rider settled into his brain before it could begin to take up the reins and try to control him. Herself's eyes were wet. There were tears on her cheeks and her face was twisted in pain. One Steed mourned for one dead and another about to be broken.

On the moss under the tree, soaked in fever sweat and urine, Garvin panted and groaned but knew triumph. RIDER, THAT WAS YOU. YOU ARE NOTHING BUT A NIGHT-MARE. YOU ARE A DREAM AFTER SEEING A HOR-ROR MOVIE. From his Rider there was no response. Nothing interfered with the boy as he slowly got to his feet and stole back to Scarecrow and Amre's house.

He took a hot bath, got a clean shirt and went to eat. He was silent in the dining hall, managing a smile for Maji, ignoring Darrel. "We're going on an adventure track tonight," the girl said, but Garvin just shook his head, tired. He stopped down at the infirmary and said good night to Amre. "Are you all right, Gavi?"

He smiled and nodded, his eyelids drooping. He tried to tell her that it had been good that day, that he had finally seen the enemy. Then he turned and walked up the hill, thinking of bed. On his way he brushed Scarecrow's mind after first making sure there were no other Select around. He gave the Guardian a glimpse of what he had seen that afternoon. He was aware of Scarecrow setting things aside, preparing for a training session with him. Garvin excused himself as he headed upstairs. He didn't get undressed, just fell flat on his face and went to sleep.

Scarecrow scanned him and chuckled. Then his own lack of sleep began to catch up with him. He turned down lights and went to lie on a couch to rest for a few moments.

Amre was on duty at the infirmary with a ranger woman in protracted labor. The woman was tough and Amre was gentle. Both patients were resting quietly by midnight. The full May moon shone down on the town and Amre felt for a moment as if she were in an enchanted village. The white of the buildings shimmered, reflecting moonlight. Night breezes made the leaves dance.

She was ready to go find Scarecrow and turn in. She remembered as she headed up the hill that something had bothered her about Garvin. Instead of going to the observatory, she went directly to the living quarters. The door of the back porch opened as she approached. Garvin stepped out, moving with the steady tread of the somnambulist. She knew better than to wake him, but she moved to follow.

His head turned. His eyes were open and seemed for an instant to have no pupils. Then something knocked the breath out of her, stunned her. Amre staggered under the impact of Garvin's mind. He turned and glided away over a moonlit field. A strong breeze, a sighing of trees in the wind brought her back, made her catch her breath. Garvin had disappeared. She felt a fuzzy probe from a half-awake Scarecrow. She formed an image of what she had seen. Then she went in the direction Garvin had taken. She hoped Scarecrow was awake and probing ahead.

It seemed that a wind went with her.

She followed the shimmering leaves and caught sight of Garvin falling down and getting up again, all in one movement. Scarecrow's mind found hers again. HIS RIDER HAS HIM HYPNOTIZED. I THINK HE IS HEADING FOR DEVIL'S LAIR.

She thought of the place, a shallow hole in the rocks near a dry streambed. Children used it to frighten each other, little children Miche's age.

PORTAL, Scarecrow's mind told her. THAT IS THE KIND OF PLACE THAT WOULD BE A PORTAL.

Then Scarecrow's mind was gone from hers, and she saw Garvin starting to stumble over rocks. The Devil's Lair was practically in the back yard. Amre, forest trained, moved forward as fast as she could. But Garvin's Rider made him plunge headlong. It obviously didn't care if every bone in the boy's body was broken. Scarecrow concentrated on Garvin, battering down the defenses the Rider had put around the boy's mind. GARVIN! GARVIN! WAKE UP!

Garvin pitched headlong toward a black spot in the moonlit rocks. He would get there before Amre could. The Rider blocked any contact with him. Amre stood where she was and shouted, "Gavi, stop!" At that moment the leaves above the Devil's Lair, the grass, the brush all rustled and sighed in a sudden breeze. Birds in the trees woke and chirped in alarm. Something ran through the undergrowth.

For Garvin it was all a dream. He moved through a magic land; every tree and rock stood out in the night. He had a sensation of being asleep and knowing he was asleep but found it too wonderful and enchanting to want to wake up. When he stumbled and fell, he didn't feel any pain, wasn't jarred out of his trance. His body moved, his mind even probed, but all of that was happening far away.

Then there was something right in front of him, something he thought he should recognize. A rip in the night, an opening into infinity, lay in front of him. A mind tried to probe his: GARVIN, WAKE UP! A voice was calling aloud, "Gavi, stop!" He thought he knew the mind, could identify the voice, but he couldn't make his legs halt. There was a portal into which he was about to plunge.

The forest sprang to life around him; the leaves moving in a strong wind flashed their light undersides. Birds and animals awoke. The Wind played around him, catching at his shirt. He felt minds calling to him, GARVIN! GARVIN! He remembered the minds that had led him through dark infinity into the Republic. He could feel them again, the children and tutors of that Select cluster group, dozens of minds calling to him.

He shook his head suddenly and rubbed his eyes. His feet and his knees were cut. He was out in the middle of the wood. There was someone running toward him. It was Amre. Scarecrow was further away but running to him also. Inside, he could feel his Rider outlined against his brain like a rat caught in a flashlight beam. He probed the Rider and felt its terror of him. Amre had him by the arm then. "Garvin, can you hear me?"

He nodded, reached out his mind to reassure them. THIS WAS SOMETHING IT SAVED FOR AN EMERGENCY. Garvin turned and looked at the shallow indentation in the rock that marked the portal. Amre didn't want to let him go. Garvin looked, reached out his mind, felt the infinity of Time, the endless worlds. They were drawing him away from Devil's Lair. Garvin allowed them to do that, but he knew he had been through portals before and that he would be going through them again.

Around them the trees moved. Scarecrow and Amre both looked uneasy. They could hear the Wind moving off in the night. There was a mind in the distance, telepathic and not Select. Scarecrow tried to probe it, but the Wind got between them. It seemed to be made of an infinity of minds.

Garvin learned to be alert when asleep. In the days just after his sleepwalk, the Rider was very small and frightened. Garvin could feel it inside him, way back in the limbic system, the ancient lizard part of the brain. I KNOW WHERE YOU ARE, RIDER. I KNOW WHAT YOU ARE. Being able to remember the moment when he had felt the Rider without a Steed, naked and terrified, had given Garvin an ability to understand and control it.

He stood one evening looking at himself in the bathroom mirror, examining his eyes for signs of the Rider behind them. Memories came back to him easily. An image came of him as seen by another. He wore a white wig, buckled shoes, knee pants, and a silk shirt. He walked slowly, carefully down a lawn between sculpted hedges. Herself was there, red hair tied back, wearing a riding costume. Several of the green ones who had performed the operation were there looking pale and watery in the sunlight.

They were called Goblins. The operation was called a jump. The immense gardens and house were the property of the Rider who was the master of the woman called Herself. A small faun scampered across the path, turned to look at them with bright animal eyes, and laughed a dry little laugh. Garvin felt dull horror as his own Rider made him walk up and down without his willing it, put him through his paces.

Herself smiled and asked, DO YOU WISH TO RIDE? TO HUNT? SANS SOUCI OFFERS MUCH. Or rather Herself's Rider asked this of his Rider. The two Steeds were only the instruments they used.

YOU ARE VERY GRACIOUS, MADAME, he felt himself replying. AT PRESENT, THOUGH, I MUST TRAIN THIS STEED YOU WERE SO GOOD TO FIND ME.

I DETECTED A STRENGTH THAT MADE ME HESITATE.

THIS ONE IS AMAZING! YOU HAVE DONE VERY WELL BY ME. THERE IS EVEN A HINT OF TIME STRIDING IN HIM. The woman's mouth quivered for a moment. She looked Garvin over for her Rider. TIME AND TRAINING, Garvin found himself telling her, WILL MAKE THIS THE GREATEST OF ALL MY STEEDS.

I WILL RETURN THIS EVENING. YOU MAY ASK ANYTHING YOU WISH OF MY STEWARDS. They passed through an arch in the hedge, and Garvin saw the huge horses, the grooms helping her into the saddle. She moved off with several servants, cantering down an avenue of poplars. A small centaur the size of a pony galloped with them for a while like a dog chasing a car. The windows of the chateau shone in the afternoon sun.

"Gavi." Outside the bathroom door at Weatherhill, little Miche called to him to come with her and be in the adventure track. He went downstairs and outside. It was after supper and dark. The cluster group was in the schoolroom. He looked over and saw Maji and Darrel holding hands. He saw that it was Darrel who had taken her hand, not the other way around. The two of them had begun their apprenticeships. They wore moccasins and leather shirts and carried small axes in their belts. Maji opened her eyes slightly as Garvin put on a headset. All the others were sitting quietly with their eyes shut.

It was a mild adventure which would go on as long as anyone was interested in it. The track came from one of the Asian states, Mongolia or Far Tibet, and had reached the Republic along some tortured trade route. The landscape was Chinese. A party of children on ponies crossed a gently swaying bridge. Their destination lay on the other side, in a red pagoda on some hills.

The figures on the ponies were the children of Cluster Group Two. Their faces shimmered when looked at too closely. They moved in a limited number of ways, looking to the left or the right, urging their ponies forward, leaning over to talk to someone else. Darrel and Maji were riding together toward the back of the column. Garvin found himself not too far away. He was picking up some of the details of the plot. Members of the cluster group looked back, shouting and pointing.

A huge balloon rose from the hills behind them. It was dark blue and caught the light of the setting sun. There was a gold dragon painted on it. Garvin looked over and saw that Maji and Darrel were paying no attention to this. He opened his eyes and saw them sitting very close, arms twined. He looked down and saw that there was nothing below the bridge. Whoever had designed the track had assumed that all eyes would be looking ahead to the pagoda or behind at the balloon. There was just the barest hint of water and rocks.

Most of the figures had cleared the bridge. Garvin reached out with his mind and touched each member of the group so lightly they were hardly aware of anyone doing it. He imposed his own mind on the track itself, urged his pony forward up the hill in front of the pagoda, made it stand on its hind legs as they all watched. When he knew he had Maji's attention, he put into her mind the idea of taking off her headset and stepping outside with him.

He took off his own headset, feeling the figure he had just occupied settling back into the crowd that galloped away from the dragon balloon. Maji was standing up, looking at him with curiosity. Garvin walked outside and she followed.

They stood in the shadows. "I have to go back soon," she

said. He wanted to show her that his life was an adventure track, a real one that was still going on. But remembering what Scarecrow had told him, he couldn't reveal himself to her. "I don't want to hurt Darrel," she said. "I've known him since . . . always."

Brushing her mind, Garvin knew he could make her stay with him, could make her do whatever he wanted. But that reminded him too much of his Rider. Darrel had come out of the school and was looking for them. "Good night." Maji kissed him and slipped away.

Alone, Garvin knew his days in Cluster Group Two were drawing to a close. Did he belong to any group? Automatically he probed his Rider. From his memory came images of the Immortals' Companions in black uniforms running over the clipped lawns of Herself's chateau. It was just after she had ridden away.

Until they arrived, Garvin's Rider had been walking him up and down Herself's gardens, putting him through his paces. Two Goblins stood in the shade of a tree and watched. In a decorative pool nearby, small mermaids dove, then surfaced to dry their long blue hair. Garvin, his body moving without his willing it, understood why the dying Steed in the operating room welcomed death.

Then there was an explosion, a gunshot, a mind trying to reach his. That's when the Companions had appeared in front of him. The clothes they wore, their hair, were like Nick's. Garvin's mind broke away from his Rider's. GARVIN, COME TO US, a mind commanded. There was an image of the Talking Suitcase and old Roger.

Garvin found himself turning around, moving away from them. His Rider snapped the contact between him and the intruders. There were servants of Herself running up the walks. Some of them were armed with very modern weapons. Minds on both sides flicked through the air. Garvin felt his Rider's fear of flying lead as it forced him to stagger away from his rescuers.

The two Goblins moved from where they were to either

side of Garvin. GOBLIN TRUCE! GOBLIN TRUCE! Servants and Companions lowered their guns. Garvin realized the Companions would not come near him if it meant coming too near a Goblin. He was being carried away into captivity. He would end up like Herself.

Garvin worked his throat, let out a strangled shout. He tore his own legs from his Rider's control. He turned and headed toward the Companions. The Goblins snarled as he passed between them but didn't try to stop Garvin.

The Companions grabbed him and hauled him toward the ornamental tower. DO NOT SHOOT. YOU MIGHT HIT THE RIDER'S STEED, the order went out from Herself's guards. Garvin felt his Rider trying to strangle him, knock him out. It was all he could do to prevent the Rider from taking over his mind and lashing out at the Companions.

They had him inside the tower. It was a comfortable twentieth-century room. There were two dead guards in wigs and knee breeches on the floor. One of the Companions' heads snapped around; his long ponytail flew into his face. He held his temples and screamed. Herself was back from the hunt.

Garvin felt her Rider reach out to his. The Companions were pushing him toward a wall. Garvin saw it flicker in front of him. THEY WILL CALL YOU ACROSS TIME, one told him. The wall turned into a tapestry of worlds and Garvin passed through the portal into Time.

Weeks later in the Republic, in District Four, outside the classroom where his cluster mates enjoyed an adventure track, Garvin remembered the minds that had led him through Time. He understood that he owed this world a debt. And that there was a place of some kind for him with the Immortals' Companions. He went back inside to join the adventure track.

CHAPTER ELEVEN

A FEW DAYS later, at a staff meeting at the Fire Gates, Scarecrow attended to the proceedings with his Umbra. Within his Keep, he sifted information from his district. The orders to report all strange occurrences directly to him was still in effect. A pair of telepathic twins had been born and Selected at Stonemount up north. A baby without a stomach had been born at the Orchards and destroyed. Then he found something.

There was a handwritten report. "Ranger Sergeant Guindon of thirty years service reports to his Guardian that on the night of May 21st I saw a figure dressed like a Hotland shaman running scared about half a mile south by southwest of Fire Station #30 and I wasn't drinking that night nor the day before."

The report was attached to a factor tape from the sergeant's commander. THE ATTACHED WAS TO BE SENT TO YOU, GUARDIAN. THE MAN WHO WROTE IT, ALTHOUGH HE HAD PUT IN MANY YEARS GOOD SERVICE TO THE REPUBLIC, WAS OBVIOUSLY MISTAKEN OR CONFUSED IN THIS MATTER. I SCANNED HIS MEMORY AND SAW WHAT HE CLAIMS WAS A SHAMAN.

I BELIEVE HE MIGHT HAVE FALLEN ASLEEP ON GUARD DUTY AND BEGUN TO RELIVE HIS OLD WAR EXPERIENCES. HE WAS RIDICULED BY OTHER CIT-IZENS. YESTERDAY, MAY TWENTY-SECOND, HE WAS FOUND NEAR THE SAME SPOT WHERE THE SIGHT-ING WAS SUPPOSED TO HAVE HAPPENED. HE WAS DEAD, WITH HIS SERVICE RIFLE BESIDE HIM. I BE-LIEVE IT TO BE AN ACCIDENT, WITH THE POSSIBIL-ITY OF SUICIDE. I AM ALCYIA LIEUTENANT SELECT COMMANDING FIRE STATION NUMBER THIRTY.

Scarecrow made a note to have a guard placed at the glade where the sergeant had died when he issued his general orders. The man had decided to prove himself by lying in wait for the Hotlander. But the shaman had been too quick for him and forced the Citizen to turn his gun on himself.

The meeting was droning on. There was a report being given on the number of burners turning up in the district that spring. THE NUMBER OF BIRDS AND SMALL ANI-MALS WITH EXPLOSIVE CHARGES IS NO LARGER THAN IN PREVIOUS YEARS. THE DAMAGE DONE HAS INCREASED BY AT LEAST THREE HUNDRED PER-CENT. WE MUST CONCLUDE THAT THIS IS STILL WITHIN THE RANGE OF CHANCE. FOR INSTANCE, THE TRANSPORT DISASTER ON THE GREAT EAST-WEST ROAD...

An orderly caught Scarecrow's attention. There was a mes-sage for the Guardian. Before he opened it, Scarecrow knew it was from Uncle. He was on his feet immediately. He had sealed orders ready to go out to every Select in District Four. His staff was to get them delivered and to assemble before dawn at the town of Axblade. Scarecrow left the meeting room, jumped into a rover, and was gone.

He passed through Axblade later that afternoon and ex-changed his rover for a horse. Once again the young Select captain came out to greet the Guardian. Scarecrow saw him-self in the other's eyes. His face was tense; there was gray in his long blond hair. Before riding off alone, Scarecrow handed the Select a metal factor case. SEALED ORDERS, he told him. THE SIGNAL TO OPEN THEM IS THE PHRASE "DRAGONS' TEETH." Then he trotted west out of town.

Out in the woods Scarecrow followed a zigzag path, inspecting each of the approaches to the town from the south. Then, before heading for the border, he cast around to see if he was being followed. As he did, he felt a mind tug at the edge of his. He brought his horse to a halt and scanned again. He caught it, tentative, elusive, prepared at any moment to do a rough imitation of a flock of finches. The telepath was coming closer, scanning clumsily ahead.

Scarecrow pinpointed his pursuer at a spot almost a quarter of a mile west of him. He probed suddenly and found fear. Whoever it was knew he was caught and moved fast, trying to block at the same time. Scarecrow scanned and knew that it was a man and that it wasn't a Select. Neither did it feel quite like Hotlands. Scarecrow caught him again and felt the pounding of the other's heart, the pumping of his arms and legs. He smashed the blocks the other mind tried to throw up. He moved in to paralyze the legs. Suddenly the mind disappeared.

All that Scarecrow was left with was the chill emptiness he always felt on thinking of a portal and the knowledge that the enemy was more afraid of a Select telepath than he was of Time. Calculating the approximate location of the portal, Scarecrow made a mental note to put that spot in his orders and hurried south.

Uncle was waiting for Scarecrow at the edge of the Republic. Together they went out over the dead ground to Hotlands. Scarecrow blocked the minds, distracted the attention of the Citizens who would have seen them. The Select who were on duty in the lookout stations and on patrol gave only the most cursory attention to the border. It was thirty years since Moriaph's great peace of the north. Except for the rash of burners, this spring had been the most peaceful in years.

It was getting dark as they cleared the open ground and went into a large thicket of twisted trees. A lizard as large as a dog scuttled away at their approach. Mole and other of

Grim Reaper's Hotlander apprentices were waiting for them just across the border.

The Hotlanders were in contact with others further back in the woods. Mole told Scarecrow on the way to the ruined town, THEY ARE COMING OUT OF THE SOUTH LED BY RED DEATH. A STRIKE FORCE OF FIVE THOUSAND MEN WITH ALMOST TWO HUNDRED SHAMANS. RED DEATH IS ONE OF RUMACK'S CHIEF CAPTAINS. Scarecrow saw images of men riding horses to death, of mercenaries driving vehicles which had been brought through portals and reassembled out in Hotlands. They were covering hundreds of miles in a matter of days. Those who fell behind were shot as deserters. The survivors were lashed on by shamans showing the image of the screaming Rumack.

As he dismounted, Scarecrow noticed smoke in the woods. Later that summer, when the burning forest choked him, he remembered this as when it had started. Brushfires glowed in the dusk. Scarecrow saw figures standing around: Grim Reaper's apprentices. On the ground lay three dead shamans.

They showed him what had happened. There was a portal in the woods near that ruined town. They had mounted guard on it for weeks knowing the Hotlanders would eventually use it. That morning they had come tumbling out of Time and died as they did. They had come from the world adjoining the Republic, a tundra that Rumack was using as a staging area for his invasion.

Scarecrow turned and went to see Grim Reaper. The old Select's mind seemed to be on fire. He showed Scarecrow images out of Hotlands and out of alien worlds. There were Hotlanders holding automatic weapons and hauling light artillery. There were shaman cadres each with a death stick topped with a human skull. There were outsiders, mercenaries, very hard men and women in the uniforms of a dozen other times and places.

In some jungle world where the sun shone bright and unclouded, Rumack rode by on an enormous horse, reviewing Hotlanders and mercenaries. Rumack cast his mind through those assembled. It was at third- or fourthhand, but Scarecrow felt it, blunt and lethal as a hammer blow.

When Scarecrow saw Grim Reaper, he realized that the man's moment was at hand. Only the eyes were alive, burning in the dim light. Even in his outer Umbra, Scarecrow found an awareness of approaching death. Images that seemed to be etched by fire and murder: piles of Citizens, soldier and civilian lying dead and stacked like wood. Lines of children tied together at the neck were led through portals. Select wept as they marched stunned and naked between lines of shamans. THAT IS WHAT I WAS SHOWN BY THE ORACLE. THAT IS WHAT MIGHT BE.

I HAVE MY ORDERS READY, Scarecrow told him. WHERE IS RUMACK?

COMING UP WITH THE MAIN ATTACK. Grim Reaper showed Scarecrow Rumack's plan as far as it had been discovered. There were two columns coming out of Hotlands on the flanks of one commanded by Red Death. They would smash into Districts Three and Five at the same time as Red Death reached District Four. They would go in at dawn when raiding parties would appear out of dozens of portals all over the three districts, disrupt the defenses, and spread confusion and panic. Rumack himself was leading a huge reserve force which would come through the portals and exploit a gap hundreds of miles long torn in the Republic. HE SAYS HE WILL TEAR US OPEN LIKE AN ANTHILL.

Scarecrow felt the old man's sadness. I LIVED LIKE A DOG BEFORE I UNDERSTOOD TIME AND WHAT IT REALLY WAS. THERE IS NOTHING I WANT MORE THAN TO DIE HERE TONIGHT PUTTING A DENT IN RUMACK'S PLANS. IN TIME THE ONLY THING WORTHWHILE IS BEING A LEGEND OR A PART OF ONE. CRUSH RED DEATH AND YOU WILL HAVE COMPROMISED RUMACK'S ATTACK.

THEN HE WILL TURN ON DISTRICT FOUR. WHAT THEN?

TIME WILL BEGIN TO TURN ITS ATTENTION TO THIS PLACE. HELP WILL COME. There was an image etched on Grim Reaper's consciousness, something from the Oracle. It was Garvin, changed, scarred, eyes flashing, an army following him.

In the dark outside, a mind reached and made contact with Grim Reaper's apprentices. They grabbed it, crushed it. Another mind probed them and another. Red Death's advance guard was upon them, casting about to find the help they expected to feel pouring through the portals. REMEMBER ME, SCARECROW.

Scarecrow rose and spoke. "Thank you, Grim Reaper. Those of us who live will not forget you." The old man nodded, his eyes still closed, his mind on what was happening to the south.

As Scarecrow mounted his horse, another shaman appeared from the portal, tumbling out of Time, firing an automatic rifle. He died before he could bring it to bear, stumbling, choking as the apprentices seized him.

Scarecrow joined Uncle, and they made good time through the woods. It was deepest night as they passed over the open ground. Scarecrow allowed himself to be discovered as he galloped up to the first watchtower he came to and sent the signal DRAGONS' TEETH to every corner of the district.

By then Cluster Group Two was already long out of Weatherhill. They had risen in the dark for an overland hike. Darrel and Maji were going to lead the others as part of their qualifying for apprenticeships. They had arranged to leave before anyone expected them to and went from house to house waking the children, getting them together on the green.

Garvin was up before they got there. In the bathroom he was shaving all the hair on his head except for the Mohawk crest and the start of a ponytail hanging down the back. That last was in imitation of the ones who had rescued him, the ones who had called themselves the Immortals' Companions. His Rider, more prominent now than a few days before, still flinched at the razor. Garvin noticed that and tied a razor blade around his neck with a piece of rawhide. That would serve to remind them both.

Amre had laid out for him a buckskin shirt and moccasins. He put them on, buckled a belt with an ax at his waist, turned, and saw her appear at the door. THANK YOU, AMRE, BUT I AM STILL NO WOODSMAN. He saw in her mind how he had begun to blend in and how he had seemed to grow in the weeks he had been there. He was at the age when he appeared to get taller by the day. The clothes he had been given at first no longer fit him. He was taller than she now. She kissed him on the cheek. They both knew: he was going away very soon.

Someone gave a soft whistle outside. Miche ran into the room wearing a small pack, and hugged her mother. The whistling continued as Darrel and Maji assembled the cluster group. Miche ran down the stairs, Garvin and Amre followed. "Take care of them all, Gavi."

He nodded and thought of Nick. Miche took his hand and they disappeared into the night.

Practice as a medic enabled Amre to return to bed and go back to sleep. She wasn't even surprised that she was awakened again before dawn. This time it was one of Scarecrow's Select aides. AMRE, THERE IS A MESSAGE FROM THE GUARDIAN. HE SAYS TO ASK YOU WHAT IT MEANS. Outside, the garrison was on the move. Troops headed out to mount guard at the Devil's Lair. Amre picked up the confusion and uncertainty in the minds of the other Select. From the aide she received the images he had found in his orders: Rumack howled, armies marched through the night, shamans tumbled out of portals into the Republic. And Scarecrow walked in his white robes into the midst of the invading army. THERE IS ALSO A MESSAGE FOR THE BOY GARVIN. WHERE IS HE?

Scarecrow fell asleep almost as soon as he reached Axblade and found the situation there in hand. He awoke a few hours later with the sun up and rifle fire sounding northwest of the town. In the predawn the garrison had swept the woods where the day before Scarecrow felt someone disappear into a portal.

They took a Hotlands party by surprise before it could organize itself after tumbling out of Time.

As Scarecrow drank coffee and was helped into his ceremonial robes, he received reports from around the district. Everyone had responded. Even if many thought Scarecrow as mad as Grim Reaper had ever been, it wouldn't do to be remembered as one who had failed to act in the face of a Guardian's command. Some of the orders they received seemed insane: to guard their own posts which were miles inside the borders of the Republic, to take up odd positions in the forest, to make strange, seemingly meaningless sweeps.

As these defensive moves were taken, Hotlanders were discovered in their midst. It wasn't just isolated wanderers but commando bands, each with gunmen headed by a trained shaman. At Fire Station #30, where the sergeant had been forced to shoot himself, the local Select commander who had ridiculed him found orders that sent her to watch over a deserted glade in the predawn. No doubt she sat there with her rangers, cursing Scarecrow and wondering who his replacement was going to be. Then Hotlanders seemed to appear from the trees. The riflemen had died along with a huge tattooed shaman whom the Select herself had smashed.

There were other reports of traps sprung and opportunities seized. Some bands of Hotlanders got through. Fire Stations #25 and #28 had been overrun in the first light of dawn. The Orchards to the north had outlying herders and farm families surprised and slaughtered. There was a Hotlander sniper group holding up traffic on the Great East-West Road. But most of District Four was ready and alive, thanks to their Guardian. In towns and farms and outposts around the district, Select scanned the woods and wondered at the skills of their Guardian. They remembered the image they had all received with their orders: Scarecrow striding through the woods to meet the Hotland invaders.

WHAT ABOUT WEATHERHILL?

There was hesitation from the aide who was briefing him. THE NEWS IS NOT ALL GOOD, GUARDIAN. THE FORCE YOU ORDERED TO GUARD DEVIL'S LAIR WAS

AMBUSHED. THE TOWN HOLDS, BUT THE WOODS AROUND IT ARE FULL OF ENEMY. AND THERE IS ANOTHER PROBLEM. Scarecrow saw an image of Cluster Group Two disappearing into the night. THEY HAVE NOT YET BEEN FOUND.

It is me they wanted, Scarecrow thought. They wanted to pin the Guardian down. He silently formed the names of Amre and Miche. Then he thought of Garvin and hoped the boy was ready.

Scarecrow drew a deep breath and stepped outside. Gunfire had started south of Axblade. Hunter parties, border outpost garrisons fell back, firing at the invaders. Some units had orders to join Scarecrow at Weatherhill. A battalion of rangers was leaping from transports and assembling around the town. A troop of border cavalry cantered past to take up their position out on a flank.

A young Select cadet flashed a message by mental Relay from south of the town. PRISONER. He sent an image of Uncle holding a rifle at Mole's back. Scarecrow ordered them brought to him immediately. He kept other Select minds away from them. TURN YOUR ATTENTION TO THE BATTLE LINE, he commanded.

A rover came bouncing into view. Two rangers sat in front. Uncle, with his rifle leveled at a tiny figure, was in back. "Brought him right to you, sir." Uncle's voice betrayed nothing. Mole's pale face was streaked with smoke and tears. The pain in his mind was so intense that Scarecrow found it hard to keep in contact with him.

In a back room with a scrambler on, Mole showed Scarecrow everything. Red Death's columns had expected to find an ammunition and supply dump. Instead, what they found was Grim Reaper and his apprentices and a wealth of booby traps. For a while that was enough to stop them. A half-track that had been brought across a dozen worlds and assembled in Hotlands blew up on a land mine. A whole Hotland company went mad, shot their shamans, and ran amok as Mole and the others seized their minds in the dark. Overshamans trying to set up light artillery had to battle for the minds of the gunners.

Hotlanders felt snakes ripping into their innards, felt hot iron in their eyes, and smelled their own flesh burning. The attack was supposed to reach the Republic at dawn, to come across the open ground at the moment when trees and rocks seem to move and shadows run away. They lost hours there in the ruined town. The whole invading column piled up. Finally Red Death himself led an attack and they came forward like a wave.

The ruins were on fire. So many guns were trained on them that Mole and the others couldn't get at all the gunners. Grim Reaper sat still, eyes closed. The Hotlanders formed a Relay around the town with two hundred shaman minds. Red Death showed them and they showed the troops. Great Rumack opened his mouth and howled for blood. The riflemen went forward. Hundreds of minds reached out. One of Grim Reaper's apprentices was cut in two by rifle fire. Another smashed his brains out on the side of a wall.

Mole watched the old man; Select and Guardian, wanderer in Time, confidant of the Oracles. Grim Reaper opened his eyes, at the same time opening his mind to Mole. Now there was firing from the other buildings of the town. A shaman tumbled through the portal and wasn't destroyed. Mole felt the old man's mind reach out and grab a shaman. Mole was with Grim Reaper as the old man went through the minds of shaman and overshaman through the Relay to Red Death.

Great Rumack's face appeared again in Red Death's mind. The mouth opened, the eyes flashed. This time there was terror in the eyes, and Great Rumack howled with fear. Red Death went rigid, eyes bulging. The shooting stopped. The whole Hotlander column caught his terror.

At that moment Mole felt his mind released by his master. GO AND SHOW SCARECROW, the old man told him. Grim Reaper's body sank into itself and Mole knew he was dead. But he could feel Grim Reaper's mind alive in the brains of every shaman in the Relay. Mole turned and escaped in the confusion as he had been told to. He came right to Uncle, who reported him as a prisoner.

There were great tears in Mole's eyes. Scarecrow stood up. Uncle would know how to safeguard this prisoner. The Guardian moved to the door. It had begun. He had to put his hopes in what Grim Reaper believed. Outside was what would have been a beautiful morning. There were columns of smoke south and west of the town and steady gunfire. The troops of the Republic, rangers and cavalry, were formed up in open order. Scarecrow arranged the defenses of his mind: Umbra, Curtain, Keep. He walked in his white robes across the town green, through the soldiers and into the woods.

CHAPTER TWELVE

IN THE DARK before sunup, Maji and Darrel led Cluster Group Two through the woods. Garvin stayed toward the rear of the column. With most of his own past open to him, he felt strong. He thought of the ones who had died when he was captured, of the ones who died rescuing him. He had an anger that made his Rider cringe. Garvin could feel the outline of the Rider in his own mind. I KNOW WHAT YOU WANT ME TO BECOME. I SAW WHAT HAD BEEN DONE TO HERSELF. IF I FEEL THAT HAPPENING, WE BOTH DIE.

In the darkness the youngest children were quiet. Every once in a while one or two put their hands into Garvin's. They could do it without anyone else knowing. As the sun came up, they lost their fear. Some of them started giggling. Darrel looked back, caught sight of Garvin, and was angry. Maji blew a long, low note on the whistle, motioned for the cluster group to fan out. The noise stopped, the children moving through the undergrowth as quietly as they could. They were several miles out of Weatherhill on a route only Maji and Darrel knew. The children formed a crescent with Maji and Darrel at the two tips. They moved through the woods like a sickle.

Garvin fell behind. There was a stream to the left of the crescent. There was a small promontory over it. On that was a single pine tree. Garvin climbed the pine, hoisting himself a lot more easily than he could have a few weeks before. But he still wasn't a match for these children of the woods. I COULD EASILY SLIP AND FALL, he told the Rider, and felt it squirm. He went up until the branches began to bend under him, until the tree began to sway. NOW TELL ME ABOUT YOURSELF.

There was nothing for a moment. Garvin hung on with one hand. Something stirred inside his mind. He waited and when nothing more happened, he moved out on a narrow branch. Through the trees below him, he could see Cluster Group Two chasing small game in front of them. They didn't make a sound. He could see Maji, follow the grace with which she moved. At that moment he didn't want to die. When he thought of Herself and her eyes, though, he knew there were worse things.

He held on to the limb with the fingers of one hand. He almost slipped. His arm ached. The sun was shining in his eyes. Then he felt something like a voice but as unplaceable as déjà vu. It came from inside him and it said, 'i will co-operate. get down from there, boy, before you kill us both.' The surprise almost made Garvin slip. His mouth went dry and he inched back to a place where he could grab the trunk securely.

Below and a distance away, the ends of the crescent were pulling together. Bushes moved in the center of the forming circle. A deer jumped, saw children, turned, saw others, spun around and around as the circle grew smaller and smaller. YOU MADE ME PARADE IN THOSE CLOTHES, Garvin told the Rider, remembering the chateau and garden, feeling his anger.

'and what have you done since you were free to decide? you are disguised as a child in a society that pays no attention to children and as a nontelepath in a place where telepaths reign. as for the clothes . . .'

YOU KILLED MY FRIENDS. PEOPLE HAD TO DIE SAVING ME. YOU KIDNAPPED ME.

'you were kidnapped by a slave trader, boy. as for death, let us see how clean you can keep your hands.'

YOU ARE A PARASITE. YOU LIVE...

A rock missed Garvin's head by inches, caromed off the tree, and hit his shoulder. "Don't worry." Darrel stood down below, looking up. "I meant to miss. Get down here.... We're going to fight."

'kill him,' the Rider told Garvin. For a moment Garvin felt himself reaching out to do just that, intending to crush Darrel like a bug. Then he remembered the Rider's career of blood. He skimmed Darrel's mind as he started down the tree. He was aware the other thought he was clumsy and a fool. He saw it all: Darrel wanting to be in the border cavalry, to travel west, to get out of Weatherhill where he had lived for his whole life. Darrel felt betrayed that Maji was so interested in the newcomer, this kid who wore a hunter haircut but acted as if he had never seen a woods. Garvin had been given the apprentice clothes that Darrel had worked for. Garvin lived in the observatory with Scarecrow and Amre, Garvin who couldn't even talk.

Garvin hit the ground knowing Darrel's plan. They would take off their shirts and belts and moccasins and fight on the ledge over the creek. The loser would end up in the water and would walk home in his shorts, soaked and humiliated. Darrel was going to crush Garvin in the only way he knew. He was unbuckling his belt, already moving to force Garvin to fight with the sun in his eyes. Garvin admired the skill with which the other did it. Darrel stood poised, waiting for Garvin to get ready.

Garvin could feel his Rider pay very close attention. He could take Darrel's mind and twist it, could terrify or cripple him in any one of a hundred ways. But he didn't want to. He did something much simpler that occurred to him.

He opened his mind to Darrel and showed him some of his own life, New York and the Mohawks and the rest of it. There was the wonder of waking up in the forest town and of the three little pigs. Darrel's head was bobbing, his mouth hanging open in amazement. There was fear in his mind, an awareness that he had tangled with something bigger than he had known. Darrel tried to speak but couldn't. He was looking down at the ground. When he dared to raise his eyes, he saw that Garvin was concentrating on something else.

There was terror. Every bird and animal showed it, every member of their cluster group. He could feel them running toward him. Cluster Group Two burst out of the woods around the clearing where Garvin and Darrel stood. They stumbled as they fled. A boy about eleven had been cut and bled down the side of his face.

Behind the children were other figures, Hotlanders, about a dozen of them, moving in a wide semicircle, herding the children. One of them had a twisted shoulder, another scuttled on dwarf's legs. In charge was a figure with tattooed face and chest. He carried a pole hung with feathers and topped with a human skull. Garvin felt the command that one gave: DO NOT DAMAGE THEM.

The Hotlanders used their rifles to prod the children to the rock where Garvin and Darrel were. Maji had her knife out, but it was knocked to the ground with a rifle butt. There wouldn't be much loot on these, but they could be sold. Some fun could be had with them that wouldn't damage them too much. A little boy was struck when he tried to stop someone from taking his pack. Hands were pulling at Maji's clothes. Darrel looked at Garvin wide eyed, wondering why he didn't act, willing to follow him if he did.

Garvin was aware of shamans in the woods all around them. Children were crying. He found the mind of the shaman in front of him. He cut through the man's rudimentary defenses. The man had learned them in a strange world outside this one. They didn't keep Garvin out of his memories. The sight of awesome Rumack, the terrors of stepping through portals and out into Time were nothing to Garvin. He held the shaman's heart and brain in his grasp, and the man knew real horror.

The shaman tried to scream and couldn't. One agonized

message went out to the rest of the Hotlanders. WIZARD. THERE IS A WIZARD HERE. He was blue in the face, his tongue lolling, his legs twitching. Most of the raiders had nondescript rifles, ones they had gotten in Hotlands. Two had new automatic weapons. One of them leveled his at the children. Garvin let go of the shaman's mind, seized that of another rifleman, and made that Hotlander shoot the other in the head.

He grabbed the shaman again and let that one's panic wash over the others. They saw their leader roll on the ground, his tongue blue and his eyes bulging. They felt his agony. They were running before he died.

When the gun was fired, all the children had thrown themselves flat instinctively. Garvin still stood panting and shaking. The other automatic-weapons man turned and aimed from the edge of the woods. Maji knocked Garvin flat with a tackle as the rifle burst went over them.

Cluster Group Two was surrounded by Hotlanders. Garvin could feel them moving in the woods. The children could sense it too. They looked to him for leadership. He stood up, aware of an uneasiness in the enemy around him. THE WIND, he could feel one shaman telling another. THE WIND COMES. Then leaves shook, branches moved. Garvin recognized the Wind. He had felt it that night his Rider had taken him sleepwalking. He could remember it being there when the minds had called him to the Republic.

Then, right where the Wind was moving the grass, a figure appeared tall and smiling. "Hello. Too late for the fun here," the Guvnor said aloud as he walked toward him. He showed Garvin a firsthand memory of Roger carrying the satchel. SENT BY THE TALKING SUITCASE TO LOOK YOU UP, he told him.

At Weatherhill, Amre had an infirmary full of casualties. The ambushed force had brought back a dozen wounded. Since then, several Citizens had been hit by sniper fire. All that morning scattered parties had been coming in, loggers and fire watchers, a Select surveyor and her party, an old semiretired botanist Select. Troopers lined the defenses; hunters hunkered down in cover around the town and traded shots with Hotlanders. The enemy was out there in force, but they didn't have the numbers to mount an assault.

Somewhere out in the woods an alien mind formed an image of children raped and butchered. From someone's mind a shaman had picked up the information that children from the town were lost in the forest. A woman, Loren's mother, slumped against a wall in tears. The Select in the town pinpointed the shaman, probed after him, felt him fall back and disappear.

There was a volley of rifle fire and then silence except for a steady sniping. Amre put her arms around the sobbing woman. "Don't you think they'd show them to us if they had them?" The woman nodded and became calmer.

The children of Cluster Group Two watched as Garvin communicated with the tall man with the strange clothes and the mustache. There seemed to be a breeze around him and nowhere else. It made them uneasy, but they had full faith in Garvin. It seemed that he was a sort of secret Select. Darrel picked up the shaman's totem stick with the skull on top. The Rider was uneasy too. 'have this clown get us out of this world immediately.'

YOU CAN CALL ME GUVNOR. EVERYONE DOES, the man told Garvin. Garvin saw images of hundreds of worlds. He saw the Old One and Roger again. He saw a two-headed woman. THOSE ARE MY CREDENTIALS, OLD MAN. NOW OUR MUTUAL FRIENDS THINK IT IS TIME YOU LEFT THIS WORLD.

THAT IS ALSO WHAT THE RIDER INSIDE ME WANTS.

AND HE IS QUITE A FILTHY BUGGER. SOMETIMES YOU WILL FIND THAT EVEN THE LOWLIEST COME UP WITH A GOOD IDEA.

Garvin nodded. He knew that it was time. He turned toward the others and told the Guvnor, THIS IS CLUSTER GROUP TWO AND THEY HAVE TO GET BACK HOME.

The Guvnor nodded and said, "All right. And we can speak

aloud if that's all the same to you. I'm afraid telepathy will never be second nature to me." He nodded to the children; the breeze rippled their hair. Garvin reached out to probe it, giving the Guvnor a questioning look. "The Wind is my friend. Your friend too. You'll learn all of that later."

Darrel stepped forward and handed Garvin the totem stick. 'congratulations,' the Rider told him. 'on your first blooding.' Garvin knocked the skull off the top. He was going to set off back to Weatherhill the same way that they had come. The Rider protested inside him. 'the children will make a target out of us.' The Guvnor at the same time thought of a large transport that had gotten ambushed about half a mile away.

Garvin probed in the direction the Guvnor had indicated. There were Hotland minds out there. Garvin and Guvnor could count at least six shamans and probably ten times that number of riflemen. "Form up your command, old man, and we'll break them," said the Guvnor.

The woods around Weatherhill were alive with alien minds. Firing was almost continuous now. A Hotlander attack had come in and been stopped. There were more casualties for Amre's infirmary. In the middle of the blood and confusion, with wounded troopers and townspeople lying in the halls and even outside the door, Amre found herself thinking of the perfect fingers of her little boy who had been Selected. She felt a soft baby nestling next to her.

She saw bloody, naked children's bodies. She saw headless children running through the woods toward her. She felt a Hotlander mind on her own. "You cowards," she said aloud. She could hear sobbing around her. A Select mind swept aside the Hotlander.

The Select, tired, harassed, with a slight wound in his leg, was still on duty but reaching the end of his tether. This Hotland raid, so unexpected, with trained shamans and gunmen appearing out of the ground, was straining everyone's ability to function.

Then there was an explosion of gunfire and a wild honking

of a transport horn. They all felt a mind reach out, huge, all-embracing. DEATH TO RUMACK AND ALL WHO FOLLOW HIM. Amre recognized Garvin. There were images in the air of shamans dying if they weren't fast enough to run. One stood stock-still with a whirlwind tossing around him before he fell facedown, dead, empty.

The horns and the firing grew nearer, coming out of the southeast, heading for the gates of Weatherhill. The shamans who had the town surrounded gave way, started to withdraw in terror. Riflemen abandoned sniper positions and fled. The garrison was firing at them as they ran. Out of the woods, bouncing on the logging road, came the transport, horn blasting, a stranger at the wheel. In the back, hanging on to the sides, children screamed their defiance as on the roof Garvin waved his captured totem stick.

Scarecrow took the report just as his forces came into contact with Red Death's. THE CLUSTER HAS RETURNED INTACT. YOUR DAUGHTER IS SAFE. THE BOY GARVIN HAS BEEN A HERO.

In front of him the level of firing was rising. There were more ranger companies in the line now. The flanks were securely anchored by whole squadrons of cavalry. Border guards and hunters who had fallen back in front of the invaders acted as a skirmish screen. There were still under three thousand troops of the Republic in line. But Scarecrow had gathered every Select who could reach him. Village commanders were there and administrators from all over the district. There were cadets, a cluster group of youths almost old enough to be cadets, scientists who had been at work in the forest. They had come, some fighting their way past Hotlanders. They had been summoned by an image out of an earlier time. A Guardian walked forward in his white robes to save his people.

Scarecrow counted on that. He had as many Select and more than Red Death had shamans. He counted on Red Death and his command being shaken by its encounter with Grim Reaper. And he counted most on surprise. Red Death would have imagined the district to be in confusion but following its old strategy of falling back on the citadel at Fire Gates. Instead he found them moving forward on an extended front, sweeping the Hotlanders back faster than they had come. Most of all, Scarecrow at the back of his mind counted on Garvin. That was his final reserve.

Amre reached the perimeter of the town as the children came running toward their families. The garrison was out and after the Hotlanders. Garvin stood with the stranger, holding the totem stick like a staff. Maji was on his other arm. There was a constant moving of the leaves behind them. Garvin and Maji kissed. He looked for Amre, sought her mind. I WILL BE BACK, he told her. Then he and the stranger turned and were gone.

Garvin felt his Rider's mistrust of the Guvnor and the Wind. But he himself trusted them both implicitly. It might just have been that the Guvnor preferred to talk and that Garvin could understand him when he did. It may be that the Guvnor reminded him of someone he had known. Garvin was willing to follow the other to a portal he knew. "I don't believe the Hotlanders have found this one yet," the Englishman told him.

The portal was a space of diffracted light between two trees. "Where does it lead?" Garvin asked.

The Guvnor laughed. "Right down Rumack's throat." And Garvin was laughing too as they entered the portal.

CHAPTER THIRTEEN

THE ARMY of the Republic was in quarter-moon formation, its concave edge toward the Hotlanders. As the firing line faced the invaders, cavalry galloped down forest paths to outflank them. Select formed a Relay, transmitting the image of Scarecrow. Doubts and confusion faded. A Guardian stood by as they had in legends.

Scarecrow's Umbra touched those of the Select nearest to him. They in turn linked with others. Scarecrow reached out, still holding the Relay, and touched the mind of a scout falling back in front of him. He sent what he found into the minds of every Select.

"Fighting every step of the way," the man was thinking. "Hotlander devils are tougher than my dad told me. They have wizards too as tough as ours. Those ones are bad; catch you and turn your mind inside out. Our Select are never around. Never a Select when the shooting gets hot."

The Relay saw as the man did: figures moved through the trees to kill him. There was a death's-head on a stick. An image of Rumack filled the man's mind and he cringed in terror. He couldn't fire his gun. Dread Rumack held him paralyzed.

THAT IS RUMACK, Scarecrow told the Relay. HE BOASTS THAT HE WILL SELL US ALL AS SLAVES. He probed and found the shaman who had the scout's mind. The army of the Republic saw the image crumble as the shaman tried to hide himself. Select had opened their minds to the Citizens near them. Their Guardian gave the signal, and with a shout they moved forward as a single will.

Scarecrow formed in his mind the image of a sickle slicing grass. Each Select in the Relay reached out for a shaman's mind. The firing in front of them grew intense. Hotland riflemen went for cover. Out on the flanks border cavalry began to edge behind the Hotlanders. The sickle that the Hotlanders found in their minds wasn't slicing grass. It was lopping off heads.

Red Death felt the shimmer of fear run through his army. The fight with Grim Reaper before dawn had put a chill into Rumack's lieutenant. This unexpected resistance when he had been told there would be friends waiting at every crossroad unnerved him. He formed the image of howling Rumack, filled the minds around him with the cry of Rumack's triumph. He felt the howl turn to fear and felt the mind of that old wizard Grim Reaper alive somewhere inside his.

RED DEATH, THEY MOVE TO SURROUND US! His army was coming apart. Soldiers threw away their rifles and fled. Shamans trying to rally them were cut down by rifle fire. Shamans seized by Select's minds went mad and lashed out at their own troops. The Hotland leader reached for their minds.

RED DEATH! As he did, he felt himself seized. The leader of the forest wizards had probed through the tangle of minds and grabbed him. RED DEATH! WE HARVEST YOU LIKE HAY. RUMACK HAS LED YOU TO DESTRUCTION. The sickle cut off Rumack's head and it bounced on the ground, eyes lolling back.

Every shaman and rifleman caught that image. All semblance of order disappeared. They bolted back down the same forest paths they had just traveled. Fire on their flanks indicated that they were about to be cut off. They threw away their guns. Shamans dropped their death's-head staffs.

In the woods south of Axblade, his aides waited for Scarecrow to order a general pursuit. The Guardian stood facing the retreating enemy. As he felt for the trace of Grim Reaper in the minds of the fleeing Hotlanders, he was aware of something else. Uncle and the Mole had joined the retreat. They were going south with the enemy column.

WE AWAIT YOUR ORDERS, GUARDIAN. A Select aide stood by.

"Follow them to the border and secure it."

THEY ARE IN OUR PALM, GUARDIAN. WE CAN CRUSH THEM.

Scarecrow shook his head. "What are the reports from Districts Three and Five?"

An aide pressed buttons on a factor. THIS IS JESSIA, GUARDIAN OF DISTRICT THREE. WE ARE FALLING BACK IN GOOD ORDER ON THE EYES OF HELL. BUT TOWNS AND STATIONS ALL OVER THE DISTRICT ARE IN FLAMES. WE WILL NEED HELP TO TURN THE RAIDERS BACK.

Scarecrow nodded. More buttons were pushed. THIS IS OLIVET. WE CANNOT HOLD OUT WITHOUT ASSIS-TANCE. JOYOUS FREEDOM'S PERIMETER HAS BEEN BROKEN. HOTLANDERS APPEAR TO BE POURING OUT OF THE GROUND.

"Guardian, a message from the Warden of the Border Reaches," a Citizen radio operator told him.

He took the headset from the woman and heard Moriaph's voice cracked and far away. "You were right, Scarecrow. The only one who knew what was happening. I will mount my counterattack from your district. I will be there by nightfall." Scarecrow thought of Amre and Miche back at Weatherhill. "Scarecrow, are you still there?" He thought of Garvin and wondered how long he could hold out.

* * *

Tumbling in Time, Garvin lost touch with the Guvnor. The hand that had grabbed his shoulder disappeared. The mind faded to a distant pinpoint. Garvin had no eyes and ears. There was no air and he had no lungs with which to breathe.

Garvin felt the Wind somewhere nearby. It was a kaleidoscope of lives floating with him in Time. Garvin was afraid. Then he felt the Rider's fear as sharp as an ice pick inside him. That made Garvin pull himself together. He had been in Time. He couldn't remember the trip to Herself's chateau. But he recalled the long fall from there to the Republic.

Thinking of that, he tried to focus on the infinite worlds that existed. When he did he was aware of a steady, muffled heartbeat. Something pulsed out beyond the worlds. From that he turned to the worlds close at hand. The one he had just left was fading. Garvin felt pain in that world, pain and death. Another was taking shape in front of him. There was little human life there and almost no pain.

Its air tested clean. Realizing that, Garvin felt his lungs start to work. The Wind flowed above him through the portal. The Guvnor had him by the shoulder. "Steady there. Slight drop." Garvin's feet came down on grass. He stumbled, gulping in air. The sun stood almost where it had before. The sky was clear, the possibilities infinite.

Figures moved on the horizon, men and horses. There were flashes of sun on metal. Garvin picked up traces of telepathy. WHERE? WHAT? Garvin asked his Rider.

'an adjacent world. that activity is Rumack's supply line.' Garvin picked up a feeling of admiration by his Rider for Rumack. 'i doubt if your new friend is to be trusted.' Garvin decided to trust the Guvnor.

As they detected other telepaths, they were detected. A mind probed in their direction. Garvin recognized a Hotland telepath and blocked hard.

The Guvnor, who had been scanning in all directions, said, "It's going to be necessary for you to pretend to be my prisoner. Is that agreeable to you?"

Garvin nodded even as his Rider told him, 'one who pretends is still a prisoner.'

Figures had detached themselves from the activity on the horizon and were approaching. Three mounted Hotlanders galloped toward them. The Guvnor signaled the Wind and extended his mind in greeting. Aloud, he said to Garvin, "They bring our transportation with them. Just block and leave the rest to me."

One of the horsemen was a telepath. Garvin deflected the mind with his Umbra defense. The Guvnor showed an image of Rumack. It was authentic and recent. THE ORDERS OF RUMACK ARE TO TRANSPORT THIS WIZARD SPAWN TO MARKET. The shaman was impressed. The Guvnor remembered Rumack standing only a few feet away. I AM EMPOWERED, the Guvnor told the horseman, TO ENLIST ANY HELP I NEED.

The three horsemen could now be identified as the shaman and two riflemen. They galloped up the little rise where the Guvnor and Garvin stood. NEED MORE PROOF, the shaman told the Guvnor.

HERE ARE MY CREDENTIALS, the Guvnor told him. At that moment the Wind moved forward and unraveled the shaman's mind from his body. It seemed slower to Garvin than it had before. But it was fast enough and deadly. The shaman's body slumped in the saddle; the death's-head stick fell from his hands.

The riflemen could not aim their weapons. The Guvnor had their minds before they could act. "Hold the horses," he told Garvin. The animals sensed the Wind and could feel their masters' terror. Garvin held them all with his mind, calmed each of them.

The Guvnor made the two riflemen drop their guns and dismount. The shaman hit the ground when his horse shied. The Guvnor had the two men pick up the body. Garvin understood that they were going to carry it through the portal. Since they weren't telepaths, they could never find their way out. They would disappear into Time forever.

He scanned the riflemen's minds. They were terrified; their arms and legs moved without their willing it. They were in the power of a great Wizard. One man was a veteran, a vassal of a Hotlander warlord. The warlord was the shaman who had just been taken by the Wind. The man thought, "I've seen death lots of times, looking at me and not looking away. I wish it had been any of the other deaths instead of the hell inside that portal."

The other rifleman was only a little older than Garvin. He had run away from a farm where he had been mistreated. He had been caught up in Rumack's army, where they had fed him. "Two weeks from home and I'm going to die," he kept repeating to himself. There were tears in his eyes as his legs moved to the portal.

They reached the portal, and Garvin intervened. "Don't kill them, Guvnor. Make them put the body into Time, but let them go."

"Can't. They'll raise the alarm."

"They're too frightened to talk."

"The next shaman on the scene will find out what they saw. They have to be disposed of." The two men started into the portal with the corpse. Garvin blocked the Guvnor from their minds, turned their movement to one of tossing the shaman's body into Time.

He made the two riflemen climb onto the third horse. He showed them the image of screaming Rumack and tore it in two. I WILL DESTROY HIM! That rang in their minds and horrified them. Their horse tried to bolt. "Which way are we going, Guvnor?"

The man looked toward the horizon. "North northeast."

He sent the Hotlanders south as fast as their frightened horse would run.

"I'm sorry, Guvnor," he said. "Killing them is what my Rider would have done."

The Guvnor took the shaman's horse. He vaulted into the saddle. "You're the strongest adept I've ever encountered. Today we'll find out just what that's worth."

It took a couple of tries before Garvin could get his horse under him. The Guvnor set a brisk pace. Garvin had trouble staying on. He watched the way the Guvnor sat, copied the way the other linked his mind with that of the animal. The

Guvnor rode like part of his horse. After twenty minutes in the saddle, Garvin's insides had been turned to jelly. "Where are we going?" he managed to ask.

"Down an appendix." The Guvnor showed him a line of half a dozen worlds joined by portals. "Some say an appendix is an idle moment in the minds of the Gods. Rumack found a very good set of portals. Or purchased a map from someone at Goblin Market.

"Portals are the highways of Time. A portal leads from one world to the corresponding place on the next. The trick then is to find another portal that will take you from world two to world three. Rumack seems to have no trouble with that."

"What lies on the other sides of the Republic?"

"Dead Worlds, unbreathable air. Nothing I could find beyond that. But the route which Rumack has been so good as to mark out for us leads to a place where I feel quite comfortable, and that's near a main Time Lane. I think you might like it."

They rode, staying parallel to the traffic they had seen. Garvin began to understand what it was. Hotlanders were carrying material to portals that led into the Republic. Return traffic was mostly empty-handed work crews. Then he made out a group of prisoners, Citizens with their hands bound, their minds in shock. WE WILL RESCUE THEM, he told the Guvnor. He could feel his Rider's protest inside him.

"If you try, old boy, I'm afraid we must part company, much as I want to keep you with me. You're going to have to learn something that took me a lot of getting used to. Minds and bodies, telepathic and nontelepathic, are the currency of the Time Lanes."

Garvin saw the Guvnor's memories of shuffling prisoners in their millions at Goblin Market. "There are tens of thousands of worlds, thousands of them inhabited." Some of the worlds the Guvnor had seen looked almost like the history Garvin could remember. Others were askew. There was a city of red brick inhabited by a race of blue-eyed Orientals. There were people in furs and Aztec feathers standing in an arctic waste.

"People are common as gravel, sad to say. And not at all unique. One man may have a thousand doubles on a thousand worlds."

"You sound like my Rider."

"Never! The difference is that it has the chance to live forever. You and I don't, old boy. Our little lives are rounded by the well-known sleep. Whatever body your Rider happens to be using no sooner develops a head cold when it leaps like a flea to the next one. You and I will survive only by our wits."

'and with the help of a wind. ask him about that.' Garvin felt the Wind above them like a large, invisible, well-fed cat. He was forming the question for the Guvnor and that took his mind off his horse. It stumbled slightly and Garvin came down hard on his testicles. For a few minutes he could think of nothing else.

A challenge from a telepath brought him back to his surroundings. Their path was converging with the supply line. Other supply lines were visible, fanning out over the tundra. A man in a flak jacket and World War Two American helmet liner stood by the side of the road and asked, BY WHAT COMMAND DO YOU GO HERE?

The Guvnor showed the image of Rumack. SPECIAL PRISONER BEING BROUGHT BACK. The man nodded and probed Garvin. He was blocked hard enough to snap his head back. HE IS A STRONG YOUNG DEVIL, THIS WIZARD SPAWN, the Guvnor told him.

"That was no shaman," Garvin told the Guvnor.

"Mercenary. Look." He indicated a group of about a hundred people in an assortment of twentieth-century military equipment. RUMACK IS PAYING WELL.

"Paying them to attack the Republic?" Garvin was angry.

"Steady on." The Guvnor smiled. "It may be the only trade they know."

'spoken like a mercenary,' his Rider told him.

Then they were approaching a scene of great activity. There

were tents and crude, temporary buildings ahead. "Hungry?" the man asked. Garvin realized that he was. "We'll dine at the expense of Rumack. Can't linger, though. Do as I say. If I mention how strong you are, give everyone a hard probe."

The supply camp was a jumble of horses and wagons, shamans and riflemen. There were piles of empty wooden crates and stacks of unopened ones. A single half-track was being loaded and horses were being shod. There was the smell of smoke and men and the sound of orders being yelled. For the first time Garvin caught a feeling which he would come to associate with being in the midst of an army. It was confusion turned to order by discipline, of discipline maintained only by fear.

The Guvnor gave him a hand down from his horse, led him to a tent. Someone laughed at the way Garvin staggered. Inside was food, hot stew and biscuits and something that was supposed to be coffee. "Army food was what drove me off my own world," said the Guvnor under his breath.

Garvin shoveled down food. He guessed that it was the middle of the afternoon. He hadn't eaten since supper the night before. He also hadn't slept much but he didn't feel tired. The tent was empty except for the two of them and some cooks. Figures appeared at the entrance. A chief shaman, his face black with tattoos, a necklace of teeth around his neck, stood with several shamans. WHO? asked the chief.

ONE ON AN IMPORTANT MISSION FROM RUMACK. The Guvnor showed his image of the war leader. The shaman blinked but was silent. I BRING A SPECIAL PRISONER, A YOUNG WIZARD. The shaman reached out to probe them both. CAREFUL, MIGHTY LEADER. HE IS VERY STRONG.

Garvin was still sore from riding and he wanted to finish eating. He put that into the probe along with his anger at seeing the prisoners and not being able to help. He caught the mind of everyone in the camp. Horses screamed, a sentry fired into the air.

The Guvnor had blocked what he knew was coming. "Steady there," he muttered. Then he leaped up, grabbed Garvin by

the collar, and yanked him to the door of the tent. EVEN
MY GREAT POWERS CAN BARELY CONTAIN THIS
ONE. I MUST HASTEN.

The chief signaled assent and held his head with tears in
his eyes. The Guvnor steered Garvin toward the portal. As
they approached, a shaman appeared pulling a rope. Attached
to it was a string of riflemen, each carrying a crate on his
shoulder. The shaman was gritting his teeth at having to
tumble through Time again and again. His riflemen were
stunned with terror. Garvin felt the Wind overhead as the
Guvnor guided him into Time.

Garvin paid attention during this tumble. The world behind
him receded in his awareness. Another one grew before him.
Then he felt the million possibilities of Time, heard the steady
heartbeat.

The Guvnor was too separate to be reached by telepathy
as they tumbled. The Wind spread itself in Time, and Garvin
reached out to probe. The Hotland shaman was the latest, the
clearest mind in the Wind. Already the hard edges of shock
and fear were disappearing as his consciousness joined the
swirl of lives.

'ask your great new friend about the wind. you are a yokel
in time and do not understand. for a man like the guvnor to
have that kind of control over a wind would be like someone
in your old neighborhood keeping a lion and letting it feed
on local children. winds are forbidden to any but the gods of
the city out of time.'

ARE YOU AFRAID OF BEING EATEN?

'no. it fears eating me. it knows that i would not be di-
gested. i would rule the wind. without me the guvnor would
have thrown you to it as a snack.'

Garvin probed the Wind and felt beyond the thousands of
lives. He found a place where Time seemed full of currents
and eddies, where there were no worlds and the heartbeat of
Time was very strong. 'the cave of winds.' From his Rider's
surprise, Garvin knew it had never glimpsed the cave before.

Then another portal was opening. Light was shining and
there were minds near. It was a world like the one they had

just left, but warmer. Garvin could tell that this was a place where the deer ate the grass and the wolves ate the deer. The buzzards ate what the wolves left and eventually ate the wolves.

Then he dropped a few feet to the ground, got his legs under him, took his first gasp of this world's air. The Wind was above them. Garvin probed for it. The Guvnor whispered, "Don't bring it to their attention."

IN THE NAME OF THE TERRIBLE ONE, I DEMAND TRANSPORT, he told all around him, showing the image of Rumack. A jeep was parked nearby. The Guvnor went to it, dragging Garvin with him. The jeep was the chief's. He wouldn't let them take it. Then Garvin probed again, hard. The chief begged the Guvnor to remove Garvin at all cost.

The Guvnor was driving away, Garvin beside him before anyone could come to their senses. "Get sleep if you can. We will run until they catch us or we reach safety."

"Where are we going?"

"A place that's rather like home to me. You might find it amusing also." He showed Garvin an Edwardian London. "Not quite my own, but it will serve."

'probe him, boy.'

HE IS MY FRIEND.

'he is a mercenary. you are a prize. because of me.'

Instead, Garvin asked the Guvnor, "Who are you?"

"Just a simple cavalry captain." The Guvnor looked around at the flat veld on which they traveled. They passed work crews of Hotlanders hauling supplies. "This would be perfect cavalry country. A few hundred hard riders could paralyze an army."

'ask him how many slaves he has sold at goblin market.'

Again Garvin refused. He asked the Guvnor, "Where are we in relation to the world I came from?"

"How long since you left your world?"

"Hard to say. A couple of months."

"What month was it?"

"November."

"Here we're well into June. You're a long way from home. They say that every twist and turn of history is represented somewhere in Time. I don't know about that. I do know your world is months away from us now."

The immensity of Time, the distance from home, made Garvin's mind reel.

"It will bother you at first. You'll learn, though, that there's no world, whether heaven or hell, that you don't have to leave eventually." Garvin was going to ask more questions when the Guvnor straightened up at the wheel and told him, "Probe. See if we're being followed."

Right behind them was a column of Hotlanders with their shamans. They had saluted the jeep respectfully when it passed. Now they were halted, picking up signals of alarm from the base Garvin and the Guvnor had just left. Garvin saw images of them, felt the chief's anger. "They know," he said.

"Damn. Damn all." The Guvnor was slowing down. There was a cloud of dust on the plain in front of them. Minds were probing at theirs. GUVNOR, a fairly powerful adept reached their minds. I HAD FEARED WE WOULD NEVER MEET AGAIN.

"That last base must have a radio. They signaled ahead. An infinity of damnations."

"They know you up ahead."

"From a previous adventure." The Guvnor turned sharply and headed off across the plain. "Those are mercenaries who recognized me just now."

"What about the Wind? It can take them."

"A few, perhaps. But its belly is full of shamans after this morning. It can only absorb a certain number of lives at a time." There was rifle fire that didn't come close. Then a mind tried to tear the Guvnor's hands off the steering wheel. Garvin batted it away. "Your mistakes behind us, mine in front. We'll drive till we lose them or run out of fuel."

"What about another portal?"

"The only portals I understand are the ones on Rumack's supply route. Those are the only ones I've ever been shown. He tried to recruit me. That's how I have that nice fresh image of him."

GUVNOR, YOU HAVE CHOSEN A DUSTY PLACE TO

DIE. Garvin punched out at that mind. Other minds moved closer. Over a rise behind them came horsemen. A bullet smashed the driver's mirror. Garvin's mind went through the horsemen and left them lying on the ground. From them he picked up an image of a cliff. It was just ahead.

He showed it to the Guvnor. They were driving up a slope. The man swerved sharply. There was a blue ribbon on their left. Garvin realized it was a river hundreds of feet below. They drove along the ridge parallel to the cliff. A bullet hit one of the rear tires and the Guvnor almost lost control.

A PORTAL, Garvin told the Guvnor. THERE MUST BE A PORTAL SOMEWHERE.

"If you find one, old man, you will have to take us through it and bring us back out of Time. I can tumble only when I know what my destination is. You found your way from Herself's garden to the Republic. That's a fair distance." They were losing speed.

Figures moved to intercept them; minds probed at them. Garvin felt a tingling in his spine. There was a portal nearby. Figures appeared on the ridge in front of them. THE PORTAL IS COMING UP FAST. Garvin could feel it shimmering, inviting. It lay beyond the ridge out in midair.

Bullets struck the jeep. It lurched and went over the cliff. Garvin's stomach dropped. His Rider was screaming. Then a hand grabbed his collar and he heard the Guvnor say, "Any old rabbit hole in a storm," as they became separated in Time.

CHAPTER FOURTEEN

GARVIN WAS alone in time. The infinite worlds he glimpsed were beyond his grasp. The heartbeat faded as he tried to concentrate on it. The world they left had disappeared, but nothing else had appeared. His Rider was afraid and so was he.

Then Garvin tried to think of the other passages in Time. They had brought him from home to Herself's estate. Of that trip he could remember almost nothing, a blur of images. With the Guvnor he had done nothing but follow. On his own, though, he had gone from Herself's to the Republic, from late summer to late spring.

He had hurtled through Time toward someone or something that called his name, that knew what he looked like. It had been like a bursting star, the dying cluster group that had called him.

When he remembered that, he remembered one other thing: the image of a mirror reflecting an empty room that he had been taught by Nick.

As soon as he had that image, a world began to outline itself in the glass. It was right in front of him, warm and alive. The life was jungle life.

He lost concentration on the mirror and the room disappeared. Garvin focused again on the mirror, made that his Keep. The room was empty and rather dim. The light was natural light. He made the room his Curtain. He summoned up the world he had just seen and made that his Umbra. Balancing all three, he found an opening into the world, a portal.

The sky was blue. There was a roaring in his ears and intense sunlight. There was a green carpet below. The air was very warm. He felt his lungs start to work. The Wind was rushing around his ears. There was a sheet of water next to him. The carpet was jungle a quarter of a mile below him. His Rider screamed. He began to fall.

Garvin felt himself yanked back by the cord around his neck. The jungle was gone and he was back in time. He tried again, summoning up the mirror, looking into the room. Counting the Republic, the jungle was the fourth world down an appendix. The Guvnor had said there were six. He also said that an appendix was an idle thought in the mind of a God. What was the thought that had produced these worlds?

Ice. The idea came to him, and the world formed in the mirror. It was a transparent outline; he could still see the room which he held with his Curtain. He held the world with his Umbra and probed. There was life, but it was thin. There was a portal, one that corresponded to the ones that hung in midair. Garvin approached it carefully. Before he felt the cold, he knew the way was closed. A glacier blocked the way. The rabbit hole was a dead end.

The Wind could tell something was wrong. It stirred and seemed anxious. The Guvnor was no more than a flick of light, a firefly. 'had you let me negotiate the passage,' his Rider told him, 'i would have been rumack's guest.'

I NEED ANOTHER PORTAL. HOW DO I GET IT?

'world spinning.'

WHAT IS THAT?

'a secret of the immortals.'

NO ONE ELSE?

'certain of their companions.' At that an image of Herself

floated out of the Rider. She was young and wore the Mohawk crest.

HERSELF WAS A COMPANION? THEN HER RIDER KNEW.

'it was not a secret which was shared.'

Garvin thought of Herself's beautiful eyes, the flick of the Rider behind them. He remembered the estate, the chateau, the operating room, the ruined tower, the ancient globe in front of the peacock wallpaper. By reflex, he still held the image of the mirror and the room in his mind. The blue and white wallpaper leaped out at him.

THAT WALLPAPER AND THE ANTIQUE GLOBE WERE IN THE ROOM IN THE MIRROR. THAT HAS TO BE IT! NOTHING ELSE IN THE TWO ROOMS IS THE SAME.

'it was left out where anyone could see it. but no one would guess because it was left out.' Garvin felt the Rider's greed and elation at learning this.

Garvin concentrated on the globe. The glacier loomed up again. The globe had yellow oceans and multicolored land. Names were written in red script. He couldn't read the language. The side he could see showed the North American Continent. He looked hard at it and the glacier portal lay before him. He did that until he was frustrated.

He wanted to reach out of the mirror and spin the globe hard. He was trapped between a long drop and a wall of ice. He jabbed at the globe with his Umbra. The glacier disappeared. There was no portal. He concentrated on the mirror, on the room, on the globe. A portal appeared. It was underground, blocked by dirt and stone.

But it wasn't the glacier. He reached toward the globe again. Another portal appeared, this one over water. With rising elation he kept jabbing at the globe and coming up to portals. When one appeared that he knew was safe, he tumbled out of Time. Snow got in his moccasins; cold went right through him. The sun shone down on ice and Garvin shouted his triumph.

The Guvnor looked at him with admiration. "Time Strider. World Spinner," he said softly.

Garvin was filled with pride. "I can take you to that world you told me about at the end of the appendix. It will be the one after next, and I can find clear portals with no trouble."

"Let me suggest something a little harder that will make things much easier in the end. Go to the next world and get us to where London would be. We can change clothes and rest there. The one who sent me for you will meet us in London. Can you do that, World Spinner?"

'who is it that waits; ask him that at least.' Garvin did.

"A friend of the Talking Suitcase." Garvin saw what seemed to be an old woman holding up a baby. She was hard to see because the illumination was flames in a dark woods. "The Thorn thinks it will take us days to travel Rumack's supply lines," the Guvnor told him. "And weeks to get from Canada to London. I can show you the city before reporting to her." He laughed at the idea. "Think you can do it?"

Garvin nodded, wondering if he could, and turned back toward Time. 'probe him. find out what he was paid.' Garvin ignored the Rider, concentrated on the mirror, the room. The image of the ice world disappeared, and the next world, full of pine forests and empty of human life, appeared. Garvin held that and concentrated on the globe.

The way to the Atlantic was easy enough, sorting through portals, finding ones safe enough to come out and take his bearings. The sun was in the western sky when the Guvnor and he stood on some rocks on the Newfoundland coast. But that was as much of the globe as he could see. The Atlantic and Europe were turned away from the mirror.

Back in Time, Garvin concentrated on the globe but still hovered along the Atlantic wall. Clouds scudded across the sun when he looked out. He stared into the mirror. If he could just move a little further across the glass, he could see more of the globe. He tried it, his vision of the room shifting slightly, a bit more of the Atlantic appearing. He glanced through a portal and saw nothing but water and sky.

He went over the ocean with the sun falling behind him

for the rest of that day. He had moved his vantage point in the room halfway across the mirror. Every trick of concentration that was his he used in holding mirror and room and globe. He caught sight of the outline of Ireland on the map and looked out from a thousand feet in the air to see the browns and greens of the land caught in the last rays of the sun.

From there it was easier. The Guvnor showed him which way to go. At each portal they passed through to look around, the man's praise grew. That kept him going. When at last in the final ray of sunlight they stood in a green river valley, the Guvnor said, "Splendid." And Garvin collapsed on the ground.

"The Thames," the Guvnor said, looking at the river. "Quite sweet still in this incarnation. We can walk from here." Garvin heaved himself up and walked.

'where? what are his plans? how much was he paid to bring me here?' Garvin showed the questions to the Guvnor, who seemed amused.

"Immediately we are going to some friends of mine. Tomorrow, if it's agreeable, we shall go over to London."

"Who is the woman with the baby?"

"The Thorn and Rose. An Immortal like your friend the Talking Suitcase."

"She'll help me? I have to put together a rescue mission for the Republic."

"Well, Garvin, that comes under the heading of politics, and I don't meddle in that."

"I have to go back and help them. I promised that I would."

"Did you take an oath of some kind? Those are very silly things. I took one to old George the Fifth in the world where I was born. It turns out there are dozens of him in different worlds. In one he was a German agent. In another he sometimes appeared on state occasions dressed as Marie Antoinette."

"Scarecrow and Amre saved me. The Rider would have broken me without them."

"Decent folk. World bound, but decent. I know you won't

believe me now, Garvin, but eventually the world-bound ones stop mattering to you. Only those who move in Time will have meaning."

"If the Thorn and Rose won't help me, I'll go back there by myself."

"The politics of Time," the Guvnor said, as if he hadn't heard, "is that the Riders herd people to Goblin Market and the Immortals try to stop the Riders. They ambush prisoner convoys, organize worlds before the Riders can get to them. They slow the Riders down, but I've never heard of them actually saving a world once the Riders set their minds on taking it."

A mind reached out and touched theirs. Garvin blocked but the Guvnor identified himself. There was joy in the night. Lights came on in the distance. "How do you like Time?" the Guvnor asked Garvin.

Despite his exhaustion, Garvin brightened. "I like it fine."

"Yes. It's the only place for ones such as ourselves. If things had turned out differently, I probably would have died somewhere leading a cavalry charge into a machine-gun nest. As it is, I was lucky enough to find my gaseous friend here. And I've fallen in with you.

"Come with me, Garvin. The whole of Time lies before us. We could have a war band such as never was before. We could range over a thousand worlds and no one, Immortal or Rider, could stand in our way. There would be victories they could tell about in all the Time Lanes. Think of it."

Minds in front of them were announcing, THE SWORD OF THE LORD AND THE DIVINE WIND.

"I'm something of a local favorite," said the Guvnor. They approached the lights and Garvin saw those were torches mounted on wooded palisades. Both the palisades and the ditch around them were new. His Rider noticed that.

Figures in pilgrim hats and dark clothes stood in the gateway. "Don't give them a hint of your secret sharer, Garvin. They had a nasty experience with a Rider." It occurred to Garvin that many people would hate him because of his Rider. 'my enemies are yours, boy,' it told him.

THIS IS GARVIN, the Guvnor told them, WHO SAVED MY LIFE THIS AFTERNOON, WHO WALKS THROUGH TIME AS EASILY AS YOU PASS FROM ROOM TO ROOM. They gasped and marveled.

A man with a Bible pressed against his chest reached out with his mind and touched Garvin's. A BLESSING, he announced. Standing to the rear were women in long dark dresses and bonnets. Men held rifles. 'repeating rifles, newly acquired. see how unused they are to holding them.'

HOW MAY WE SERVE YOU AND YOUR SAVIOR? they asked the Guvnor.

"Hot water and food would do nicely. And do you have those clothes I left behind?"

A little later Garvin soaked in hot water in a metal tub. the Guvnor was in another tub blowing cigar smoke rings in the air. "They'll let me have anything I want," he was saying. "Except women. I haven't asked, but one can tell."

Garvin sat putting things together. "You saved their lives from a Rider?"

"I needed a base of operations awhile ago. Don't look at me as if I were a hero. I'm not. Campi Romani, the Roman Fields, are the place for heroism if you're interested. Girls too, for that matter. It would be quite close for you."

Garvin felt a stir of interest on his Rider's part. He was quiet for a moment, then continued his line of thought. "You were there when I arrived in the Republic, weren't you? The Thorn and Rose were there too." He showed the image the Guvnor had shown him of the woman in the dark. "That light is the burning transport."

The Guvnor nodded and closed his eyes. Men came in with more buckets of hot water. Garvin continued, AND THE WIND TOOK ALL THOSE KIDS, THEIR TEACHERS TOO. THAT WAS THE BEACON I SAW IN TIME. YOU KILLED ALL OF THEM. MY RIDER IS TELLING ME MY WHOLE PATH IS MARKED WITH BLOOD.

The servants left. "The Thorn assured me that an Oracle proved to her that those children would all have died quite surely and quite horribly anyway."

'ask him what reward she promised him.'

"How much is she paying you, Guvnor?"

"Enough to raise a company of mercenary horse in a nearby world."

'there is more. probe him. you can find out everything.'

Garvin shook his head. A servant announced dinner. The Guvnor reached for towels. "Don't let the Thorn know where I am until I tell you it's all right, okay?" Garvin said.

The Guvnor stood up and wrapped himself in a towel. He looked Garvin right in the eye and nodded. 'his word is worthless. go into his mind.' Garvin ignored the Rider.

There was a huge dinner at which Garvin began to realize how tired he was. Elders told in words and mental pictures the history of their colony. It began in the early seventeenth century with Brother Johnathan By-The-Will-of-God-Thou-Shalt-Be-Saved Smith. He had a vision of a green and pleasant land. The Lord also provided a gateway. Garvin saw images of Brother Johnathan dragging figures in dark clothes holding muskets and spinning wheels through a portal into Eden.

For centuries the colony prospered in isolation. Then the world of Mammon burst upon them. An invading band appeared, burning, raping, and enslaving. The invasion's leader overmastered the elders. He went into every mind and broke the people. They were in chains, awaiting transport.

Their savior came out of the rising sun. The Lord had sent an angel. The Guvnor and several score of very hard-bitten types rode in at dawn with the sun behind them. The invading soldiers were cut down as they ran. Their leader was Beelzebub, king of pests and lord of flies. He cast forth his mind against the forces of the Lord. And fell dead with a look of idiot horror on his face.

When they reached that part of the story, people stood and cheered, took up a hymn. When the excitement had died down, someone asked, "Please tell us how the Lord sent you the Wondrous Wind." The Guvnor lighted a cigar and looked down the table at Garvin. He blew a smoke ring.

Then he showed them a wrecked world, a ruined city. A crew of tattered soldiers moved carefully down a street. "A mixed unit is what we were, some Coldstream Guards, a few sappers, a body of naval cadets from Osborne, a Welsh machine-gun crew, and other odds and ends. We were the army of His Majesty George the Fifth, or the largest part of it still fighting in the capital, as far as we knew."

The few civilians that they met scuttled past them, wordless, terrified. "There weren't many of the enemy, really. That's all that kept us alive. Because when they found us, they killed us very quickly." He showed planes and helicopters and the image that flowed wherever they went: the Royal Family bowed down to the tall man with the clouded eyes and empty face.

"The only thing that held our little band together as long as it held was that somehow I could block those images." The Guvnor showed tanks moving through the streets. His little band was cut up and driven away. Minds closed in on the Guvnor as he was cornered in the ruins of an alley.

Then the enemy minds were trying to hide themselves. The air stirred. The guvnor felt his pursuers' minds caught up in the Wind. He felt it pass over his head. It passed through the Guvnor and he became part of it. "I was ready to go at that moment. I had seen my enemies die before I did. What more was there for me? But that wasn't to be. The Wind let me go, stayed in the air above me, and when I moved, it followed. It has ever since."

Later, after hymns and brandy, when they were going to their bedrooms, Garvin asked, "Why does it follow you, Guvnor?"

"My double is the only reason I could think of. That once it took one of my doubles and so recognized me when it saw me again. It's not much of an explanation, but it's the only one that's occurred to me."

"Your double?" Garvin was ready to fall asleep.

"We all have them on the worlds that are much like our own. When doubles meet, one always dies, they say. Good night, old man."

Long after Garvin was asleep, a figure left the sleeping town, stole out of the place without the sentries being aware.

It was the youngest son of one of the elders, a fair telepath. The Wind stirred and the youth made a prayer to it and God, who sent it. He headed in the direction the Guvnor and Garvin would take the next day. With a prayer and a shudder, he slipped through the portal and was gone.

At that moment in the Republic, worlds distant and several seconds earlier in Time, Scarecrow thought of Garvin. Then he put the thought as far away as he could, burying it in the recesses of his Keep. He had sent Amre back to the Fire Gates with the children and wounded who could be moved.

Lights were set up on the green at Weatherhill. Engine noises grew closer in the night. Airships snapped on their landing lights and came down one after another. Scarecrow stepped forward as the Border Warden's staff leaped from ships, lowered the stairs, arranged themselves. Moriaph appeared and he reached out to help her. For a moment she didn't recognize him. Behind her in the doorway, looming over her, was Gepeto, the Deep Select.

CHAPTER FIFTEEN

GARVIN SAW the summer sun try to break through the smoke and fog. He felt the railway station floor pulse with the power of the steam engines. Around him were the seven million minds of London, tearful and arguing, old and young, in love and indifferent, brave and afraid. Troop trains were loading up, bound for the port cities and South Africa. Garvin remembered New York.

The Guvnor strode out of Time, his hat at just the right pitch, his boots ringing on the pavement. Garvin followed in clothes that didn't quite fit, a large cap pulled down to hide his haircut. 'he is leading us to my enemies,' his Rider told him over and over. The Wind stirred feathers on the hats of officers' wives. YOU ASKED ABOUT THE WIND, AND HE EXPLAINED THAT.

'he offered a tale to those gaping . . .'

GOOD MORNING, CAPTAIN TAGENT. A man with a thick mustache and wearing a bowler hat linked minds with the Guvnor. IS THIS YOUR LAD? The man made a clumsy probe toward Garvin. The block he received shook him.

"Mr. MacInnes," said the Guvnor. "This is Garvin, a long

lost nephew. Garvin, this is Mr. MacInnes of the Royal Psych-
ical Society. They like to keep tabs on things."

"You will be responsible for the lad, Captain?" MacInnes
tried no more probes.

"And vice versa, I dare say." The Guvnor led Garvin past
screaming sergeants and conductors looking at their watches.
Soldiers in khaki kissed their girl friends, an officer was seen
off by a friend from the Guards in scarlet and black. "The
Boer War is in full swing. Germany has come in on the side
of the Afrikaans." The Guvnor spoke in a low voice. "A
certain number of these soldiers will get diverted, end up in
the Time Lanes as mercenaries or prizes. 1902 is a great
favorite of the gods; not enough technology to be dangerous
and plenty of young men spoiling for a fight."

"MacInnes called you Captain Tagent."

"Always, when I find a world like this, I become Captain
Tagent. First I have to make sure that there isn't one already.
That could be messy. On worlds like this the name Tagent
means something."

They were out on the street; the Guvnor hailed a cab.
Garvin asked, "Is Tagent your real name?"

"My mother's family name. My father's name is not one
that necessarily would go down well on these worlds. But
even if things are only remotely similar, there are always
Tagents. And they are always well placed."

A cab halted. The Guvnor gave directions, turned in the
door as he was getting in. "I say!" Across the street a woman
was being helped down from a carriage. She was very beautiful and used to being watched. "Marie Bright is her name,"
the Guvnor said. "An actress. I wouldn't be surprised if she
had a friend. Shall I put thoughts of us in her mind?"

Garvin hesitated, embarrassed. The Guvnor sat down; the
carriage started up. The Guvnor said, "I asked you to think
about a partnership. Have you considered it?"

"I have to go back to the Republic, Guvnor, with an army.
I need your help."

The Guvnor ran through the minds around them as if he
were sifting a handful of sand. "The only way to get to the

Republic is through this world. Now this world is a hub. You can get to half a dozen worlds from here. Because of that, it's important to the Riders. They maintain a presence here. Your friend will tell you that.

"The Immortals are around also. Both sides are undercover right now because that suits them. But the Riders have the advantage as they always seem to. This is a good world and I'm fond of it. My old nanny used to describe one like it to me. But I don't relish being here when it goes. Nor do I want to be caught down at the end of a blind alley with your friends."

The carriage had speeded up. Garvin felt it turn a corner and then another. The Guvnor reached out his mind, ready to stop the coachman. "Will you come away with me, Garvin?"

Garvin shook his head, sick with disappointment. The carriage turned again. The Guvnor looked at him. "Your powers are godlike, but I'm afraid you have much to learn." They were in an alley so narrow the coach doors almost scraped the walls. Garvin felt minds all around him. The Guvnor smiled and said, "Never trust anyone, old boy. You can't afford it."

Garvin batted away the minds that probed him. He reached out for the driver and his horses. Then a mind more powerful than any he had ever felt seized his consciousness. 'your friend has led us into a trap,' the Rider was howling inside him.

Garvin shook off the other mind, using the image of the room. He thought of the mirror surface and invoked his Keep. The peacock design was his Curtain, the globe his Umbra. The other mind was dark and ancient. It took the image of the room and began to put out the light. Garvin swept the dimming aside and restored the room.

The ancient mind attacked once more. Garvin turned that mind back until it split in two. One part dimmed the lights. The other began to chant, HERE WE SIT/IN THE DARK/ WITH A SECRET./CAN YOU GUESS IT? The second part of the other mind was as clear and open as a child's. It caught

Garvin's attention. He wanted to reach out for it. Night began to fall in the image of the room. There were faces at the carriage windows.

The doors opened. Garvin saw Immortals' Companions. As the room blacked out and the child mind continued to chant, the Companions grabbed Garvin. The carriage rolled indoors. His Rider was frantic inside him. 'my enemies. you have given them one of their greatest victories.' Garvin couldn't move, couldn't reply.

"There he is, signed, sealed, and delivered," the Guvnor was saying. "I'll take my payment immediately. It's not through any of your doing that I got here to collect my perks." He showed Garvin's abilities in moving through Time and around worlds. "He brought us both back here alive. I'll have my force assembled by tomorrow morning. Two hundred of the finest rogues still unhanged. And you'll bring them where I say."

AGREED. That was the ancient mind. It relaxed its hold on Garvin. He opened his eyes. Two Companions held him up. The Guvnor stood talking to what Garvin recognized as the Thorn and Rose. They were inside a warehouse. He could feel a portal and the infinite possibilities of Time nearby. The space was lighted by lanterns. Garvin looked carefully at the Immortal. The Thorn was handsome but weathered and grim. The Rose, small, smooth, looked right back at him bright eyed.

Garvin said to the Guvnor, "You lied to me. You betrayed me. You're no better than the slave traders!" He lashed out with his mind. The Guvnor blocked clumsily. The Thorn restrained Garvin.

"Time Strider. World Spinner," said the Guvnor. "His only trouble is a certain innocence. Tell them what you've come for, Garvin."

I CAME TO GET HELP. Garvin showed them his promise to the people at Weatherhill. WITHOUT IT THEY WILL BE CRUSHED.

IT IS NOT WISE TO FOSTER HOPE WHEN YOU CAN DO NOTHING, the Thorn told him. THE ORACLE HAS

BEEN FULL OF YOUR PROBABILITIES FOR YEARS. YOU WERE TO BE THE STEED THAT DESTROYED RIDERS. IT SHOWED YOU LEADING ARMIES. INSTEAD YOU ARE A SINGLE CHILD WITH NO CONTROL OVER HIMSELF OR HIS RIDER. YOU ARE COMING WITH US. WE ARE GIVING UP OUR HOLD ON THIS WORLD.

AND RUNNING? Garvin asked. THE TALKING SUITCASE GAVE UP THE WORLD I WAS BORN ON. The Companions had let go of him. Garvin felt the portal at the back of the warehouse. He went for it. I AM GOING BACK BY MYSELF. AT LEAST A RIDER WILL DIE WITH ME.

'no. no. that is not the way, boy,' his Rider told him. The Thorn's mind began to smash his mental defenses. Garvin kept on walking. Then the Rose's mind was inside his. GARVIN, STAY. His motor control failed. He staggered and stopped.

"Offer them something worth their lives," the Guvnor suggested. "The Thorn and Rose will bloom and die forever and ever, but they probably would like a victory now and then. In fact—"

ENOUGH. The Thorn silenced him.

Garvin reached out to the Companions. They were young. None were from this world, but most came from Rider-infested worlds. They were tired of running. They wanted the Thorn to make a stand.

Garvin showed them Nick and his initiation. The Companions looked toward the Thorn, who ignored them. The Rose blinked and stared at Garvin. He showed them the beacon in Time. Telepathic children cried his name in the belly of the Wind. WHY DID YOU KILL THEM? WHY DID YOU BRING ME TO THAT WORLD JUST SO YOU COULD ABANDON IT? he asked the Thorn.

THE ORACLE SHOWED YOU THERE. I HAD NEVER EVEN BEEN IN A MIND THAT HAD SEEN THE PLACE. She showed him Grim Reaper. THEN I FOUND HIM. She showed him what the shamans would have done with the childrens' bodies, what the Riders would have done with their minds. IT SHOWED ME WHAT WOULD HAPPEN TO THEM WITHOUT YOU.

AND YOU WILL LET THEM DIE FOR NOTHING? Garvin was angry.

There was a sob and every mind filled with images of the owl flying, exploding. THE OWL, THE BAD, BAD OWL. The Rose started to cry.

'a plan. you have a plan. let them see me.' Garvin did and there was a shudder from everyone in the room. The Rider showed the Thorn and Rose raising all the forces they could and reinforcing Scarecrow. But first the Immortal transported the Guvnor and his mercenaries to the veld world, the one he had described as perfect cavalry country. They would harass Rumack's supply lines. All summer Garvin would raise and send reinforcements for both forces. At the end of summer he would return, roll up Rumack's supply line, and crush him.

There was silence for a moment as everyone contemplated the plan.

"Interesting," said the Guvnor. "Something is unexplained, though. Why would I risk my life and my mercenaries?"

"Glory," said Garvin.

'at the time the republic is relieved,' the Rider told him, 'you will have a force of a thousand mercenaries paid for a year and transport anywhere in time.'

The Guvnor nodded, amused.

THIS IS A RIDER PLAN, the Thorn told them. WE WILL BE TRAPPED IN AN APPENDIX NEGATING OUR GREATER SPEED AND MOBILITY IN TIME. THERE ARE TOO MANY HOLES IN THE SCHEME. THE BOY MUST COME WITH US. She reached for Garvin's mind.

LET US MAKE A STAND, the Companions were asking. HE IS ONE OF US. DOES NOT THE ORACLE SHOW HIS TRIUMPH?

PROBABILITIES. IT SHOWS ONLY PROBABILITIES. The Thorn came up against Garvin's Umbra defense. She waited for the Rose to distract him. There was a pause.

I LOVE GARVIN, the Rose declared. She didn't move against him.

HOW CAN WE TRUST A RIDER? asked the Thorn. But it was like a ritual now. She was testing Garvin.

Garvin tore open his collar and showed them the blade. "I will answer for its loyalty."

AND THE ARMIES? WHERE ARE YOU GOING TO RAISE THEM? There was rising excitement from everyone.

'campi romani,' his Rider told him.

THE ROMAN FIELDS, said Garvin.

The Thorn nodded as if she had seen it all already. YOU WILL BE MET THERE BY ONE YOU KNOW.

At the end of the appendix, in the Republic, Scarecrow sat in the Weatherhill observatory and faced Moriaph. Through a window behind her he could see a flight of gunships returning from a run over District Three. One of them was very badly shot up. Their appearance raised the level of activity on the landing field set up on the town green.

The old woman picked that up too. "A hundred gunships," she croaked. "Every one the Republic can still put in the air." The town, the woods around it were alive with troops. Moriaph had assembled the nations' army in District Four. "Let me show you the latest report from the Eyes of Hell."

She reached out and fumbled with a factor. When it was on, Scarecrow received the impressions of Jessia, the Guardian of District Three. THE HOTLANDER ASSAULT IS IN ITS FOURTH DAY. Images were red tinged with fatigue. The mind that had formed the report was battered by the constant bombardment of Hotlanders mortars, the constant probing of the shamans. An image of Rumack's howling face appeared.

Around the mountain fortress was the litter of war, burning vehicles and ruined buildings, unburied dead. In the air were minds, Hotlander and Select. AGAINST ALL WE HAVE HELD. IN THE LAST DAY THE ATTACKS HAVE LESSENED PERCEPTIBLY. Scarecrow felt, as Jessia had, the

Hotland attack run out of steam, the fading of the besieger's Relay.

Moriaph laughed. WITH THE ELEMENT OF SURPRISE GONE, she told Scarecrow, THE HOTLANDERS ARE THE SAME BARBARIANS THEY ALWAYS WERE. Scarecrow saw the situation map the old woman kept in her head. Raids had held garrisons in place all along the thousand-mile Hotland border. The main attack had come in District Five, where the citadel of Joyous Freedom had fallen, in Four, where Scarecrow had won, and in Three where the Guardian Jessia held out.

Howling Rumack himself was in District Five to the west of them. A lieutenant pursued the siege in Three. THANKS TO YOUR VICTORY, SCARECROW, WE HAVE RUMACK CUT OFF FROM HIS OTHER COLUMN. WITH THE ATTACK IN THREE WEAKENING, I AM GOING TO CLEAR THEM OUT OF THERE, THEN GO AFTER RUMACK HIMSELF. DIVIDE AND CONQUER. Scarecrow saw in her mind the gunships flying, the mechanized columns snaking through the woods. He saw the Hotlanders swept away like pieces off a chessboard, a fitting finale to an old war leader's career.

He saw it all and knew it was nonsense. Rumack was not the one who was cut off; Moriaph was. She was fighting a war in three dimensions. Rumack had a fourth: Time. The siege of the Eyes of Hell was bait to draw Moriaph. Rumack had convinced her that he was stuck in District Five. He had tricked her into believing she held the upper hand.

Moriaph was speaking aloud. "The plans are formed, Scarecrow." Her voice was rheumy. "We march this evening. We will be in District Three by dawn. Scouts report that Hotland security is very lax. They won't expect us to try to raise the siege so quickly. I will have to command from the air because of my legs. There are twenty thousand ground troops, five hundred vehicles. I want you to command them."

Scarecrow had known this was coming. "The plan is suicidal."

WHY? She was staring at him. Her mind felt like steel.

IT IS A TRAP. He drew a deep breath and showed her portals and Hotlanders tumbling out of them all over District Four. He showed her Rumack and he showed her Grim Reaper.

Then she broke contact with his mind. Her mouth worked before words came out. "I carried your name in my Keep as one that I loved. I was told what your reply would be, Scarecrow, and I was told what reasons you would give. But I don't believe it."

The room was guarded from outside minds by Scramblers. Someone entered the room behind Scarecrow and started to flash images at him. They were of Uncle and Mole. Someone had seen them join Red Death's Hotlanders and go south. Many had seen them earlier talking to Scarecrow before the battle. A HOTLAND "CAPTIVE" AND THE ONE WHO CAPTURED HIM ALLOWED TO REJOIN THE ENEMY. It was Gepeto, the Deep Select, who stood behind Scarecrow. THE ENEMY COLUMN ITSELF WAS THEN ALLOWED TO ESCAPE.

There were images of Garvin. First it was glimpses of him that Gepeto had lifted from the minds of ordinary citizens, memories of him in the cluster group, or making his triumphant departure. Then they became much more precise: Garvin found in the woods, Garvin learning to speak again, Garvin touching other minds with his.

"What explanation do you have for this, Scarecrow?" Moriaph asked. She wanted Scarecrow to provide reasonable answers, excuses she could accept.

Scarecrow turned away from her. He realized that Moriaph was doomed. If he thought about it, he would feel pain. Instead, those images of Garvin had all his attention. They had come from Amre. She had tried to keep far away from Gepeto. She had gone with the children when they were evacuated to the Fire Gates. WHAT HAVE YOU DONE WITH HER? He got up and moved toward Gepeto, who smiled and made him sit down again.

The Deep Select had the same smile on the night of the following day. He was leading Scarecrow out into the woods toward a portal. They left behind noise and panic in Weatherhill. Hundreds of minds repeated to themselves at regular intervals, MORIAPH IS DEAD. Again and again they saw the images remembered by the eyewitnesses, Moriaph's gunship falling to Hotland ambush.

WE HAVE SERVED EACH OTHER'S PURPOSES WELL. BOTH OF US WONDERED HOW WE WOULD AVOID HER FINAL FOLLY, Gepeto told him.

Scarecrow felt an emptiness inside when he thought of Moriaph going off so bravely to her death. Gepeto, with his mind hooked inside of Scarecrow's Curtain, noticed that and was amused. Scarecrow flashed the images of Goblin Market which he had gleaned from Grim Reaper. HOW MUCH TIME HAVE YOU BOUGHT YOURSELF?

A LIFETIME. THERE IS ALWAYS A NEED FOR WILLING AND ABLE ADMINISTRATORS. RUMACK DOES NOT WANT TO KILL THE GOOSE, ONLY TO KEEP THE GOLDEN EGGS. RIGHT NOW IN NEW LIBERTY THERE ARE PLANS TO SEND HIM TRIBUTE. Scarecrow caught images of cluster groups of children, Select and Citizen alike, given over to the Hotlanders.

YOU HAVE MUCH TO EXPLAIN, SCARECROW. He felt himself walking. There was no hope. Gepeto controlled him, led him to Rumack. Amre was back at Weatherhill under guard. He faced his own death and that of everything he loved. Yet, just as he had when he first went to Grim Reaper, he felt a certainty. He was playing a part in a great project, and that part was not over.

SHOW ME WHAT YOU KNOW ABOUT GARVIN. Gepeto swept aside Scarecrow's Keep defenses and looked out through his eyes and heard with his ears. Scarecrow screamed as the air was forced out of his lungs and Gepeto held his heart still for two beats. Then Gepeto was in the midst of his dreams and fears.

"Scarecrow." There was a voice calling. "Scarecrow." It was Amre. Gepeto loosened his grip just a hair to go after her with his mind. Scarecrow started to wrench free. The trees moved. Another telepathic mind snapped the connection between him and Gepeto. The Wind caught Gepeto and took him. Scarecrow felt the whisper of the other's terror. Then his fat body fell facedown.

Amre rushed to Scarecrow and held him. A man stood behind her. "Garvin sent him," she said.

"These are my credentials, old man." Scarecrow saw Garvin very recently saying, "Scarecrow, this is the Guvnor, an ally. Give him four hundred light-cavalry horses. Hold until the end of summer and I will be there."

CHAPTER SIXTEEN

GARVIN TRAVELED through a thousand worlds to get to Roman Fields. It took him days of sifting Time until he found what had been described to him. There were dead worlds and worlds that vibrated with life. Some he would have investigated if the memory of his mission hadn't kept him going. He held the image of the room; he looked into the mirror. He slept in inns and in a motel. He came to a stretch of airless worlds, lifeless rock.

"A little jewel in a wasteland," the Guvnor had described Campi Romani. Garvin found it, green and living. He moved the globe to North America. South of the Great Lakes, he approached portals. Each was a mile or two apart and each had a village near it. Garvin probed for telepathic minds and moved on when he found one.

Some portals didn't feel right to him, and he passed them by. Then he found one, approached it several times, held it in the mirror, probed. He tumbled through and hit the ground in the middle of a grove of trees. The town lay before him across meadows nestled on the banks of a river. He cast his mind toward it as he began walking.

People dropped what they were doing and watched. They

felt his mind. It had been years since the village had a Pontifex. Garvin had been given a uniform by the companions. He wore the boots and pants with the buckskin shirt that Amre had given him. The shirt was open; the razor on his neck caught the sunlight. He carried no weapons.

A single figure walked out of the town toward him. It was a man in his late forties or early fifties. He wore a World War One British helmet and a flak jacket with an eagle emblem and the legend *Navy of America*. Garvin touched his mind and found that his name was Milus. He was the town centurion and servant-in-waiting for the priest. He held a rifle in port position.

When he felt Garvin's mind, Milus fell to his knees and pledged his loyalty. The people gave out a great sigh. Garvin caught the word Pontifex. They looked like Romans and they looked like American Indians. Bronzed men and handsome women sank to their knees in awe. The youth were all wide eyed. The priest was one of them.

"Please don't kneel. Stand up." They couldn't understand English. In his mind he formed an image of them rising, and they stood. That they couldn't understand what he said was further proof of his right to rule them. They followed respectfully as Milus led them, rifle held like a ceremonial mace, to the Pontifex's house.

This was a stone building on a hill in the middle of the wooden town. It was large and ready for use even though it had been nearly thirty years since the last Pontifex. People hurried to prepare a feast. The finest linens were brought for his bed, oils for his bath. The days of wonder were upon them; everyone knew that.

That night when the excitement and celebration had died down, the young Pontifex and his people slept. Everyone, young and old, male and female, shared a dream deep in the night. It involved a girl with hair like the Pontifex's, and it took place in a forest. It was intensely erotic. They knew it as an omen that a line of priests would be founded there and rejoiced.

One afternoon Garvin rode a mare he called Cream out of

the town. He felt the animal move under him. Each hoof struck the ground with just a moment's hesitation to make sure it was solid. He felt the warmth of the sun on her flanks, the instinct to run free blocked by careful training. He had his choice of any horse in the stables, and he had chosen this one. Or perhaps she had chosen him, raising her head and watching him as he walked in.

The first few times he had made sure that nobody saw him ride her. He remembered his ride with the Guvnor. As he got more confidence, he also realized that it didn't matter. If he had ridden backward, it was all right. He was the Pontifex, the priest, the emissary of the Gods. He could do no wrong as far as his people were concerned.

As yet he didn't know what to do with this knowledge. He guided Cream with his mind, his hands, and his legs. Figures in the fields looked up from the corn and rye. In an open pasture tents had been set up for newcomers. Garvin saw figures approach a plank bridge over a stream at the edge of town. A sentry stopped them. Garvin reached out and found they were young men and women from a village that owed allegiance to the Pontifex at Two Eagles.

They wanted to give their oath. BY COMING HERE YOU HAVE DECLARED YOUR LOYALTY, Garvin told them. Then, aware that they could see him, he turned Cream gracefully and rode into a stand of trees.

As he guided the horse, the Rider guided him. 'those volunteers will have to be fed and housed.' There were images of barracks being built. 'tell milus.'

His Rider flooded Garvin's mind with ideas constantly. It showed him images of something called the Armory of Night. 'there is a need to arm these people. as word spreads of your presence, other telepaths will want to challenge you. every manner of weapon can be obtained there.'

The Armory was on one of the dead worlds adjacent to the Roman Fields. It bothered Garvin that this was all his Rider's idea. The Guvnor and the Thorn had shown him nothing about it. His Rider filled his mind with images of endless corridors, mile-long indoor firing ranges, storerooms with everything from crossbows to lasers. He let Cream gallop along the path, his head narrowly missing branches. The Rider curled up inside him and was still.

Something moved beside a tree. Cream started. Just a week before, Garvin would have fallen off. Now he held on and probed. He caught an image of himself. The sun caught a fine blade on a gold chain that now kept the razor at his throat, the gold band that held his ponytail. His hair stuck up like a crest. There was nothing left of the kid who had stood on the high school steps.

A girl stood still as a deer as he opened her mind. Her name was Thelia. Garvin saw the old women of the village dressing her, anointing her, leaving her here where he would pass by. Garvin caught her outline under her shift, saw her long legs and dark hair, her huge eyes. He felt the beat of her heart and was aware of his own. Cream caught the excitement and skittered. He controlled her with a flourish.

THE TWO EAGLES PONTIFEX! THE TWO EAGLES PONTIFEX! Garvin found an image of horsemen riding across the fields. Infantry followed in open order. The horsemen were after the new recruits who had just come to join him. Instinctively, Garvin headed toward the trouble. He caught Thelia's awe as Cream jumped a low wall and galloped out into the open ground.

'get down, you fool,' the Rider screamed in his head.

In the town Milus struggled to pull the muster together, to form up the new volunteers for battle. As Garvin appeared, sentries, field-workers, recruits were running in all directions. BEHOLD THE WRATH OF THE PONTIFEX, a mind was telling them. Half a dozen horsemen were chasing Garvin's followers. He scanned them to see which was the Pontifex.

A half-trained mind detected this. INTERLOPER, it broadcast. THERE HE IS, one of the horsemen told the others. THE ONE WHO LURES AWAY MY VILLAGERS. HE WILL MAKE A SUITABLE PRIZE FOR THE GOBLINS. Garvin caught the mind in all its arrogance, ran through its defenses in seconds, and had the Two Eagles Pontifex by the ganglia.

Horses and men caught their leader's panic. Several of the horses spilled their masters. Infantry began to edge away.

WHAT ARE YOU DOING HERE? Garvin's mind rang in all of theirs.

SEEKING HOW BEST TO SERVE YOU, the Two Eagles Pontifex told him, slipped from his horse, and threw himself to the ground. Garvin read in the Pontifex's mind how angry he had been at the loss of followers to an upstart priest, a mere boy. He had gathered his muster and marched the ten miles between their two towns, thinking to take Garvin by surprise.

Now he crawled on the ground to kiss the toe of Garvin's boot. Paulus was his name, thirty years old, son of a priest. Garvin caught all the details of the life of a village Pontifex. It was boring. He tried not to remember what the Guvnor had told him: that in the end only those who moved through Time would be interesting.

I AM YOUR MOST LOYAL SERVANT AND THESE ARE YOUR VASSALS, Paulus told him.

'they are your prisoners, boy. not worth an awful lot, but useful perhaps for barter.'

YOU ARE MY ALLIES, Garvin told Paulus and his muster.

'if he had not been so intent on taking you prisoner, i could have been shot as you sat there!' Garvin saw the rifles dropped by the Two Eagles muster and realized that was true.

'ask him about the armory.' Garvin did.

THE ARMORY OF NIGHT? I HAVE HEARD OF IT. MY OLD LIEGE, ALAQUIN, PRIEST OF A HUNDRED TOWNS, HAD DEALT WITH TRADERS FROM THE ARMORY. Garvin saw that Paulus had never been anywhere very much. IT IS SAID THAT OVER ALAQUIN IS A GREAT PONTIFEX IN A STONE TOWER THAT TOUCHES THE SKY. . . .

'you must arm these people or they will be worth nothing in battle.' Garvin shut out both the Rider and his new vassal. He turned and saw Thelia standing at the edge of the field. He dismounted, went over, and took her arm. He felt the crowd's joy. Garvin walked back to the town with her beside him.

Behind them marched the Two Eagles muster of over two hundred men, half of them armed with rifles. They were led by Paulus, who was happy as a puppy that had found an owner.

His people wanted to carry Garvin on their shoulders to his house. He refused, gave Cream's reins to a groom, turned to go up the hill with Thelia. The crowd buzzed. He turned their minds to thoughts of a feast of celebration. Inside all was prepared, food, wine, linen, and oils.

Garvin fumbled with the knots on Thelia's shift. His hands trembled so much that he couldn't undo them. Thelia saw the Pontifex with his tongue between his teeth, struggling with the knots. She took her heart in her hands and kissed him. Her hands trembled less than his and her shift fell to the floor. Together they got his clothes off too and were on the bed.

The old women had instructed her. She knew that a Pontifex could take whatever form the Gods chose. That this one came as a young boy eager but clumsy was a mystery that she would never think of examining. Outside in the growing dark, a bonfire was being lighted. There was a chest of jewelry in the house, he remembered. Garvin found a box of gold rings. The first one he tried on Thelia fit perfectly.

Garvin took fencing lessons one morning from Milus. THREE THOUSAND FOUR HUNDRED AND SIXTEEN ANSWERED THE MORNING ROLL, Pontifex Paulus told him. Garvin wondered if this was enough.

'troops of this quality must exist in immense numbers to have any worth at all.'

Garvin put on a helmet and mask. Milus positioned himself a few feet away, demonstrated a parry position.

SIX MORE PONTIFICES HAVE SHOWN THEIR LOYALTY, BELOVED OF THE GODS, Paulus reported.

Milus moved deliberately on to the attack. Garvin parried clumsily as his Rider winced.

In the mind of the old soldier, Garvin found his instructions. "Keep your sword up, one foot back for balance. Shift the weight. Keep the sword up!" Milus had half a dozen old companions in arms, centurions from the wars of the Arch-pontifex Laydia. They had begun to turn the volunteers into some form of army.

'divide them first into centuries, then into cohorts, each made of six centuries. a pontifex can command each cohort. though some of them have almost no telepathic capacity to speak of and several are even more complete fools than pau-lus.' Garvin turned a thrust and almost got cut.

"We ask permission," a townsperson was saying, "to hold market twice weekly. Farmers and merchants wish to come here to do homage to you."

'let them. and levy a tax on everything to support this useless rabble.'

GRANTED. Garvin gave the Rider's suggestions as his own order. The presence in his mind kept up a steady commentary.

'seven half-trained telepaths, none of whom has been near the armory of night. no wonder they command half-armed mobs.'

Garvin dropped his guard for a moment, and Milus nicked him on the arm. The Rider froze. The man was horrified. IT IS NOTHING, Garvin told him. All marveled.

There was a commotion out on the edge of town. A Pontifex galloped toward them. ALAQUIN IS WITHIN STRIKING DISTANCE. There were images of well-trained troops occupying a village about five miles away. Everyone looked at Garvin.

'this one rested as near to us as he dared.'

A defensive alignment passed through Garvin's mind from his Rider. He couldn't assess it; there wasn't time. He showed it to them. They would defend along a stream east of the town. There were woods on the right to shelter the levy armed with spears and bows and arrows. The rifle-armed troops would hold the center. There would be some infantry and all the cavalry on the exposed left flank.

'make alaquin bring the battle to you and slip the noose on him when he does.'

Garvin's stomach was tight. The rescue of Cluster Group Two, the defeat of Paulus had begun and been over before Garvin could think about them. His tension increased as he put the troops into position.

Thelia bought him food, bread and cheese, water and wine. He drank the wine but didn't touch the food. She stayed with him just behind the center of his army. GO BACK, he told her. She looked up at him. He was on Cream and getting used to giving orders. She turned and went off, looking back several times. He felt very alone when she was gone.

By then there was death in front of him. A wounded horse ran screaming toward his lines. A skirmisher writhed in pain and died off to the left. Garvin's vassal Pontifices were not trained to form a Relay. He reached out his own mind and found each of them. HOLD YOUR GROUND. He probed to his front where he could see enemy troops moving.

'alaquin will come up fast, hoping to break you quickly.'

There was lots of firing on the right, lots of pain. Garvin probed that way, found Alaquin's subordinate commanders amid the tangle of their soldiers' minds. The telepaths tried to mingle their consciousnesses with those of the men. Their attack lost its cohesion.

CHARGE! FOR GARVIN PONTIFEX MAXIMUS! Out on the open ground to his left, Garvin could see horsemen trotting forward. Paulus led them. Horses began to splash through the stream in front of his position. Alaquin's troops stopped their advance, drew aim, and fired. Some of them had repeating rifles. Horses and men went down in a tangle in the water. Garvin reached for Paulus. GET BACK! GET THE MEN BACK!

He caught the Pontifex's mind. The desire to win glory in the eyes of his lord turned to stunned confusion. Paulus had taken a bullet in his chest. Garvin felt Paulus hit the water, his horse falling on top of him. The man lost consciousness. Cavalry bolted in all directions.

Firing had started right in front of Garvin. There was a

flash and roar. 'light artillery. get under cover.' Garvin's line had turned into a band of pain and confusion. He passed his mind quickly over his own troops. 'they are here to die, so you have time to find alaquin. now find him.'

Garvin probed forward. There was a mind directing the advance. Garvin reached for it, felt the telepath duck and try to hide among its own troops. Garvin was among them, spreading panic. ALAQUIN! WHERE IS ALAQUIN? One telepath was sending a message to another. Garvin grabbed for the mind receiving the message. On his right he was aware of his spear-armed levy beginning to run in front of gunfire.

Garvin ran down the other commander in the rear of Alaquin's center. NAME? he asked. The answer was an image of a flag with a sickle-moon-and-star symbol held aloft in the trunk of a caparisoned ivory elephant.

It was Alaquin. Garvin obliterated the image. He found that the image was on a flag held aloft in the trunk of a caparisoned ivory elephant. He went after it again and obliterated it. The other mind drew back a bit and revealed that moon, star, elephant were symbols on a larger flag held by another elephant. Garvin sat on Cream hypnotized, peeling away larger and larger flags. A man took a bullet a hundred feet in front of him.

'the flanks are crumbling. finish him off.' Garvin tore away another flag. 'your people are dying.' Garvin felt the pain of the battle. He pulled back from the flags, formed an image of the room, the mirror. An image that powerful had to be in the mirrored room. He felt he could remember a small ornament on a table. An ivory elephant, beautifully decorated, held aloft a flag with a sickle moon, a star, and a small elephant holding up a flag with smaller moon, star, and elephant. Alaquin froze when he saw that.

Garvin was in Alaquin's mind. He found a childhood which had taken place in a city in southern Africa. It was a Moslem city on a wide blue bay in a world that was all Moslem, a city of magic on the Time Lanes. It was useful to the Goblins, and for many centuries the world had prospered. All that ended in fire and slaughter when Alaquin was still a young man.

Garvin saw Alaquin go through a portal with nothing but the clothes on his back and a few spells of magic he had learned from an old wizard. He had come to the Roman Fields by a long, hard route. But he found there another place useful to the Goblins and prospered.

I CAME SEEKING VASSALS IF POSSIBLE, ALLIES IF NECESSARY. I FOUND INSTEAD A MASTER, Alaquin told Garvin. Firing from Alaquin's army died down almost at once. THERE IS NO ALLAH AND NO PROPHET, AS I LEARNED LONG AGO. THERE IS ONLY THE CITY OUT OF TIME AND YOU. He showed Garvin what had driven him: an army with automatic weapons and mechanized artillery moving fast behind him.

Two thousand rifle-armed troops surrendered with Alaquin. The defeated commander walked forward. Garvin rode out to meet him, shaken at the pain caused by the battle. A quarter of an hour of firing had left dozens dead and many more wounded. Alaquin paused as he forded the stream, amazed at the youth of his conqueror. Garvin looked down to where Paulus lay dead, his face in the mud and his lungs full of blood and water.

CHAPTER
SEVENTEEN

THAT NIGHT Thelia awoke beside Garvin. In the faint light from the window, lying naked on the sheets, he could have been any boy from the town. Then he twitched and she caught a bit of his dream. A wolf looked down on a village of little pigs. Garvin and she were two of the pigs. She caught his feeling of helpless entanglement.

He was still for a few moments. Then there was another dream. It was less flowing and soft than the other. It was of a world of metal and stone, with rooms as huge as a pasture. THE ARMORY OF NIGHT. The name hung in the air, and Garvin pressed his face into the pillow as if receiving a message he didn't want to know.

The next morning he told Milus to call for volunteers and to prepare what was called in the Fields a Pontifex rope. HOW MANY CAN I TAKE AT ONCE? he asked his Rider.

'it depends on capacity and daring. the mortals take only twenty because that number guarantees that none will slip away. but once with a steed of modest powers in no way comparable to yours i took a string of sixty men at arms and made it through five portals losing only twenty-eight.'

Garvin's vassal Pontifexes stood awaiting orders. Alaquin

was a fat man in his forties with gray in his beard and tired eyes. Garvin had decided to leave him in charge. SHOW ME THE DEFENSIVE ALIGNMENT WE SHOULD USE, Garvin told his Rider.

It appeared inside him and he shared it with the others. It was more or less the same as before but with the addition of Alaquin's force and the new recruits who were still showing up. I WILL RETURN IN THREE DAYS. Alaquin nodded. He understood although even he had dealt only with traders who had second- or thirdhand knowledge of the Armory.

Milus stepped forward. "The volunteers have assembled." There were hundreds of them. Garvin got them down to sixty very quickly. He showed each mind a little taste of the emptiness of Time. The ones who flinched felt themselves step backward. He showed the others a little more. Then he had his sixty, which his Rider told him was a good number. Some of them were old veterans who knew Milus; some of them were kids a little older than Garvin himself.

Milus was one of the sixty. He held a roll of thick purple cord. Garvin was secretly glad to have Milus walking to his right and just a pace behind him. He crossed the meadow, back the way he had first come, to the grove of trees. Garvin didn't like what he was about to do. He felt Time grow closer as he approached the portal.

'without weapons from the armory of the night, the army will be mangled by the one coming up. automatic weapons will cause immense damage before you can reach their leader.'

Alaquin's brief fight had proven that. The Fields was like the drop of water Garvin once saw under a microscope in lab: organisms ate and were eaten.

He had to have an army ready. The contact the Thorn mentioned should be there soon. He had to win here in order to rescue the Republic. There were a thousand other endangered worlds. Garvin's head spun. Milus had unraveled the cord. Each of the first batch of twenty took hold of it with both hands. Then Garvin grabbed the ends of the rope with both hands and stepped out into Time.

He looked into the mirror, noting the details of the room.

The elephant stood on its table. Garvin scanned the worlds around him. The ones near the Fields were all dead, a burned ring. He felt the Fields as green and pleasant as a garden.

'it is a garden for the growing of people. think of where we are going as being the toolshed.'

Garvin picked out the Armory of Night, perched on the edge of one of the dead worlds. It felt like a speck in his eye. He wanted to turn away. Then he felt the faint echo of the twenty lives on the cord with him. Garvin remembered the thousands who awaited him with Alaquin and found a portal. He felt thin air, steel, and concrete. There was life beyond the portal but no one who lived there.

He tumbled through and banged his knees on the edge of a loading dock, a huge metal ledge. Stretching in front of him was a line of lights on top of ten-foot poles. Garvin pulled the rope and brought the twenty volunteers through the portal after him. They stood gasping and feeling their hearts to make sure they were beating again. Old Milus looked at him first, and then they all did.

They depended on him absolutely. Garvin spent a moment reassuring them, then stepped back into Time. He invoked the mirror, the room, and the globe, shuffling the portals back and forth until all sixty of the volunteers shivered on the loading dock. They were suffering from shock and a slight lack of oxygen. They calmed when Garvin stepped forward to the line of lights. WHO? something asked him mentally.

It reminded him of Scarecrow's factors. He knew it must be a machine. Without breaking stride, he showed it what kind of force he had left behind in the Fields and how he had won it. As he did, his Rider sent a brief message. Garvin caught a flash of a Chinese woman in a gold dress. She stood before an empty throne.

He hesitated then. WHAT DID YOU SHOW? His Rider wouldn't respond. Garvin thought of the blade at his neck. But the volunteers were right behind him and Garvin had to think of their morale. Also, at that point he could not put a plan together. It was all up to his Rider.

They passed a dozen lighted poles and came to a huge

metal door. As the column approached, a small side panel slid open and the machine told him, PLEASE ENTER. Again Garvin hesitated, but there were light and noise and human minds inside. He entered with the volunteers following and found himself in a huge lighted interior as large as half a dozen football fields.

People looked small under the arching, lighted dome but there were many of them, telepaths and nontelepaths. Minds linked and blocked, probed and broke apart. People shouted aloud in the Latin dialects of the Roman Fields. A cohort formation of infantry dressed in jungle gear marched past singing cadence and holding aloft new high-powered rifles. Tractors pulled flatcars loaded with guns and ammunition. A large section of the great door slid open and some self-propelled guns rolled out into the dark.

Garvin could pay no attention. His attention was focused on a seven-foot-tall figure of metal that strode across the great hall toward him. There was a human head at the top of it. People turned aside and watched.

Light gleamed on the metal. The legs clicked as the figure walked. The face looked very small. The hair was gray; the eyes empty. WHO? asked the figure. Garvin recognized a fellow steed. He gave his name. SAM, replied the other. Garvin tried to go within the other mind. He felt Sam's Rider immediately. There was almost nothing of the man. The Rider was everywhere in that mind. Garvin shuddered and started to pull back. Again his Rider used him to send images.

Sam gestured for them to follow. The yokel volunteers huddled together and looked to Garvin. He followed Sam and they followed him. Trade in arms slowly resumed as the Master of the Armory of Night led them out of the hall and down a long metal corridor. Far enough away so that the minds on the trading floor were fading, Sam showed Garvin a dormitory. The volunteers stayed there as Garvin continued on with Milus and Sam.

They followed the Armorer down endless corridors, through storerooms that looked like museums of weaponry. Garvin tried to make contact with Sam and found very little of him.

Most of his physical functions were handled by machinery. Sam looked at him with unblinking eyes. Images leaped between the two Riders. Garvin caught a glimpse of a palace in flames, of a field with thousands of bound captives. 'what do you wish,' Sam's Rider asked. It indicated the riches of the Armory, all of them available.

The answer came from Garvin's Rider. 'lasers. thirty portable laser rigs and a couple of days' instruction.'

Sam's Rider understood. Sam threw open a door to a comfortable-looking room. When Garvin indicated that he would sleep with his command, Sam stood blank faced. His Rider did not respond.

Garvin tried to work out a plan of action. But something, perhaps just the dead unreality of the Armory of Night, made that impossible. Every hour he felt a little piece of himself die. A few hours later he stood beside the giant on the practice range, watching the volunteers learn how to handle their new weapons. Following his own instincts, Garvin would have left, gone back to Thelia and the town where he was like a God. But what would happen to Thelia and the rest if he came back empty-handed? What would happen to Scarecrow and Amre?

Sam's mind had brushed his at that moment. There was a flicker in the other's eyes. There was a second's worth of image of a jungle and ragged men in some kind of formation stumbling through it. Planes sounded overhead, enemy planes. Sam's eyes fell; contact between the two minds was broken. The troops looked like Americans.

"Sam, do you speak English?" Garvin asked. There was no response.

'pay attention to what you are being shown,' his Rider told him.

The sheer size of the room they were in daunted the volunteers. It was as large as the arms trading floor and empty except for them. During the instructions, Sam almost seemed to come alive. He positioned the men carefully. They were divided into thirty teams of two each. He indicated with almost human gestures of his metal hands the interlocking fields of fire they could achieve. Then he placed Garvin in the center of them. That was the first day's training.

Garvin had trouble sleeping, turning over and over in the arbitrary night. The next day he found it hard to focus on what was happening as Sam put them through another practice session. The weapons were activated this time, and Sam stood beside Garvin. There were thirty lasers and thirty men carrying small but fairly heavy transformers.

With a two-man team the weapons were portable. With a little training the thirty teams could lay down a field of fire that spanned 180 degrees. After hours of running through the maneuvers, indicating who would fire at which point, who would hold his fire to avoid hitting other teams, the weapons were turned on. Wooden targets hundreds of yards away burst into flames and were consumed.

That afternoon the teams were in a semicircle designed to give a wide field of fire and still have flanks and rear protected. Garvin held the minds of the teams as if he had reins. Targets were set up, weapons were turned on. Something flashed between Sam's Rider and his own. Garvin thought he saw the green of Goblin flesh and became distracted from the teams at practice.

Like a spasm, one of the laser operators on the left turned sideways on his heels and cut the two teams next to him down. Two men died instantly, burned in half. The others writhed on the ground screaming out their agony. Garvin immediately made every operator shut off his laser and drop it.

As he did that, he felt Sam sorting through the minds of the injured, assessing them. Before Garvin was aware of what he was doing, Sam reached a decision, or his Rider did, and shut off the oxygen to their brains. Their screaming ceased and they died.

"Touch another one like that and I'll turn the lasers on you!" Garvin faced Sam and started yelling. "If they get hurt, they're to be cared for, understand!"

Sam's eyes remained blank. Garvin could feel Sam's Rider turn the man's attention away from Garvin. His own Rider told him very calmly, 'it is the way sam has been trained to behave. it is the estimate of his rider that the cost of saving those two lives would have been prohibitive.'

Garvin ordered the four bodies put in body bags and kept in a freezer. After that it was time for a meal. He sat a little apart from his stunned men and drank a glass of what was supposed to be wine. He didn't like the way wine tasted anyway, but this was worse than usual.

Garvin had lost his sense of hours and days. Sam's Rider indicated that it was sleep period and that lights would be out shortly. Garvin felt as if he were in a dream where everything seemed to be out of his control. The men put their weapons in a locked armory. Garvin wanted to go back right then, but he was too tired. He wanted to catch Sam's mind as the metal Steed led them through huge empty rooms to their dormitory. He kept bumping up against Sam's Rider, who was as cold and opaque as his own.

Garvin kicked off his boots and was asleep before the lights went out. There were no other people nearby; they were miles from the trading floor. He woke up to feel fear all around him. He was out of his cot and floating. His arms and legs wouldn't move. There was light ahead of him. He was going toward the door of the room headfirst.

His volunteers were half awake. He saw himself in their eyes. He was being carried by Sam. They were stunned. Their Pontifex was being taken from them. Someone leaped through the air, heading for Sam's head. Milus had jumped from his bed. In one hand was a knife. Sam let go of Garvin with one hand and smashed an arm right into Milus. The knife clattered to the floor. The arm had bashed in the front of Milus's head.

Then Sam had Garvin through the door and slammed it locked. Garvin started to get free. The metal arms closed on him. He felt his ribs crack.

'not yet. do not kill him quite yet.'

As Sam carried him down metal corridors, Garvin felt his Rider's glee. He reached for Sam's Rider and felt himself blocked. His own Rider was strong and made it hard for him to probe.

Goblins. Garvin could feel the Goblins before he saw them. 'an army awaits me back at the fields and a world awaits me in the republic. our period together is one that i would like to forget, boy. but it was very profitable.'

Sam walked with a steady clicking. Doors opened in front of him. "Sam, you can be free. You can defeat that maggot inside you." Garvin thought he saw a flicker in Sam's eyes. "I've learned to fight mine. You can do the same." Garvin's Rider tried to fill his mind with terror. He blocked inside with his Umbra. He probed toward Sam's mind. Sam's Rider rose up to stop him.

Garvin blocked with his Curtain. With his Keep he showed Sam something he remembered from when he was a kid. It was a tiger in the zoo kept in a tiny cage. It had roared and Garvin had felt its agony. Both Riders tore Garvin away from Sam's mind.

A last door opened in front of them. Garvin saw green skin and operating tables. There was a figure lying drugged and brainwashed. It was a Pontifex of the Roman Fields. A Goblin moved toward Garvin with a syringe.

'you will die slowly, and just before you do i will be gone. i will take your head back to show your followers.' Garvin felt his Rider up in the stirrups, eager to leap.

Green hands reached out. Garvin tried to break his Rider's hold. It was using up all its strength holding him. He heard a siren. It grew louder. He felt himself fall. He hit the floor on his hands and knees. His Rider's boldness turned to confusion. The Goblins stood frozen.

The siren sound became a howl. Sam stood above him with his mouth open and his head thrown back. Metal hands tore at metal chest. An image, crude and gray, formed of a tiger knocking the door of its cage open and springing. Wires hung out of the chest; a tube leaked down Sam's side.

For a moment Sam's hands stopped as his Rider began to get back control. Then the hands came smashing together into the face. Blood spurted out and there was a piercing mental scream from the Rider. There was also a flash of what felt like a buried dream that had seen day. Sam's metal body slammed to the floor. He was free for the instant before he and his Rider died.

GOBLIN TRUCE, GOBLIN TRUCE, the green figures chanted, and hurried for an exit. The Pontifex on the operating table rolled his eyes and tried to focus his mind. Garvin felt his Rider shrink in terror inside him. After a while he got up and went looking for his people.

CHAPTER EIGHTEEN

GARVIN BROUGHT back the first group of volunteers. Fighting had begun outside the town. Cheering started when his first arrival was announced. There was a series of images from Alaquin: a bloody delaying action at a bridge, a cohort of partially armed troops cut down by machine-gun fire.

THEY ARE TRYING TO TURN THE LEFT FLANK, Alaquin told him.

Garvin automatically reached for the mind of Milus until he remembered Milus was gone. He deployed the teams himself and went back through the portal. His Rider was shrunken and silent inside him. It was afraid again after the death of Sam's Rider.

The rest of the volunteers waited on the loading dock. The Pontifex to whom Garvin's Rider had planned to leap was with them, stunned and confused. The Armory of Night was empty. After the death of Sam, Garvin had swept through the trading floor in a rage and chased everyone out into Time.

Twenty more of the volunteers attached themselves to the rope and followed Garvin through the portal. There was smoke coming from the battlefield, pain, and death.

I WILL HOLD AS LONG AS I AM ABLE, from Alaquin.

Garvin turned and went back again. The portals of the Roman Fields turned under him. Within each one people grew, waiting to be harvested for war.

On his third trip back he brought the bodies of the accident victims and Milus. He left two laser teams with the Pontifex. ADMIT NO ONE BUT ME OR SOMEONE WHO CAN SHOW YOU ME GIVING THEM ADMISSION. The man nodded and Garvin was back in Time. He wanted to get away from the Fields and never see it again. He could hear in the silence of Time the high, metallic screaming from Sam's throat. It sounded as if his vocal cords hadn't been used in years.

The five corpses they carried were nothing. Death was everywhere around when he arrived with the last of the volunteers. THE DAY IS ALMOST LOST, came from Alaquin. Garvin had to act fast or his army would surrender to the enemy. The other side was keeping its telepaths in the rear, clearing the way with fire power.

Garvin deployed the laser teams as he had been shown. The training, he realized, was intended for his Rider. Fugitives from the firing line ran past them as the laser formation went toward the town at a trot. Thelia ran toward them leading Cream. Garvin kissed her and got up on the horse. He never took his mind or his eyes off the battle in front of him. He started to reach for his Rider's advice, then stopped himself. He didn't want it.

A unit of Alaquin's cavalry appeared as Garvin came out of the town. They were shaken but still intact as a unit. They formed up just behind and to the right of the laser men. Garvin rode Cream in the front line. Deserters felt Garvin's presence and stopped running. They were in an open meadow. He could see some of his own men fleeing toward him and movement behind them.

Armored cars, at least three, and infantry with automatic weapons appeared. Garvin halted his laser teams. His army was beginning to jell around him. He could see more enemy troops. They were about to harvest his army.

YOU WILL ALL DIE IF YOU DO NOT HALT, he told

any Pontifex with them. Garvin reached for their minds, crammed images of laser fire into them.

Then he saw himself very clearly. Someone had him in his gun sights. He sat on Cream, who danced with excitement. Whoever saw him pressed the trigger. The sight hairs were crossed on Garvin's chest. The horse threw up her head at that moment. Cream took the bullet and her skull exploded. Garvin felt himself falling and wrenched out of the way.

All the pain of the last few days came back to him: the smell of burned flesh, his cracked ribs, the high scream as Sam crushed his own head. He broke contact with the enemy. He felt for the laser unit and it was in his mind like a gun in his hand. He was looking at Cream, her body still convulsing.

A shell fell near them and a couple of men were wounded. FIRE! Everything in front of them burst into flames. Grass, trees, men, machines all went up in a white heat. They turned to hot black ash, and where they had been was a vacuum.

Garvin turned the unit left and right. Armored cars were sawed in two. Trees burst into flame. Before them minds were blinking out as people died. Garvin concentrated on the minds of his unit. He looked at Cream. He blotted out what was in front of him.

MIGHTY ONE. It was Alaquin. THE ENEMY BEG YOU TO SPARE THEM. THEIR HIGH PRIEST IS DEAD.

Garvin disengaged his unit from their lasers. The agony reduced itself to a dull throb. Garvin looked at the fire and carnage, the writhing wounded. His Rider was still in shock. It told him nothing at all. Garvin couldn't blame the Rider for what he had just done. He threw up, then threw up again.

Everyone stood helpless. Thelia ran up and took his arm. He let her lead him back to town. The women bound his injuries, offered him medicated wine. He could feel their awe. "THIS IS NO PONTIFEX," said a thousand minds. "THIS IS A GOD." He shut his mind to all others. Thelia led Garvin back to the house. The laser men took up guard around the place. They were heroes; they were all in profound shock.

Thelia sat down beside him on a couch. She was frightened

by what she had just seen him do. But she took his hand and that made her less frightened. She put her arms around him. Garvin closed his eyes and said, "Thelia, I'm not a God or a hero or anything. I'm just about your age and maybe not as smart as you. Sometimes it seems like I'm going crazy. At first I thought I was doing the right thing, but I'm going to end up worse than Hitler. I don't even know which ideas are my own any more."

All she understood was her own name. He talked on for a long while and they held each other. Eventually they went to the bed and the reality of their bodies and the fact that they were very young made them forget a little what had happened.

Late at night they slept. More than once the town, the encamped armies, the wounded, the shell-shocked, the drunk, saw fields and men burst into flames and die. They felt the air turn into a deep wound. Each time he had that dream, Garvin would lie awake in the dark for a while.

Just before dawn Garvin felt the burned earth and injured men become a distant sorrow. The sleeping army became a song. It was a kind of lullaby of Time in which every horror was balanced by happiness, every war by peace. Garvin slipped into deep sleep.

He was awakened at midmorning by Alaquin probing him very hesitantly. Alaquin showed Garvin figures walking toward the town. It was a unit of Companions formed up in open order around Roger. The old man wore a tunic now, but the satchel he carried was the same.

The cracked ribs made it hard for Garvin to get dressed. Thelia helped him. He knew he was going to miss her. Garvin brought his laser teams to attention. He summoned Alaquin and the other Pontifices. He wanted to get it all over with quickly. HOW MANY ARE UNDER ARMS?

TEN THOUSAND ANSWERED THE ROLL THIS MORNING, MOST TERRIBLE ONE, Alaquin replied. MORE ARRIVE HOURLY.

CALL FOR VOLUNTEERS. TELL THEM THEY WILL TRAVEL FAR IN TIME AND THAT THEY MAY NEVER

COME BACK. BUT I WILL BE GRATEFUL TO EACH ONE OF THEM.

Garvin stepped outside. Roger and the Companions had stopped at the foot of the hill. The laser men were drawn up behind Garvin. Alaquin and other Pontifices arranged themselves around him. Garvin searched the faces and minds of the Companions.

The Suitcase understood. NICK IS LOST.

AND YOU ARE THE ONE THE THORN SAID WOULD MEET ME HERE.

THE ORACLE SHOWS ME LEADING YOUR RECRUITS ON TO THE REPUBLIC.

WHAT DID IT SHOW ME DOING?

I WAS NOT SHOWN THAT. The mind of the Immortal was a thing of paradoxes, loops, and twists.

Garvin realized that it awaited orders. He thought a moment. HOW MANY CAN YOU TRANSPORT?

I CAN HOLD TWENTY COMPANIONS, EACH OF WHOM CAN HOLD TWENTY VOLUNTEERS. I CAN LEAPFROG DETACHMENTS FORWARD.

IT TOOK ME ONLY A FEW DAYS TO GET HERE.

IT WILL TAKE ME FAR LONGER TO BRING AN ORGANIZED FORCE THERE. IT HAS TAKEN MUCH OF THE PERIOD SINCE WE LAST MET TO REACH YOU.

GET AS MANY TO THE REPUBLIC AS YOU CAN BEFORE RUMACK CLOSES DOWN THE APPROACHES. That much Garvin remembered from his Rider's plan. But he was forgetting something and the Rider was comatose inside him. He wanted to get away.

Then he remembered. TRAINED LIGHT CAVALRY FOR THE GUVNOR. He turned to Alaquin. RECRUIT LIGHT CAVALRY VOLUNTEERS. YOU ARE IN CHARGE OF MY PEOPLE HERE, ALAQUIN. OBEY ONLY THOSE WHO COME WITH MY DIRECT COMMANDS. I DON'T KNOW WHEN I WILL BE BACK.

YES, TERRIBLE ONE.

Garvin took Thelia's hand. He indicated to the laser teams that they should come with him.

MIGHT I WALK WITH YOU ALSO? It was the Suitcase. The mind of Time loops and paradoxes sang a song of worlds gone and friends lost.

YOU CAME TO MY WORLD LOOKING FOR ME, RIGHT? Garvin asked.

As an answer the Immortal showed Garvin an image of his mother, Claire standing in a butcher shop. It was Klazewiski's on First Avenue. His mother was being very friendly to the man, teasing him into not charging her. Mr. Klazewiski was admiring her breasts. A very young boy saw it all. Both adults froze, embarrassed. Both felt another's mind. THE ORACLE SHOWED ME THAT.

Garvin let Roger walk with him. The Pontifices, the soldiers, the people of the town watched him go over the fields, the laser men trailing behind. I MUST HAVE BEEN SEVEN OR EIGHT WHEN THAT HAPPENED.

WHEN ONE GOES TO THE ORACLE, the Immortal told him, A QUESTION IS ANSWERED. THE QUESTION IS KNOWN ONLY TO THE ORACLE. YOU ARE AN ANSWER THAT HAS OCCURRED AGAIN AND AGAIN.

Garvin felt a distortion and pain in senses he didn't know he possessed. He saw the sound of steel scraping metal, smelled green light, and tasted bronze melting. THAT IS THE AURA OF THE ORACLE, the Immortal told him.

It showed Garvin more. He saw afternoon light in his mother's bedroom. It fell on the picture of his father. He must have stared at it for hours. The street, the house was very quiet. The room grew dark. He felt traces of the agony the Talking Suitcase had undergone to consult the Oracle.

IT SEEMED A HEAVY PRICE TO PAY TO INTRUDE ON AN UNKNOWN BOY'S OEDIPAL URGES. BUT IMAGES LIKE THOSE APPEARED AGAIN AND AGAIN WHEN IMMORTALS AND COMPANIONS ENCOUNTERED THE ORACLE. IT SEEMED THAT EVEN THE ORACLE WAS NOT CERTAIN WHERE THESE THINGS WERE HAPPENING. WE SEARCHED BETWEEN OUR OTHER DUTIES FOR YEARS UNTIL WE FOUND YOU.

AND GAVE ME TO THE SLAVERS.

THAT TOO WAS SHOWN. The Talking Suitcase revealed to Garvin the image of Herself dealing with the cloaked and hooded figure. Banners flapped above them as the slaver held Garvin upright.

WHY? WHY DID YOU DO THAT TO ME?

IT IS ONLY THROUGH THE ORACLE'S AID THAT WE ARE ABLE TO SURVIVE AGAINST THE GOBLINS AND THEIR RIDERS. I HAVE COME TO BELIEVE IT SHOWS US THE THINGS EVEN THE GODS OF THE CITY HIDE FROM THEMSELVES. IN YOUR CASE IT HAS SHOWN US A STEED WHO BREAKS RIDERS, A SON OF WHOM ANY FATHER WOULD TAKE SPECIAL NOTICE.

They were inside the grove of trees around the portal. Thelia started to cry. Garvin took the lasers from the team and thrust them deep into Time. ARM THE VOLUNTEERS UP TO THE LEVEL OF RUMACK'S FORCES. BUT NO LASERS.

He turned to the laser men. YOU ARE THE SPECIAL DEFENDERS OF THIS TOWN. GUARD IT WELL AND BE HONORED. He kissed Thelia. She knew she would have his child. He wanted to take her with him but understood that it would be impossible. "Thank you," he said. "I will never forget."

HOW DO I FIND THE ORACLE?

LOOK FOR IT AND IT WILL FIND YOU, the Suitcase told him.

Garvin nodded and was gone.

At dawn a few days later on the veld world, the camp at the portal was just coming alive. The crew of Hotland laborers was lining up outside the cook tent for breakfast. A troop of mercenaries, French Revolutionary by origin, were there on the way to Rumack. Security was minimal. As far as they knew, they were the only people on this world. There had been no disturbances since the strange man with the young captive had come through, stealing the commandant's precious jeep and driving it off a cliff.

Thus the volley of gunfire from west of the camp was a great surprise to all. The shaman commandant himself was just waking up from last night's drinking bout with the mercenary captain. Hotlanders rushed for their weapons; men collided with each other running to the firing line. The commandant standing at the door of his tent probed and found only a few minds out there, snipers.

He was probing for them, intending to crush the life out of each one when he became aware of something behind him. A line of hard-riding horsemen were coming out of the east with the rising sun behind them. They gunned down sentries, lost formation as they swept through the tents of the camp. TO ME! TO ME! the mercenary captain was broadcasting, rallying his troops. And then he was no more. His mind disappeared as if a switch had been flicked off.

The head shaman was a fairly powerful telepath. He probed toward the attackers. "Fire at the horses," he ordered the Hotlanders who had rallied around him. One man on a huge bay was the raiders' leader. The shaman probed that one and found a familiar mind. THE ONE WHO STOLE MY JEEP!

The Guvnor could have summoned the Wind, but he came in hanging off the side of his horse to make a small target. He was firing from horseback. THE VERY SAME, he told the commandant and shot him in the head.

Then it was all over. Hotlanders ran in all directions. The mercenaries surrendered and joined the invaders. The Guvnor burned what he couldn't carry away and booby-trapped the portal. He felt the satisfaction of having done something crisply and well. He estimated he had bought Scarecrow and Garvin an extra week.

Scarecrow looked into the minds of recent refugees from District Three. He saw what they had seen: Moriaph's body dead and stuffed. Rumack used it as a footstool to get on his horse. Once aboard, he howled at the top of his lungs. He put his mind inside that of the terrified Citizens. TELL SCARECROW THAT HE WILL BE ENVIOUS OF THE TREATMENT THIS HAG RECEIVED.

Rumack's grip was closing around District Four. The only way out was to the north along the Great East-West Road. Scarecrow gave orders that all who wished would have a chance to leave. With the ones that were left, he formed an army to defy Rumack.

He took the remnants of Moriaph's forces as they came streaming back through Weatherhill from the ambush. He added troops from other parts of the district. There were barely half a dozen gunships left, no more than a few dozen transports. Fuel supplies were low. Units were shattered, their morale gone. He fleshed out the structure of the army with Citizens and Select who volunteered to stay in the District.

Orders came from New Liberty, the capital. OPEN NEGOTIATIONS WITH RUMACK. OFFER HIM HOSTAGES AS PROOF OF OUR GOOD FAITH.

Scarecrow had seen in the minds of refugees the lines of prisoners, Citizen and Select, heading for portals and slavery. Scarecrow destroyed the radios and the factors on which the messages arrived.

STAY WITH ME, he told the army. THERE IS A CHANCE WE WILL DIE HERE. BUT IF WE FAIL THERE IS A CERTAINTY THAT THOSE WHO SURVIVE US WILL LOOK BACK ON THE DEAD WITH ENVY.

Then with Amre and the children of Cluster Group Two of Weatherhill, he went to the Fire Gates. On the plateau backed by a river and ringed with open ground, he had stockpiled children. Even before the night that Moriaph and Gepeto died and he had seized power in District Four, Scarecrow had been sending children there.

They had come from his own district and as refugees from Three and Five. There were dozens of Citizen cluster groups. There were also hundreds of Select, children from ten to sixteen, sent out for the summer to the border regions. They and their tutors had spent anxious days since the disaster waiting for orders. Now they were told to return to New Liberty. Their nation was falling apart. They felt helpless and wanted to do something.

Scarecrow and Amre brought Darrel and Maji and the rest

into the hall. Their own daughter Miche was there. Scarecrow showed the Select Goblin Market and lines of prisoners. He showed them screaming Rumack. Then he introduced the children. There was an impatient stirring in the audience. Select did not pay attention to Citizens.

Scarecrow invited them to probe the minds of these Citizens. They saw Garvin, saw him start as the most inept woodsman and end as one who chased shamans in front of him. Some of the tutors at the back of the hall began to protest. Scarecrow silenced them. He showed them all Grim Reaper and explained who he was. He showed them Garvin as he had found him on the grass next to the burning transport.

THE REPUBLIC IS IN PANIC. IT HAS LOST ITS ARMY AND ITS HERO. WITH YOUR HELP I MEAN TO STAND HERE UNTIL GARVIN RETURNS. WHO WILL JOIN ME?

Again tutors protested. But some of their own number silenced them. ALL WHO WISH TO LEAVE WILL LEAVE TONIGHT. ALL WHO CHOOSE TO STAY COME FORWARD. One by one, then in whole clumps, Select children got up and walked forward. More than half of them joined. Many of their tutors did also. That night the others went north by convoy into a Republic that was collapsing around them.

The others stayed. GARVIN! GARVIN! was the chant. Citizen children found it in the air around them and shouted it aloud—"Garvin!" And from somewhere that night came another name. No one knew who had thought of it first. WARCHILD! rang in every mind. "Warchild!" was a mighty shout against the dark.

CHAPTER NINETEEN

GARVIN TRIED not to think of what he was doing as running away. Some things had to be understood before he was of any use to anyone. Besides, he hurt too badly. Death stalked across open fields in every dream he had. His Rider lay still, traumatized by the death of the Armorer, in awe of Garvin.

That was good. It allowed Garvin to wander. The worlds he first sifted after the Roman Fields were empty of all life, the next ones empty of all human life. Then came places lightly settled by desperate refugees and fugitives. The Rider stirred. 'time lane,' it told itself as Garvin sifted a couple of worlds that seemed scarred.

The Time Lane was like a ribbon of pain winding through Time. On the world where Garvin crossed it, he found a Chicago. It was small but wide open, complete with a citadel and a slave market. There were Time traders and their strings of slaves, merchants with guarded town houses, drifters, fugitive slaves, spies, and police. Garvin watched a line of exhausted women and children led under guard into a wooden pen.

He tensed, ready to free them, until he wondered what he'd do with them afterward. From the citadel, Garvin picked up a flash of Goblin mind, flat and alien. He recoiled from it, tried to shake the feel of the place out of himself as he went back through the portal into Time.

Beyond a few empty worlds, life began again, worlds of low population. 'these people are doubtless exploited. most are probably unaware of it. only a few leaders need know. . . .' Garvin cut the Rider off even though the information was offered respectfully. He didn't want to be reminded at all of the Rider's existence.

He knew that the Rider was starting to think of him as a new creation of the Gods of the City Out Of Time. 'perhaps as more than that,' it repeated to itself. Garvin spun a world beneath him and came out of a portal near a lake on a summer evening in 1991 in Nouvelle France.

"Alors!" Canada was still French. He scanned the minds of the kids who were staring at him. A dozen of them, boys and girls, sat in and on and around several cars parked at the water's edge. All were dressed in silk shirts and pants. Their hair was elaborately curled. They had been making out in back seats. Music played like a low, lazy growl on the radio.

They spoke to him in French. He entered their minds to understand the questions.

"Where did you just come from?"

"Who are you?"

"Indian?"

"With blond hair?"

"An Anglo?"

Then he showed them who he was and where he had been. They knew nothing of telepathy. They were his absolutely. They would have done anything he suggested. He stood there like the realization of all their dreams of freedom. Parents were strict; society was rigid, according to these rich kids of New France. "We are not even allowed to listen to the music we love in our parents' houses," one girl was telling him.

He listened to the music then. WHAT IS IT? he wanted to know. It drew him in. There was an organ and drums and what he realized was guitar music. He felt the kids moving to it, their hearts beating with the music.

"Creole rag," they told him. He saw in their imaginations the black countries of the Carribbean. The radio stations in Port-au-Prince and Nouveau Orleans sent out the low, insistent music. "Grand Royale is singing."

In their minds he saw a young black man with long hair and burning eyes. On the radio the music became something between a whisper and a wail and then disappeared. There was a moment of silence, then guitars and women's voices. "Les Diaboliques," they told him. He saw three black women in tight white shirts and pants. Garvin nudged a boy's mind and the radio was turned up.

While he was in that world, Garvin's nights were full of music. He wore the boys' clothes and learned to drive their cars on the highways in the forests around the lakes. The girls shared him in turn. Garvin was their secret, kept from other less favored cliques of kids, from servants, and from family.

There was always someone whose parents were away. Garvin stayed in their houses, swam and sunned himself, listened to the music drifting up from the south, drove down backcountry roads through villages inhabitated by Indians and mixed bloods. The kids' fathers were executives in mining and timber companies; the mothers kept salons at Montreal. 'the industrial revolution has here been channeled, exploited to keep the population small. . . .' Garvin put his foot to the gas pedal of the car he was driving. It belonged to the father of a girl named Thérèse.

She screamed as he blasted down dusty back roads. "You are a savage of the highway," she told him. She pretended to be angry but was delighted at first by the excitement, the story she would have to tell. The Rider shrank away to nothing as Garvin took turns on two wheels and Thérèse's mock anger turn to fear. She was sobbing by the time he stopped at a filling station at a crossroads.

It was a hot, still afternoon. The attendant was a tall young man with Indian features, black hair, and blue eyes. He bowed in deference to them, but Garvin could feel his resentment and anger. In the office the radio picked up the same station from the south that played on the car radio. Thérèse dried her tears and looked away from him.

The next morning Garvin was in another girl's father's bathroom. He shaved his head around the Mohawk, trimmed the ridge of hair. The ponytail was past his shoulder blades now. Then he noticed hair on his upper lip—not down but beard. He examined it carefully, then lathered up and shaved it off for the first time. He realized that he was deep into summer on this world. He thought of Scarecrow and Amre and the rest. He thought of the Roman Fields and realized that it was awhile since he had awakened from dreams of lasers and death. He still squirmed at the thought, but the pain of the memory had healed. Time was wasting. He had to be going.

I WILL NEVER FORGET THIS PLACE OR YOU, he told them that night when they gathered at their spot at the lake. They all kissed him good-bye as the radio played the Diaboliques singing about a magic night. Garvin made them all look away, walked into the woods, found the portal, and was gone. They talked about him for the rest of the summer.

The next world he found was almost a duplicate of the one he had just left. There was a lake, cars, music, and kids. He didn't probe closely enough to tell if they were exactly the same. He wanted to think the kids he had known were unique.

Garvin was curious about New York. He summoned the mirror, the room, and the globe. He found many New Yorks. The first was a small city at the bottom of Manhattan. 'a provincial capital,' his Rider offered hesitantly. Garvin gritted his teeth and looked around.

There was no street plan in this New York, no Twenty-fourth Street, no high school, no First Avenue. The phone book did not reveal Claire or any other names that were familiar. Music came out the open door of a pub. "Bulldog Rant," sang a hoarse voice with an English accent. Garvin was caught for a moment by the insistent drumbeat in the background.

Nothing there held him, and Garvin slipped back into Time. Leaving the lightly developed worlds, he found himself in a patch of primitive places with nothing but a scattering of tribes. Next were empty worlds. And one from which he recoiled.

'a sure sign of a developed technology.'

THEY WERE WIPED OUT. A WHOLE WORLD DE-STROYED BY GOBLINS AND RIDERS. Garvin plunged blindly through Time.

'i am like a man who thought he was getting onto a spirited young horse only to find he had mounted a dragon. i find myself to be a servant. i wish only to assist you. understand, garvin, that there has never been a steed like you. there has never been anyone like you in time.'

Garvin ignored this and his own suspicions of who and what he was by examining burned-out worlds that appeared before him. On one there were still traces of human life. Garvin hung in Time, wanting to know what the people were like, yet not wanting to.

WHEN A WORLD SEEMS LIKE IT MAY BE GOING TO CAUSE TROUBLE FOR YOU, THEN IT GETS DE-STROYED.

'it is all the will of the gods and goblins. we riders are no more than tools.' Garvin knew the Rider's tone had changed. He still didn't trust it. After the way he had been manipulated at the Armory of Night, he didn't even trust himself.

He called up the next world in the mirror, reached into it, and found a place empty of human life. Cities remained, stripped of their populations.

HOW MANY OF THEM DIED ON THEIR WAY TO GOBLIN MARKET?

'it is the will of the goblins and the gods.'

YOU COULD DISOBEY THEM.

'what would become of us? we need the goblins' expertise to make the jump from one steed to another.'

AND BILLIONS OF LIVES ARE A SMALL PRICE TO PAY.

'as one lives, the habit of living grows. if one is not brave, it is because bravery is the prerogative of the very young.

without the goblins we would be hunted down by the immortals.'

Garvin saw it as the Rider did. The Immortals, with their superior mobility, would isolate and destroy the Riders unless the Riders had greater numbers and technology. Those could be obtained only through trade with Goblin Market and the City Out Of Time.

The Rider was trying to shift blame. Garvin spun worlds impatiently. The next one was a sad place where the population was falling. But it felt almost familiar to Garvin. He wanted to find something like his own world again. He wanted to see Claire even if she wasn't the same one who was his mother. Garvin had a vision of the Gods creating one world after another, trying like he was now to find something that they remembered.

The next world had a New York that was almost right except that it had too many bridges and the air was full of huge blimps. The year was 1998. The next New York had more skyscrapers than Garvin remembered. The year was 1967; the air was charged somehow.

He sifted through Time again, and the next world looked a lot like his New York. It was grimmer and more battered. There was bomb damage and a blackout. It was 1948. He sifted again and the city looked wrong. The year he picked out of passing was 1923.

'this is what is called a progression. each world will be a little earlier or later than the ones beside it. the span of years falls in a pattern known only to the gods.'

Garvin went back to 1948. His mother wouldn't have been born yet, but he found his old neighborhood and most of the houses where he had lived. They looked off to him, both newer and more beaten up than he remembered. In the dark not too many people noticed the way he looked. Those who did had their attention turned away.

On the 1967 world it wasn't necessary to hide. He hovered outside a portal. Some of the minds he scanned were ordinary enough; others were charged, distorted. A few were bizarrely telepathic. One word was on those minds: ACID.

Garvin tumbled out of Time onto a street corner. Almost immediately he was surrounded by kids dancing around him in the light of a street lamp. Their hair was long and tangled, their clothes a bright jumble. Some of them had their faces painted. ACID was the word on each mind. Garvin probed, and some of them knew he was doing it. Their minds were soft, unfocused. All around him in the city that night he could feel minds like these. "Like wow, the hair," said a boy whose frizzy hair stuck up a foot and a half from his head.

"That dude's clothes, far out," said a girl with red and yellow paint on her cheeks and a pointed witch hat on her head. Garvin saw himself elongated and wavering in their eyes. WHO ARE YOU? was the question.

He showed them and they followed him for the rest of his visit there. They were near his old neighborhood. He walked down streets that didn't look right. He saw adults turn and stare at them, felt some of them, revolted, thinking, "Damn hippies!" Others were envious: "Nothing but singing and screwing."

More kids appeared, joined the ones following him. It was like a pilgrimage to East Twenty-fourth between First and Second avenues. When he got there, Garvin saw nothing he recognized. The block and the ones around it had disappeared. A huge apartment complex stood on what would have been his old neighborhood.

He found a telephone book in a booth decorated with garish distorted letters reading, OUT WITH LBJ/FASCIST PIG. There was nothing under any name he could think of. He made calls but the numbers were wrong. He cast his mind in ever-widening circles. Inside that strange telephone booth Garvin felt homesick.

The kids were aware of what he had done with his mind. "Fantastic, man. You should go down to Washington and make them understand." Hands reached out for him, led him away. They smoked a joint, passing it from hand to hand as they walked. Garvin felt his mind slipping in and out of theirs.

They headed toward what they called the East Village. On their way they passed the building where the Mohawks met on Garvin's world. It was semi-abandoned and falling apart. Garvin realized that he didn't want to see any more. He could spend a lifetime wandering from world to world. I HAVE TO BE GOING, he told them. They wanted him to stay. But in their strange way they understood how he felt. Garvin knew they would be doomed if the Goblins found them.

A radio was on; a guitar wove sound. HENDRIX was the name on every mind. "That's 'Third Stone From The Sun,'" someone said.

"That's this planet," someone else said. "Please tell us where you're from."

They followed him over to Tompkins Park. A portal lay right where the one had been on his world. Garvin felt a twinge of terror as he approached it. There was a circle of kids somewhere in the dark, OMing. A sharp rhythm section riffed in the band shell.

Garvin didn't want them to see what he was going to do. He took the music and the night and whirled them through the minds around him. "Come back and visit us again when we've achieved peace and understanding," someone said. "Third Stone From The Sun" echoed out of an apartment window, and Garvin took the sound with him into Time.

Garvin plunged back through the worlds of the progression. The span of years between each one grew longer. Minds concerned with history disappeared and then ways of recording years. Human minds were no longer present, and Garvin hurtled through a place of empty worlds. Somewhere out in Time people were dying in his name. Garvin turned over worlds faster and faster. IF YOU SEEK THE ORACLE, IT WILL FIND YOU. He remembered the Talking Suitcase telling him that.

'there is no oracle. the gods of the city themselves tell us so. i myself have never known anyone who has experienced it. it is a fool's errand.'

WHY WOULD THE IMMORTAL SEND ME LOOKING FOR SOMETHING THAT DOES NOT EXIST? WHERE DID IT FIND OUT ABOUT ME EXCEPT THROUGH THE ORACLE?

'there are many whys and wheres in immortals' stories.' Garvin realized that for the first time he was talking to his Rider, arguing a point with it. The heartbeat of the City seemed clearer, louder than it had been. 'who brought you to herself? who brought you that quickly from november to high summer? you have wandered for weeks now in time. see how immense it is. who travels that quickly?'

Garvin was stopped by that. NOT EVEN THE IMMORTALS. MAYBE THE GOBLINS. BUT IT WAS NO GOBLIN THAT HAD ME. Garvin tried to remember his trip from his own world to Herself's. It was the one piece of his memory that wouldn't come back. Then from somewhere far off in Time he felt a far-off flash of pain. Somewhere a world full of people was dying. He remembered what the thing inside him was. WE WILL ASK THE ORACLE WHEN IT FINDS US.

'the oracle does not exist. . . .'

Garvin was about to spin worlds instead of replying, to throw himself into danger once more to scare his Rider. Suddenly he tasted fire and saw music tear through his chest and smelled a laughing green sun. For a moment Garvin thought he was going to die. He put up his triple line of defenses.

These weren't even swept aside. They were ignored. Where Garvin had set up his Umbra, there were images of an infinite number of New Yorks. The confusion of Garvin's senses was disorienting. He could feel his body even though he hung in time. ORACLE!

Garvin heard hot lead and touched the texture of fear. He put up his Umbra defense and caught sight of himself spinning through worlds, heading for the City Out Of Time as fast as he could.

The pain and the confusion of senses almost made Garvin break contact. Instead he shifted to his Curtain. His Rider gave a long, uninterrupted wail inside him. Garvin's eyes filled with the sound of metal scraping on metal. But the Oracle showed images of him heading away from the City, speeding back to the Republic with an army.

Again he almost broke contact. 'get away from this quagmire,' his Rider pleaded. Garvin smelled nuclear fission; his ears ached with harsh lights. He filled his mind with the idea of the Gods of the City Out Of Time.

The Rider was trying to yank him away. Garvin caught one series of images: grass, cows, people. There was another: telepaths, Winds, Oracle. He heard a hunger that shook him. Then he saw the City. It hung in Time, like the Armory of Night but thousands of times larger. It pulsed like a heart, but it was impenetrable. Then the food chain of telepaths, Winds, and Oracle appeared again and the City split open and light from inside it, ordinary daylight, flooded the darkness of Time. The infinite worlds disappeared in the dawn.

Garvin smelled pain as he broke contact. He understood that the Oracle wanted to feed on a Wind. But the thing that had caught his attention was one of the images it had used. The Wind it had shown was the Guvnor's as it turned in the air while the Guvnor sold Garvin to Herself.

The Oracle was gone. Garvin hung alone in Time. 'we cannot trust that thing,' his Rider told him. It had been too frightened to catch all of what the Oracle had shown.

Garvin wanted to keep it off balance. I AM GOING TO THE CITY OUT OF TIME. SHOW ME THE WAY. He didn't know what would happen there. Everything seemed open to the Oracle but the City and the Gods. He had seen that he would go there and emerge.

He wanted to move fast to keep his Rider away from another mystery, one he didn't want to think about just yet. The Oracle's images made him realize that the Guvnor looked more than a little like the picture of his father. SOMETHING I NEED TO KNOW IS IN THE CITY, he told his Rider and felt it hasten to work out their route.

CHAPTER
TWENTY

JUST BEFORE dawn Scarecrow assembled an attack force behind his own front lines. They were north of Axblade. The town had been taken and burned after a heroic defense the week before. The story of Scarecrow's resistance went out by radio and factor to hundreds of isolated towns and forts in the Republic. It was their source of hope. And the drain Scarecrow and his defenders put on Rumack's resources and attention let the rest of the nation survive.

From the capital at New Liberty came nothing but confusing orders and strange images on the minds of those who fled the place. Hotlanders appeared out of nowhere, shot people in the streets, and disappeared before the Select could act. A single madman had appeared on the lawn before the chambers of the Council of Councils and threw himself up against the windows of the place. Despite a hundred trained minds trying to stop him, he had blown up, leaving the chamber a wreck and the Council itself a bleeding, dying mess.

Of all this Scarecrow was aware as he reviewed the units under his command. He had Moriaph Division, the survivors of the troops she had led. Eight thousand strong, they were the shock troops of Fortress Fire Gates. Behind them, Scarecrow could feel Amre with the children of Warchild Cluster.

As he walked forward to his front lines, he felt his secret weapon taking its place in the formation beside Moriaph Division. WE ARE READY, announced the Thorn. FOR GARVIN WARCHILD, added the Rose. For the last few days the two-headed Immortal had ferried her Companion-led reinforcements into Scarecrow's position. There were trained telepaths and able fighting men, and the Guardian was thankful for the help. Somehow, though, he didn't want to come too close. The immensity of Time, the horrors that came out of it, disturbed him too much.

Scarecrow's front line was no more than a thin string of sentries placed at intervals in the woods. He held a position thirty miles in diameter, and every yard of the perimeter had to be watched at all times. At the center was Fortress Fire Gates. Scattered through the forest, a dozen portals were guarded against Rumack's forces on the adjoining world. Lives had to be traded for ground and ground for time. Foot by foot and hour by hour, he held on for Garvin.

He reached into the dark, mind drifting like a night bird, and encountered the mind of a Hotland sentry. The man stood half asleep at his post. Scarecrow's mind drifted on, found another sentry and another. They suspected nothing. A mind recognized his. He tensed. Then he picked up the word "Guardian."

It was Uncle. Scarecrow crept forward past his own sentries. In the dark he couldn't see the old man. But in the other mind he found the Hotland deployment. "There are three Hotland units, big ones, behind his sentry line. Rumack's massed them planning to push you way back here, put a big dent in your perimeter. Only thing is, one of them is Red Death's outfit. Mole is with them, ready to go to work."

Scarecrow indicated that he understood. The old man's mind faded back into the Hotland mass. Behind Scarecrow, Moriaph Division and the Immortals' Companions started to slip forward. The sky lightened in the east. Dawn and dusk, the moments of uncertain light, were best for surprise attacks.

Rumack had the advantage of being able to make pushes wherever he wanted on Scarecrow's perimeter. Twenty thousand troops were massed for this one. Even including the children of Warchild Cluster, Scarecrow had a bare fifteen thousand in this sector. Under most circumstances that would be enough to hold the line but not to attack.

Scarecrow reached into the minds of his commanders. FORWARD FOR MORIAPH! FORWARD FOR THE THORN AND ROSE! His line exploded in fire. A light-artillery battery behind them opened up on the Hotlander position. SCARECROW? The mind that touched his was powerful and old. But it had an aura that was young, innocent. He saw the two heads of the Immortal in the eyes of the Companions. YOUR PLAN IS STILL IN EFFECT?

RED DEATH'S UNIT IS IN THEIR CENTER. HIT THEM AS HARD AS YOU CAN. THE CHILDREN WILL BREAK THEM. Scarecrow saw the Republic as a bubble floating in a dark sea, ready to burst at any moment. But he put that image aside and turned his mind to the attack.

Through the eyes of his advance troops, Scarecrow could see the burned stumps and black earth that marked the Hotland advance. He moved up with a battalion of assault troops. The Hotlanders hadn't built defensive works. They were surprised by the attack, but some of them were starting to fight. It was random fire at first that intensified fast.

Hotland shamans ducked into the general mind mell of their units, avoiding the probes of Select and Companions who went at them like hawks. Their own artillery was coming into action. Scarecrow felt a blazing pain off on the left where a barrage hit the Companion unit. Hotlander defenses were firming up better than Scarecrow had expected.

From the Companion unit floated an image of Garvin heroic in torchlight. Warchild Cluster picked it up, whirled the image through the dawn. Garvin raised his arm in triumph, stood with his foot planted in Rumack's neck. Rumack howled with pain.

Suddenly a huge image of Rumack reached out his paws and smashed Garvin like a firefly. In front of the advancing troops, the shamans linked to one another and formed a crude Relay. Red Death's command took shape in the center. WE HAVE SEEN THE WORST THESE FOREST WIZARDS CAN DO, he told them. NOW FOR RUMACK—KILL! KILL! KILL!

Hotland artillery poured fire into the advance. Rumack's face, huge and howling in triumph, hung over Scarecrow's troops. Then Garvin's image appeared again. WARCHILD! WARCHILD! The Select and Citizen children of Warchild Cluster ran forward behind the advance.

At that moment in the mind of Red Death appeared the ghost of Grim Reaper. The leader and all the thousands who had been with him remembered that night out in Hotlands. They saw the image of Garvin smiling in triumph. They saw howling Rumack reflected in the blade that hung on Garvin's neck. They saw Rumack, arms and legs once stiff and unwilling, now begin to dance.

The disaster the month before at Axblade leaped to their minds. At the same time they felt the forest Wizard and shouting children. They saw the image of the two-headed woman carried in the minds of her Companions. They were doomed. The fight went out of them.

The unit broke, scattering to the rear. Shamans from Red Death on down lost contact with their troops and ran. Riflemen threw aside their weapons. Scarecrow and the Thorn and Rose sent their units into the gap in the Hotlander line, sent them forward to slaughter the gunners and fall on the flanks of the other Hotland troops. With them went the image of Garvin by torchlight. I WILL BE BACK BEFORE FALL, he promised.

Rumack's horse pawed the ground a few miles from where the battle had taken place the previous day. The horse was huge but Rumack made it look small. He leaped out of the saddle, his Rider loosening briefly the absolute control with which it held him. The giant's shoulders thrust up behind his head. The head was stuck forward. A low roar came from the back of his throat. In Rumack's hands, seeming not much larger than a knife, was a short, curved sword.

Red Death faced his chief, eyes full of terror, mind crying for mercy. He let his sword hang in one hand. Red Death's command, what was left of it, was drawn up behind him, minds linked in a Relay. Rumack's Rider ran his Steed's mind through the thousands before it. Grim Reaper was alive in the Relay. The Rider could detect the trace of a forest wizard. THE ENEMY HAS POSSESSED YOU, it used Rumack to tell them.

YOUR DAYS ARE NUMBERED, RUMACK, was the reply of the ghost in the Relay. For a moment the Hotlanders saw Rumack as a dried husk. Rumack howled and strode forward. Red Death was a big man, well over six feet. Rumack glowered above him, swung his sword, and bashed Red Death's sword aside. He sliced sideways into the right of Red Death's neck.

The head toppled to the ground. Blood spurted forth. Rumack screamed and kept the body upright by hacking first one side then the other. A bloody pile of flesh, bone, and organs sank to the ground.

Shamans and overshamans fell down begging for mercy. The troops felt Rumack's mind in theirs. They moved forward and seized the officers. Rumack, blood covering him, beheaded each of the unit's telepaths. THE FOREST WIZARD IS GONE. THE UNIT IS DISBANDED. YOU WILL BE ASSIGNED IN SMALL BANDS TO GARRISON DUTY. The soldiers fell to their knees and praised Rumack. He broke the death's-head staffs of the shamans and turned his back on the disgraced units.

He walked to a stand of trees that still stood. A woman with red hair dressed all in green sat her horse. 'you see the enemy's desperation,' Rumack's Rider told Herself's.

'and yours' was the reply. The beautiful green eyes never blinked as Rumack walked closer. As the two Riders communicated, their Steeds moved on loose leashes. 'that enemy just led you to destroy a whole section of your command.'

'two defeats that unit cost me. the only ones i have suffered.'

'your supply lines are another problem. i am given to understand that you wish me to secure them.' Herself's Rider indicated troops coming through a portal. 'i brought my own household troops and reliable mercenaries. i have come over thousands of worlds. what am i up against?'

'this.' Rumack's Rider showed images of defeat. Camps burned and transports lay wrecked. Survivors fled in terror. Images of the enemy leader were distorted by the fear of those who had seen him. 'he calls himself the guvnor.' At his Rider's telling him the name, Rumack stamped and howled with rage.

For an instant Herself's Rider seemed interested. Rumack stared at her with mad eyes. 'i will defeat this one for you,' Herself's Rider told Rumack's. 'but here is the cost to me.'

'your steed spent years with the immortals. they are here helping scarecrow. you owe me this help.'

Herself's Rider was impatient. 'my steed's companion training was what brought me here before you could strangle to death. and i will have my share of your spoils.'

Rumack's mind was a thing of wild surges. His Rider unleashed him a bit more and the giant moved toward Herself. At the same moment his Rider showed hers what looked like flat, puppet images of what had happened at the chateau. Garvin lay in the operating room seen through Goblin eyes. The Companions rescued Garvin with the Rider aboard. 'it would seem,' Rumack's Rider told the other, 'that you were outwitted.'

'the steed was dying. i needed another quickly. i obtained what seemed a good one from a trader i knew well.'

Rumack was close to Herself now. His Rider told hers, 'we should breed these two and raise a line of steeds. beauty and strength, size and time striding.' Rumack bounded forward like a bear. Red Death's blood stuck to his clothes, skin, and hair. He stank of it.

Herself, given a slack rein by her Rider, spun her horse to the side, came past Rumack, and laid her riding crop across his shoulders. He howled and lunged. She moved her horse away. Her Rider told his, 'i think i will not breed her. she is the best and most beautiful steed i have ever ridden. her effect is stunning.'

Rumack rubbed his shoulder and growled but didn't move toward her again. 'all was going as planned,' complained his Rider. 'new liberty was ready to surrender. they hesitate now, waiting to see what happens here. the thorn and rose has brought reinforcements. this guvnor cuts my supplies.'

'we will crush them,' Herself's Rider told his. 'the thorn and rose shall be dropped in the deepest water we can find. you expect riches and you shall have them. and i shall have half.' Rumack growled, but his Rider silently agreed. 'i will move out immediately,' Herself's Rider announced.

In the next few weeks the circumference of Scarecrow's lines shrank steadily. Towns and forts were held until they were reduced to ruins. Then the ruins were booby-trapped. As the Hotlanders advanced, they burned the forest. There was always heavy smoke in the air. Days of heat and battle turned into nights red rimmed with Hotland-born nightmares. Scarecrow's mobile force was Moriaph Division, and Thorn and Rose's Companion outfit. They took casualties constantly.

Mole and Uncle still operated in Rumack's army. Uncle had slipped up to the perimeter one evening with news of Rumack massing troops and artillery. There was to be a feint attack from the south and a main attack from the east. "Guns and the mercenaries to use them been coming through the portals the last few days," Uncle told Scarecrow. The Guardian nodded. He had received messages from the Guvnor saying that he couldn't get near the supply routes any more. He planned to fall back in front of Rumack, then to counterattack.

After he had gotten back to safety, Scarecrow received a message from the Thorn. He moved toward her, probing. In her encampment was a young Companion, a woman bruised and exhausted. On her mind were images of the Guvnor and the Talking Suitcase. The Guvnor was saying, "Reinforcements coming through. Perhaps the last you'll get before Garvin himself returns. The portals this messenger will use link up with the only ones still in my possession."

The images of the Talking Suitcase showed it tumbling out of Time with Companions in tow. They in turn led an assortment of figures in everything from armor to flak jackets. These were wild eyed, chanting the name "Garvin" to dull their terror of Time.

The Thorn looked at Scarecrow. The Rose slept, leaning against her. IN THE NEXT DAY OR TWO WE WILL BE RECEIVING THOUSANDS OF REINFORCEMENTS THROUGH THESE DOUBLE PORTALS RIGHT HERE.

Scarecrow looked where she indicated. It was right in the path of what Uncle had just told him would be Rumack's main attack. CHANGE THE ARRIVAL POINT. I AM ABOUT TO GIVE ORDERS TO FALL BACK FROM HERE. He showed the Rose what he had been shown.

WE CANNOT, SCARECROW. THE OPERATION IS ALREADY IN PROGRESS. THEY ARE COMING FROM MANY WORLDS AWAY TO WHERE THE GUVNOR IS HOLDING ON. THE PLAN IS TO TUMBLE THEM THROUGH TIME AS QUICKLY AS POSSIBLE FROM THERE. IT IS TOO LATE TO CHANGE.

RUMACK MUST KNOW SOMETHING LIKE THIS IS GOING ON. Scarecrow felt himself trapped by events on worlds he didn't know or care about. He was exhausted. His forests were being burned foot by foot; his people were dying.

GARVIN WILL COME BACK, the Rose told them all while she still slept. I LOVE GARVIN.

So it was that during that day Scarecrow, instead of preparing to fall back in front of Rumack's attack, put all his reserves into line. The feint attack in the south was ignored. "Flesh and blood against artillery," he murmured to Amre. "I hope the troops coming out of Time are as good as the ones that are going to die."

They were alone in a medical tent. They were embracing tightly. He could feel in her mind the endless repetition: antibiotics, anesthetics, fresh foods, clean water. She thought of Miche, who was back at the Fire Gates. "She wants to see you," Amre told him. On her mind was the thought that each time he went away he might never return.

Outside, Warchild Cluster was marching to the battle line. Maji and Darrell were there with other kids of the old Cluster Two. All were dressed in bits and pieces of uniforms. All of them wore their hair as Garvin had. Select and Citizen children dressed as much alike as they could to confuse enemy snipers. They were excited to be going into battle.

"They may be getting their blooding today."

"They're eager for it." She knew enthusiasm was what they had, and it was to be used like any other resource.

"We fight to save them, and I wonder how many of those children will be left. We fought to save the forests, and how much of that is left?"

"Enough to last till fall." She would have made a better commander than he, Scarecrow realized.

He thought of that again when the fighting grew intense. The double portals lay behind his front lines. Moriaph Division was on the left, the Companions on the right. On either side of them were units scraped together from elsewhere in the line. Artillery, what they had, was in the rear. Warchild Cluster was the ready reserve.

Firing began at the same moment all along a six-mile front. There were thousands of troops facing them, many shamans and riflemen brought from all over Hotlands. Many more mercenaries had gotten through since Rumack's supply lines had reopened. A lot of them were telepaths. Rumack's guns raked the Companions' position. ANTIBATTERY FIRE, Scarecrow ordered. His guns were outnumbered and he had to save ammunition for the final defense of the Fortress Fire Gates itself. But they had to distract Rumack for a while.

In a short while an artillery duel went on overhead. Ground fire intensified. Scarecrow scanned the front line. He caught the minds of his own skirmishers, riflemen taking aim and firing. They had lots of targets as Rumack's forward elements came over the open round. Scarecrow saw one man bring down a Hotlander, felt him take aim and shoot another.

Hotlander fire wasn't as effective. Then a man arose from where he had crept. He was a shaman who dashed at them. RUMACK THE DESTROYER. HE BURNS THE FOREST TO ASHES! The man staggered under the weight of a pack. He was hit twice, fell, and got up again. He took a few steps and was hit again. He crawled toward them in the dust. WE WILL EAT THE BRAINS OF YOUR CHILDREN IN RUMACK'S NAME. A sniper put another bullet into the man. And the Hotlander's pack blew up.

Scarecrow heard the sound through the ears of a skirmisher who died when a piece of the shrapnel from the bomb tore into his heart. Half a dozen other explosions followed in rapid succession. Scores of his people were injured and killed. He saw the Hotlanders coming through the trees. They were dark troops who carried stone images of Rumack around their necks. They hurled grenades as they came forward to close with the Moriaph Division.

Scarecrow reached out for their minds. As he did, a powerful mind grabbed at him. FACE ME NOW, SCARECROW. The mind was Rumack's. The deaths it could feel in the air strengthened it. ONE ON ONE WE WILL FIGHT. It took the pain from the front line and hurled it at the Select's relay.

On the right mercenary machine-gun units were backing up a Hotlander attack from higher ground. The attackers died as they came forward. But defenders died too. Scarecrow probed toward the portals. Nothing was coming through them. NOTHING YET, the Thorn told him. ACCORDING TO THE ORACLE, THE OLD ONE COMES BECAUSE HE MUST BE HERE. At her mention of the Oracle, Scarecrow felt her memory of her tongue scalded by a high scream.

The heat of the day grew, and the burning. Scarecrow could feel the smoke-choked death and confusion of his front line. Behind him his artillery was being blown out of position. SCARECROW, FACE ME! SCARECROW, COME OUT! Rumack was raging up and down behind his lines. The shamans and mercenary captains had taken up the mind chant. Rumack was a homicidal maniac. Scarecrow thought his mind might be as powerful as Garvin's.

It was after noon that his artillery was silenced. At about the same time the unit to the right of the Companions dissolved. Rumack had broken through; he could sweep around the flank of the Thorn and Rose. The only reserve was Warchild Cluster. They were running to the spot before Scarecrow could stop them. Their Select projected the image of Garvin triumphant slaying Rumack.

Scarecrow reached for the Thorn and Rose. EXTEND YOUR LINE. GET TROOPS INTO THE GAP. WE CANNOT USE CHILDREN THIS WAY. Hotland artillery shells had begun to fall in the Companions' position. There was an explosion not too far from the Thorn and Rose. Scarecrow lost contact with them.

Then there was a mental wail. Scarecrow caught an unbearable anguish from the Rose. Through the eyes of a Companion, he saw the Thorn, glassy eyed, open mouthed, killed by a shell fragment. The Rose linked her mind with Warchild Cluster. FOR GARVIN. She showed them his face shining in the torchlight.

It was replaced by another image. It was very real. Garvin lay naked and helpless on an operating table. Green hands held him as he cried aloud. YOUR HERO IS A STEED, A HORSE. AND HE WILL BE DOG FOOD.

Then another mind seized the image of Garvin, and he was clothed and grim and striding through worlds, spinning Time before him. Scarecrow felt for the source of the image and realized that troops were pouring out of the portals behind him, yelling the name of Garvin. A tall old man strode into the world carrying a satchel. The image of Garvin was huge. It crushed Rumack like a bug. The Hotlander attack faltered.

CHAPTER TWENTY-ONE

GARVIN COULD have followed the Time Lanes, gone along well-charted paths. They smelled of Goblins, though, and even the thought of those repulsed him. He followed summer through a thousand worlds. The heartbeat of the City Out Of Time grew fainter sometimes. But the closer he kept to the height of summer—the days before the heat broke, the nights before the first hint of autumn in the air—the stronger it grew.

He slept a few times, in motels and inns, sometimes alone, sometimes with someone else. He had no money with which to pay for board or food. But he gave his hosts the very best dreams that he could. When he came to Time Lane worlds, he would probe and if he found traces of Goblin minds, he withdrew quickly. It was the same reaction other people had to rats and spiders. He glanced past worlds and felt the Rider stunned by how fast he did it. The kinds of worlds changed around him.

First there stopped being worlds where people were innocent about telepathy and Time. Some, like the world of Nouveau France, were left relatively unharmed. Then there were more and more that made their living as links in the

Time Lanes. And there were lots of others emptied of human life.

On one world where Garvin stopped to get his bearings, it was a dull, drizzling afternoon. He found himself standing on an abandoned parking lot. Grass grew through the cracked blacktop along with a couple of small trees. There were a few piles of rust that had once been cars. Across a river was a huge city of skyscrapers. There were no signs of life in it. Nearer at hand, on his side of the river, there were human minds, several of them semitrained telepaths.

There were also Goblins. 'allow me to deal with them.' It was a request, not an order from his Rider. 'i have come to understand them. they must be dealt with if we are to enter the city out of time.' Garvin ignored this and probed softly.

They weren't very far away. One of the Goblins had been communicating with the human telepaths. The images were like a puppet show, a cartoon. The Goblin showed what looked like stick figures digging very carefully in a certain spot. The telepaths then instructed the other people mentally, showing them exactly how the digging was to be done. The people didn't even hate the two Goblins. They just feared them, each hoping that if the Goblins got hungry someone else would be eaten.

'probe one of the telepaths and have him tell the goblins you are here. i will show them who and what you are.'

I CAN DO THAT MYSELF. The scene he had observed made his anger rise. Garvin went directly into one of the Goblin minds. What it did wasn't quite blocking. It was more that he was ignored and avoided. He felt something like repugnance from the Goblin. At the same moment it alerted the human telepaths that Garvin was there. The image used was of a skulking stick figure, form bent and snarling like a feral dog. Garvin understood they were being told he was a danger to all, something to be destroyed.

Before the telepaths could order the other humans after him, Garvin seized an image and swept all of the minds, human and Goblin, with it. He showed them a pair of human hands grabbing a shovel and smashing in a Goblin's skull.

He felt terror from the humans and something like disgust from the Goblins. As he stepped back into Time, there was a wail from his Rider. 'they will hunt you down like a mad dog if you do that.'

BOOM! The heartbeat of the City almost knocked Garvin off course. He righted himself in a cold fury. The Rider had withdrawn into itself. Garvin summoned the room. Even though each beat jarred him, he passed world after world before the mirror. As the City grew closer, it became harder and harder to stride in Time. The worlds themselves were now totally barren except for thin strips of life that lined the portages between one portal and the next.

BOOM! The heartbeats knocked him backward unless he devoted all his attention to moving forward. 'you will have to pass the goblins before we can enter the city. please let me show you how to behave.'

Only a few worlds remained between Garvin and the City. Succeeding layers of worlds had fewer and fewer portals. Finally there were only the ones that were on the Time Lanes. Garvin skirted the worlds near the City.

'we must approach the gates and ask admittance,' his Rider pleaded.

Then the City was before him. He couldn't see it in Time, but he could feel it. The City reminded him of the Armory of Night: an intrusive, alien thing. It was Goblin work and ringed about with dead worlds. Telepaths, even highly trained ones, could never hold on in Time this near to the City. They would be driven back or forced to tumble through a portal and approach the City on foot.

Garvin was right next to the City. There was no portal in its Goblin-built shell, no way for him to get any feel for what lay inside. He scanned the worlds adjacent to the City. BOOM! He was knocked off course. For a moment he had a vision of a world like a park, a tame expanse of grass and trees, touched life that seemed almost human. He reached out for this but couldn't catch it. No portal seemed available. BOOM! He was knocked away and couldn't catch the vision again.

He fell back to the nearest Time Lane. He would try the City by its gates. 'they will not admit you unless you bring spoils of some value.'

Garvin tumbled out of Time and onto a world. I HAVE YOU.

Before him was a vast open ground. Rising beyond that, as high and as far as Garvin could see, was what looked like a slab of solid silver. There were doors at its base. Here and there on its surface were windows. 'we approach the silver gates.' Garvin could feel the Rider's excitement.

A dozen portals emptied people onto the world. A line of Oriental mercenaries tumbled out of Time carrying primitive telepaths tranquilized and trussed like hogs. People bore gold and art and drugs and microchips. And prisoners. Thousands of naked slaves were being dragged twenty at once through one of the portals. A sobbing woman in full golden armor led a band of beautiful children dressed in white. They came as tribute to the Gods of the City.

Each one who tumbled through a portal had to pass guard stations. In this warm weather there were tables set up on the flat ground outside. At the table near Garvin sat an official with a shaved head and a black and silver robe. Half a dozen guards with automatic rifles stood nearby. The official scanned minds quickly and issued badges.

'this is the first checkpoint. let me act here,' his Rider begged.

APPROACH THE ACCOUNTING TABLE. The official was a fair telepath. WHO ARE YOU AND WHAT DO YOU BRING TO GOBLIN MARKET?

'a rider requests admittance.'

Garvin cast his mind over the throngs coming out of the portals. There were others leaving the City. Many were telepaths. He caught the mind of another Steed, constricted, enslaved by the Rider inside him.

'i wish to stay only briefly. and i promise a future donation to the goblins,' Garvin's Rider continued.

His anger rose again. The Rider was going to try to sneak them into the City on its own terms. I AM A STEED WHO

MADE A SERVANT OF HIS RIDER, he announced. The official brought the guards to alert. Garvin reached out and seized her mind. She was a gate magistrate, a tired, defeated person from a world Garvin didn't recognize. She lived in fear of Goblin Market.

Garvin knew he wasn't getting into the City this way. He took the minds of the magistrate and guards, reached out to the ones entering and leaving the City. Goblins watched from the Silver Gates. WHO AM I? Garvin repeated the magistrate's question. He showed them the Armory of Night and Sam's dying. He showed them the image of a shovel coming down on a Goblin head.

Minds reached out for his. He felt Goblins in the distance. Jerky puppet people moved on Goblin orders. Garvin swung the guards around with their weapons leveled. Thousands of people fell flat. Garvin stepped back through the portal.

'we are ruined. they will hunt us now.' The Rider was in despair.

THERE MUST BE ANOTHER WAY IN. Garvin understood from the Rider that there were four gates which looked out on the four seasons. All were guarded and all the guards were warned. BOOM! The beat of the City knocked him through Time. Even in the Rider's distress, it too thought that there had to be some other way.

'there has never been a fortification of castle, bunker or rat's nest without a bolt hole. but what good will it do to get into the city as an enemy of the goblins?' Garvin saw that the Rider's whole existence lived in hundreds of Steeds had depended entirely on the mercy of Goblins.

BOOM! The heartbeat drove Garvin away from the Silver Gates. The City hung in Time before him. Then he caught again that world like a park, the minds that seemed almost human. BOOM! He was knocked away but he found his way back. He felt no portals but he could still reach into this world.

On it was a hill, trees in sunlight, a group of human figures, naked and long legged. He saw them in each other's eyes, felt them ready to bolt. Their minds reminded him of those of deer. Garvin knew they were waiting for a signal from him. He showed them his life, worlds he had seen. They were mystified, suspicious. He let them feel his Rider. They were edging away.

The beat of the City almost knocked Garvin away. He showed them Time and the way he used the mirror. At the sight of that, there was a spark. He showed them the room. In all their minds an idea formed. They were almost ready to let him in. Hanging on with part of his mind, Garvin showed the furniture, the globe, the elephant.

It was the elephant that did it. Many of them remembered having seen it long before. They were going to let him in. They ran down a hill, laughing and whooping. They reached the bottom and began to dance in a circle, their feet hitting the ground in unison. They flashed among themselves a hundred different faces, old and young, male and female, all the identities of the Gods. Garvin felt his Rider's nervousness. 'be very careful; we are intruding.'

As the people danced, a portal began to reveal itself. A piece of the earth fell away; a rock rolled aside. BOOM! Garvin was knocked out of touch with them. He groped about in Time, caught their minds. They waited, expectant, knowing that the rock would roll back into place in seconds, the earth would close up again. Garvin latched on to their minds and dove through the portal. The rock grazed the backpack he wore.

Long arms pulled him up as earth filled the pit. They laughed and touched his clothes. One touched the blade on Garvin's neck. She cut the end of her finger and held it up for all to see. They were tall and honey-brown, their bodies hairless except for their heads, where it grew long. They marveled at the way Garvin looked. They had never seen this identity before. 'they think you are one of the gods of the city.'

DO YOU THINK THAT THEY ARE RIGHT? There was no reply. His Rider couldn't place what was happening in any kind of a context. In the simple minds of these almost-humans, there was no thought of Gods, just of the Master of

Many Faces. As tiny children they had seen him often. Sometimes he came still to this place where they lived. There were about a hundred of them, ranging in age from fourteen to what seemed about thirty. They knew where the Master wanted to go. They thought of themselves as the Swift Ones.

Off they went toward the falling sun. The land they traveled was like an endless, overgrown park. They traveled quickly, pausing at twilight to gather berries near a stream. On flat rocks was food, cheese and loaves of rough bread. Garvin ate, aware that he was starving. Some of the Swift Ones leaped into the water and splashed around. With their hair wet, Garvin could see their sharp, pointed ears. He realized they had been clipped.

He stripped and stuck his clothes in his backpack. He swam for a while and dried himself on the bank. The moon came out. Garvin understood that they were near his destination. He felt comfortable surrounded by the Swift Ones. He showed them the room again, and it delighted them as much as it had the first time. They showed him things they remembered, corridors and nurseries and playpens. They neither wondered at nor attempted to make sense out of this.

Garvin dressed in a clean Companion uniform he had in his pack. They set out by the light of the moon. After a few miles of moving across overgrown lawns, there was another light visible in the sky. Garvin understood that it was on top of a hill where the Swift Ones were not allowed to go. They led him to its foot, where he saw a line of round stones. There the Swift Ones stopped. Garvin showed them the elephant with the flag one last time. They laughed and watched him walk away. He could feel them forgetting about what had happened as they turned back.

Garvin went up the hill as fast as he could. What he had learned with Cluster Group Two helped. Remembering them, knowing that they were holding out somewhere far off in Time, made him mad that he hadn't tried the City sooner. He probed ahead, withdrew quickly. The human minds he encountered were ordinary, gamekeepers of sorts, humble servants of the Infinite Gods of the City Out Of Time. Two other things were also up there: a portal and a Goblin.

'it is useless to ask that i handle this!' his Rider began.

In answer Garvin stepped out of the trees into a clearing in front of a rambling stone building. He had the blade off his neck and held in one hand. "It is They!" exclaimed the servants of the Gods.

They didn't doubt that was who Garvin was. No one else could have gotten through. They pushed forward to look at Garvin. The Gods had never before appeared in this guise. "The clothing of the Companions!" Servants were waking up, running forward to catch a glimpse of him. The Gods rarely come this way now. They bowed low before Garvin. He stood in the main hall of the building.

The portal was close at hand. A door opened at the far end of the hall, revealed green skin. There were yellow eyes. A Goblin stared at Garvin unblinking. The portal lay just beyond it. Guards with guns were approaching. The Goblin showed Garvin an image of the building of the City Out Of Time. Garvin saw the immense shell half finished, lighted by some mysterious source. There were no worlds flashing like stars. There was nothing but the half shell covered with Goblins and machinery. Light fell on it as if through an open door from an adjoining room.

The Goblin stood in the door, awaiting some kind of response. What it had shown Garvin was like a password. If Garvin was the God, he would add something that would complete the image. Instead Garvin crossed the room in two strides. He grabbed the Goblin's throat with one hand. It felt like a leather glove full of twigs. With his other hand he pressed the blade against the green throat and forced the Goblin toward the portal.

The reaction of the servants was stunned shock. The Goblin's reaction was revulsion. Garvin thought it was going to die from the sheer horror of having been touched. The portal shimmered. No one made any effort to stop Garvin. The Goblin itself did no more than try, ineffectually, to bite his hands.

The Rider was uttering a long wail. 'we are now outcasts in all of time. you are not the gods nor will you ever be forgiven.' The Goblin was light, almost insubstantial. Garvin pushed it before him through the portal and into Time.

The next portal lay right in front of him. It was at the end of a kind of tunnel. There was nowhere else to go. Garvin cast his mind ahead and found pain and fear, light and noise. He tumbled forward and came out in what was a small booth on a catwalk. Above him was an immense lighted dome. Below him was the selling floor of Goblin Market. From where he stood, he couldn't see the walls of the place.

His Goblin hostage had gotten away in Time. Garvin looked down on the endless floor of the slave market. People of every race and world walked on the floor doing business, or were in pits sunk into the floor. They were traders and merchandise, buyers and slaves.

Some pits were huge, big enough to accommodate hundreds of captives. Others were small, with room for only one or two people. Some were open, unguarded, too deep for anyone to climb out of. Others were girded with electronic detection equipment, ringed with scramblers to hold telepaths. Voices called, minds reached out for each other. On the floor were mercenaries and guards, Riders and Steeds and Goblins.

The sheer size of the place almost overwhelmed Garvin. I UNDERBID HIS OFFER OH MIGHTY ONE. I OFFER YOU TWENTY FINE ADEPT CHILDREN AT A RIDIC- ULOUS PRICE.

... MEN AS SUITED FOR FOOD AND FUEL AS FOR FIGHTING AND HEAVY WORK.

"Is it possible that I am to be cheated by this dog!"

ANNOUNCING A FINE BARGAIN IN PIT 27-128!

Garvin found the minds of technicians up on catwalks that ran along the roof. He came out of the booth that contained the portal and went down the stairs toward the trading floor. Above him a technician under his control moved toward a bank of switches. As he hit the floor, he seized as many minds as he could reach. I AM GARVIN. I RULE THE RIDER TRAPPED INSIDE ME. I HELD A BLADE AT THE

THROAT OF A GOBLIN TO GET HERE. DEATH TO THEM ALL!

At that moment the technician threw switches. Others tried to stop him and couldn't. Half the lights in the ceiling went out. The scramblers and restraining devices on hundreds of pits were off. RESCUE ME! a mind from a pit begged him. RESCUE ME AND I WILL KILL THEM AS THEY WOULD KILL ME. Another mind reached out to him. THEY DRAGGED ME ACROSS A THOUSAND WORLDS AND I CAN NEVER GO HOME. There was pandemonium on the selling floor as Garvin broadcast the image of the Goblin with a blade at its throat.

Garvin grabbed another technician's mind and shut off more lights. A huge man, a slave who was being escorted across the floor, turned on his guards and knocked them flat. A captive telepath caught the mind of one who was selling him and made that one scream in agony.

Goblin orders were flashing through the air. Stick figures closed in on the intruder. Garvin recognized himself, a red-faced figure with a cock's comb of hair. He could feel other minds trying to wrest control of the technicians from him. Traders were running away, but he could see guards forming a wide circle around him. There were a dozen Goblins on the scene. One of them flashed an image of Goblin mouths tearing at his flesh.

The lights were coming back on. The circle began to close in. Garvin started to lash out. 'let me explain to them,' his Rider was pleading. 'we will be in those pits soon enough if you do not.'

Then Garvin saw figures in black and silver running across the floor. THE MERCIFUL MOTHER! A MESSAGE FROM THE MERCIFUL MOTHER! Garvin recognized them as city officials like the Gate magistrate. The circle parted to let them through. On their minds was an image of a woman with white hair and a patient smile. LET THIS ONE BE BROUGHT TO ME, she told them.

CHAPTER
TWENTY-TWO

SCARECROW FOUND Amre looking at the leaves of a tree. She stood in a small hollow which had remained untouched by battle. Some branches had yellow and brown leaves; a few were tinged with red. Autumn was coming. He felt her thinking of Garvin. "He will be back," she told him.

It was easier for the Citizens to retain their faith. In the Republic they had followed the orders of the Select, which were often mysterious. Even if, like Amre, they knew there was nothing particularly mystical about the Select, there was the habit of obedience. For the other Select there was reliance on Scarecrow, a beacon in the midst of chaos. But for Scarecrow himself, what was there to rely on? Just the fading memory of someone who might have forgotten them.

"We may not see it, but he will come back." Even Amre's optimism had shrunk just as their position had. It was five miles in diameter now, and the sick seemed to outnumber the effective and the dead to outnumber both. "We are not important. This place is," she told him. And it was true that they still tied down Rumack's main army. Towns and forts elsewhere still held out because of them.

He wanted to say to her, "These people are dying. This

land is dying. My people, my land." But he didn't. She believed because the Citizens always somewhere deep down inside believed in the Select. And the Select who had joined him had decided to renew the simple beliefs of their own childhoods. There was a long silence between Scarecrow and Amre.

Then a low whistle sounded. He turned and left the hollow. A sentry had sighted Uncle near this spot a few hours before. Now he had been sighted again. Amre followed Scarecrow at a short distance.

It seemed almost impossible to Scarecrow that Uncle could still be alive and functioning. He wanted to believe it, though, because the old scout was a link to Mole. And Mole had studied with Grim Reaper, who was the past, the Republic, the old forest. And that was what Scarecrow believed in, what kept him fighting on in an ever-shrinking circle.

The front lay downhill. The woods were damaged by shells and flames. Trees were splintered and burned. Scarecrow passed a unit of volunteers from the Roman Fields. They were cooking their evening meal. They gave their lives daily to defend his home, Scarecrow knew. He appreciated them but knew they also represented the end of his world.

Scarecrow passed a trench. In the evening shadows he was out of his own lines. He saw a figure crouched low coming toward him. It was Uncle, moving strangely. Something was wrong. Scarecrow reached out to Uncle. Another mind was making Uncle walk. The old man was nearly dead. Suddenly Scarecrow felt Rumack. SCARECROW! LOOK WHAT I DID TO YOUR LITTLE FRIEND.

Scarecrow saw Mole pulled in half as two saplings on which he was tied both sprang upright. Then he realized what was left of Uncle was running toward him. He tried to tear the man's mind out of Rumack's grasp. For just an instant Uncle got free. "Dynamite" was the word on his mind. There was an image of it strapped to him. Scarecrow threw himself flat as the old man blew up. There was a searing in Scarecrow's left leg as if a hot knife had plunged in.

Firing broke out all along that section of the line. Hotland minds reached everywhere. Rumack sought Scarecrow. STILL ALIVE? COME OUT AND MEET MY CHALLENGE. TRY TO MAKE ME WALK INTO YOUR LINE AND BE YOUR CAPTIVE. AND I WILL DO THE SAME. The mind was powerful and drunk with killing. Except for the part which was as cold and bright as a diamond.

RIDER! Scarecrow felt the urge to crawl toward Rumack's lines. There was metal in his leg that made him want to scream. Bullets were hitting nearby.

END THE DYING IF YOU CAN, SCARECROW! He was passing out. Rumack's mind was overwhelming. Then he realized he was moving. It was toward his own lines. He was aware of Amre's arms as she hauled him back to cover.

BOW TO THE MERCIFUL MOTHER, a court telepath told Garvin. He stood at the foot of the Palace stairs. At the top stood a tall old woman with long white hair and a thin, still-beautiful face. She wore dark blue robes and a small crown. Behind her were guards and officials in silver and black, Steeds with Riders in their skulls, Goblins in yellow robes.

Garvin's Rider was trying to force him to his knees. 'you are in the presence of one of the gods. fall down and beg for mercy.' Garvin continued to stand looking up the stairs. APPROACH. That was the command of the Merciful Mother. The touch of her mind was soft and so quick that he had no idea what she was like.

She held her hands out to him as he approached. WHAT ARE THE CHARGES AGAINST THIS BOY? she asked the officials who accompanied Garvin.

DISRUPTING GOBLIN MARKET, ALL-FORGIVING ONE.

IS THIS TRUE? Again the touch was so light that Garvin was only just aware of it.

YES.

WHY? Although she asked the question, Garvin felt she already had taken the answer from him. He could see her eyes looking right into his.

TO ATTRACT YOUR ATTENTION

AND IN THAT YOU HAVE SUCCEEDED. Smile lines appeared on the smooth white face. HAS TRADE RESUMED AT THE MARKET? she asked one of his escorts.

YES, FOUNTAIN OF ABSOLUTION.

THE PUNISHMENT FOR DISRUPTING TRADE AT GOBLIN MARKET IS OF COURSE TO BE SOLD AT GOBLIN MARKET. The smile had disappeared. BUT SINCE IT CAUSED NO PERMANENT LOSSES, I FORGIVE YOU. There was a stir in the ranks of the court. ANY OTHER CHARGES?

ENTERING THE CITY WITHOUT PERMISSION, WISE MOTHER.

THAT, OF COURSE, IS IMPOSSIBLE. The Mother of Mercy extended her arm to Garvin. He took her arm and walked beside her. She was as tall as he and sturdier than she looked. SPECIAL GUARDS OF MY OWN GAVE HIM PERMISSION TO ENTER. IS THAT NOT SO? she asked Garvin. He caught a brief image of the Swift Ones and nodded his head. Arm in arm with the Goddess, he walked through the doors of the Palace.

They were in a hall of glass. Garvin could see the City stretching out in all four directions. From the dome of the City miles above, light shone down on half and the rest was in darkness. He didn't think the Merciful Mother's hand had ever left his arm. But when he turned toward her, he found a man with a slightly battered Roman nose and a long scar down the left side of his face. He had short white hair and a robe of gold and black. He stood a head taller than Garvin.

'the master designer.' The Rider was awestruck. 'another of the faces of mercy.' There were fewer people in the hall than there had been outside. Two of them, a man and a woman in pearl-gray silk, stepped forward. Their Riders stirred behind their eyes. They reached for Garvin's Rider, which made no effort to meet them. Garvin batted their minds away. There was a discreet intake of breath among the people in the room who felt this. The Goblins present remained impassive.

DESIGNER OF THIS CITY AND OF TIME, one Rider made his Steed ask, MAY WE APPEAL TO YOU?

RIDER EMBASSY MAY ALWAYS APPEAL. The quality of the God's mind had changed. It seemed to leap and disappear like lightning.

WE BEG FOR THE FREEDOM OF THE RIDER IMPRISONED WITHIN THIS ONE.

A RIDER IS PERMITTED TO LIVE AS LONG AS ITS WITS LET IT. THIS STEED WILL NOT DIE BECAUSE A RIDER MISJUDGED HIS OWN STRENGTH.

The woman Steed now was made to step forward. Garvin ached to see her mind manipulated. He was about to reach out to her when he felt the God's hands on his shoulders restraining him. The images the Steed showed were Goblin ones from the Armory of Night.

He saw himself as a stick figure with a cock's comb of yellow hair standing goggle-eyed as Sam the machine smashed himself to pieces on the floor. HE HAS INCITED A STEED TO REBEL AND KILL ITS RIDER, ALL-ENCOMPASSING ONE. WITHOUT RIDERS, TRADE TO GOBLIN MARKET WILL FALTER AND DIE.

YOUR REQUEST?

IF YOU WILL NOT LET THIS UNFORTUNATE RIDER MAKE THE JUMP, THEN LET IT DIE ALONG WITH THIS STEED. IN THE INTEREST OF TRADE, IT—

YOU RIDERS ARE CREATURES OF THE GOBLIN AND YOU HAVE SERVED THEM WELL. PERHAPS THIS NEW STEED WILL LEARN TO SERVE ME AS WELL AS YOU SERVE THEM.

Garvin felt the Master Designer's hands on his shoulders steering him toward a door. His Rider, which had thought it was looking death in the face, kept repeating over and over, 'the honor. the incredible honor.' If it had controlled Garvin, his eyes would have overflowed with tears of gratitude. Not even the fact it was betrayed and abandoned by its own kind mattered if it was going to live.

Garvin could feel the courtiers' amazement and the other Riders' anger. Doors opened in the hall of glass, and he found himself descending a flight of stairs. He felt the large hands, the scarred knuckles of the God on his shoulders. Some court officials and servants were still with them. So were the Goblins, who seemed to glide down the stairs.

A door opened on to a room of dark polished wood and deep carpets. There were chairs and couches and, set before tall windows, a table with food and drink. Outside was a twilight park. Deer moved beneath the trees. The hands of the God never left his shoulders. Garvin was aware of movement behind him. Turning his head, he found a beautiful woman. She had dark hair and eyes. Her hands were beautifully slender. Servants were carrying away the dark robes. She dressed in a thinner white one.

The Goblins stood in a group, watching. From someone's mind Garvin caught the name MISTRESS OF LAW. He turned around and faced her, probed as hard as he could. The God blocked him so quickly and easily he was hardly aware of its happening.

A dozen Goblins stood in a group, watching. One stepped forward, blinked his yellow eyes several times, then showed them stick figures. Garvin recognized the angry little creature that was supposed to be himself. He felt the Goblin's disgust as he broadcast threats against them at the Silver Gates. Then the creature actually touched one of them, grabbed and shoved it. There was shock in Goblin minds at the thought of that.

From the back of the group, another Goblin stepped forward. It stared ahead through yellow slit eyes. From it came a feeling of shame and repugnance. Garvin realized that this was the one he had pushed through the portal. It spread its hands before it and looked at the Mistress of Law.

YOU HAVE BROKEN GOBLIN TRUCE, she told Garvin. THE PUNISHMENT DECREED IS THAT YOU WILL BE EATEN BY THE OFFENDED ONE. YOU WILL BE ALIVE WHEN THE PUNISHMENT BEGINS.

The Goblin came forward. Garvin realized that sentence had just been passed. Garvin slammed at the Goblin with his mind. At the same time he took out the long razor blade and crouched. The Goblin stopped, enraged. All the Goblins tensed

and looked at the Mistress of Law. WHAT MADE YOU
BREAK THIS LAW?

I WANTED TO GET NOTICED BY THE GODS.

YOU HAVE SUCCEEDED, AND NOW YOU ARE
ABOUT TO DIE. There was a touch of sadness in the beautifully balanced mind that brushed his. Every Goblin stepped
forward, and Garvin knew he couldn't stop them all.

So he showed the Mistress of Law the secret he had kept
from thinking about, the idea that had brought him here. He
showed her the picture of his father. I THOUGHT I COULD
FIND HIM. The Goblins were almost within arm's reach.

The Mistress's brows went up. She clapped her hands three
times and the Goblins stopped, amazed. JUST AS NO ONE
MAY LAY HANDS ON A GOBLIN, SO ALSO NO GOBLIN
MAY HARM ME OR ANY OF THE MANIFESTATIONS
OF THE GODS. THIS ONE CLAIMS A SPECIAL RE-
LATIONSHIP WITH US. EXAMINATION WILL SHOW
IF HE TELLS THE TRUTH. IF HE DOES, WE WILL NOT
FORGET WHAT WAS DONE TO HIM BY GOBLINS IN
A RIDER OPERATING ROOM. SENTENCE IS SUS-
PENDED.

The Goblins stood still, looking at the Mistress of Law.
The repulsion Garvin felt at being this near to them was almost
overpowering. He wanted to lash out at them. The God caught
that. YOU WILL NOT SO MUCH AS TOUCH ONE OF
THEM EVER AGAIN. IS THAT UNDERSTOOD?

Garvin glared at the Goblins. 'say yes for both of our
sakes,' his Rider pleaded. Garvin made no response. 'for that
backwoods world full of your friends then.' Slowly Garvin
nodded his head. IT IS UNDERSTOOD.

EXCELLENT. A door slid open on the far side of the
room. The Goblins stood with mouths agape and minds blank
with shock as Garvin followed the Mistress of Law out of
the room.

Servants closed the doors behind them. They were in a
carpeted hall. Garvin knew he had never seen it before. But
something about it haunted him. He had intended to keep his
attention on the Mistress of Law so as not to have her change

without his noticing. But the moment of déjà vu distracted him.

Suddenly the servants were holding her robes. He looked and it was too late. The woman was gone. A man in his fifties with short curly gray hair smiled and motioned Garvin toward a room. He wore black silk shirt and pants, with just the hint of a white collar. He looks like an Irish priest, Garvin thought, with more than a little trace of Irish cop.

They went into what looked like a study with deep chairs and a dark-wood desk. There were paintings and books and a fire burning in the fireplace and reflecting on the windows. A servant remained who drew the curtains against the night outside. THAT WILL BE ALL, THOMAS.

"Yes, Reverend Lord." The servant withdrew. The God sat at the desk and indicated a big leather chair for Garvin. He opened a silver box on his desk and offered Garvin a cigar. Garvin shook his head. He indicated a decanter on a sideboard. Again Garvin shook his head.

YOU ARE HERE TO CLAIM A RELATIONSHIP WITH THE GODS?

Garvin showed the Reverend Father his memories of the photo in Claire's room. Then he showed the Oracle's images of him traveling to the City and returning with an army.

The smile left the face of the Reverend Lord. THERE IS NO ORACLE, GARVIN. AS FOR ANY POSSIBLE CONNECTION TO THE GODS OF THE CITY OUT OF TIME, YOU MUST PROVE YOURSELF. IF I LET YOU BACK INTO TIME TO DO WHAT YOU INTEND, YOU MUST DO SOMETHING IN RETURN. He looked Garvin right in the eye. His mind was impossible for Garvin to fix. It almost shimmered. YOU MUST BRING BACK THE WIND THAT ESCAPED. TO DO THAT YOU WILL HAVE TO KILL ONE CALLED THE GUVNOR.

NO! Garvin jumped out of his seat. ANY QUARREL I HAVE WITH HIM IS PRIVATE.

The Reverend Lord's mouth worked. "Someone thought it would hurt us," he said. The God had a brogue. "That's why they sent you here with that worm planted in your skull."

The eyes picked up the blaze from the fireplace. "I am telling you to take revenge for both of us."

"No!"

Inside him the Rider was screaming, 'remember the ones you promised to save!'

Garvin caught the mind of something running past the door. He had noticed the study was shielded from outside minds. He assumed it was something like Scarecrow's scramblers that did it. The hall was within the shield. He knew what the mind was. He leaped up and tore the door open.

There was a honey-colored child of perhaps two or three running toward a set of doors at the end of the hall. One of them was only half closed. Gray afternoon light seeped through it. Garvin saw through the little girl's eyes before he saw it himself.

She laughed, delighted, and ran inside. He came to the door, stopped, and hesitated before he put his foot on the carpet. The little elephant stood on its inlaid table. Across the room the globe rested before the peacock screen. There were things he hadn't noticed: cherubs on the ceiling, the velvet cords that held the curtains open.

The child stood in the middle of the room, her delight at having run away fading. Garvin stood and looked at the room reflected in the mirror. It was all there: the fireplace with the fire prepared but not lit, the table where they would bring the tea things. The naked child looking up at him. All that wasn't there was Garvin himself. He cast no reflection in the mirror.

He felt his Rider's fear and trembling, but all Garvin himself felt was trapped. He didn't want any part of this. He wished he had stayed in the Republic and gone down fighting. He clenched his fists. The little girl started to cry. Instinctively, he knelt down and held her. He touched her hair with his hand and noticed that she had the pointed ears of the Swift Ones. He reached into her mind to comfort her.

Through the little girl's eyes he caught sight of the figure in the doorway. The man with the face of the picture in Claire's room wore an expensive tweed suit. He had on a blue shirt that caught the color of his eyes and a tie that caught the light and dark of his hair. He smiled and said, "How's your mother, Garvin?" There was the hint of Irish in the voice still.

Garvin stood up and turned to face him. "All right, unless she's been eaten by your Goblins or sold into slavery." The man took a few steps toward him, but Garvin stood where he was. This one cast no reflection in the mirror either. "It took you awhile to change out of the Reverend Lord outfit," he said.

His father's eyes danced. "One of my finest effects."

Garvin thought of what this would have meant to him a few months ago. Just to have found his father would have been beyond all his dreams. Now he didn't trust what he saw. And he had vital things to do. "You never had much time to waste on us," he said.

The God nodded. "Anonymity was your best defense. Some of my enemies managed to see through that. My guess is that they won't bother with Claire. As for the rest, how dry have you kept your own wick? And have you stayed around to assess the results?"

He looked at the mirror image of a room with the little girl staring up at nothing. "We are two of a kind, my lad. I take it you're anxious to be going. I can't let you out of here now without the two promises. You know too much and understand too little."

'obey him in all things,' pleaded the Rider.

"They tried to break my heart with that thing inside you," said the God. "I can do nothing to the Goblins who did this. If you think I am all powerful and they are some kind of servants, I tell you it's a partnership and not always one that's equal for me.

"All of this: Palace, Market, City Out Of Time, the infinite worlds, is nothing but a way to raise the Winds." The God who looked like Brian Garvin closed his eyes and said, "The Goblins do that in their own awful way. You will not lay a hand on any of them again." SAY IT!

That rang in Garvin's head. He choked back his defiance.

His voice came out in a whisper. "I won't lay a hand on any Goblin again."

"One of my precious Winds has been stolen."

"I'm not going to kill the Guvnor for you."

"Blood is thick and sticky, Garvin. I'm sure he'll explain all of that to you when you meet again. I want the Wind back and I want my stepbrother. However you bring him, alive or dead, it's all the same. It will be your introduction to my side of the family. Now tell me you agree."

Garvin felt his Rider tugging at him, begging him to agree. 'only by making this promise can you redeem your earlier ones.'

Garvin felt himself trapped. It choked him. "You will get back the Guvnor and the Wind, dead or alive."

The God sighed. "The parasite inside you wants you to give the right answers. But if I could, without harming you, I'd cut that out and let it die."

Just then the Rider seemed nearer to Garvin than this father standing there. "Pimp." Garvin bit the word out. "Butcher. Damn you, how many billions have you slaughtered?"

Suddenly he was looking at himself through the God's eyes. He stood there with his fists clenched, half looking as if he was going to cry. The little child got frightened again. She started to sob. The God scooped her up in his arms. "I love people more than you can believe. I love them more than I ever would have thought possible."

Garvin turned away. There in the mirror he saw the child laughing now, floating alone in midair.

CHAPTER
TWENTY-THREE

MICHE WHIMPERED in her sleep. In total darkness Scarecrow felt for her mind. Hotlander nightmares floated there: bats with the faces of wolves. Scarecrow's left leg throbbed. Amre had cut out the shrapnel but had few antibiotics. Scarecrow filled his daughter's mind with an army of bright little pigs who built a wall too high for flying wolves to get over.

Then he isolated the pain in his leg, put it out beyond the Umbra of his mind. He used a crutch to pull himself up. Amre was out on night duty. Miche turned over and slept quietly. He went to the door of the bunker and looked out over the plateau of Fortress Fire Gates. The perimeter had come down to a small strip of woods, the open ground, and the Fire Gates themselves. Only here at the very center were the defenders outside the range of shaman minds. Rumack's artillery had stopped bombarding in these few hours before dawn.

They would start again when the sun came up. The Fire Gates was a commanding position only so long as it had artillery superiority over the besieger. After that, it was just a target. As Scarecrow stumbled to the door of the bunker, an orderly staggered to his feet and helped him on with his white robes.

The Guardian cast his mind out over his people. Most of them slept, however badly. A song of soft bedding, of rocking gently in the air and waking up to hot food and good coffee touched each sleeper. It was the Talking Suitcase. The Immortal mind, never sleeping, kept up morale as it lay in its satchel next to the snoring Roger.

Scarecrow cast his mind out to the west into the last patches of woods that he still held. Warchild Cluster was out there on the firing line. Scarecrow reached for the mind of the Rose. He found her awake, her mind hovering like a night bird over the children. She had taken command of them after the death of the Thorn. IMMORTAL ROSE, AWAKEN YOUR COMMAND BEFORE DAWN AND HAVE THEM FALL BACK TO THE EDGE OF THE OPEN GROUND! He was still selling District Four, inch by inch.

WE MUST HOLD SCARECROW. IN THE NAME OF WARCHILD. He saw the Immortal through the eyes of a Select child. The head of the Thorn, tightly bandaged, seemed to grow smaller every day. In the dim light of campfires, he picked up the Warchild Cluster as it woke itself up, saw itself. He recognized some of them, Maji and Darrel, gaunt faced, filthy, hard eyed.

At that moment all the cluster's minds were filled with the image of a huge, grinning Rumack squashing Scarecrow like a bug. GUARDIAN, WHERE ARE YOU? SCARECROW, ANSWER MY CHALLENGE. EVEN CRIPPLED YOU CAN FIGHT MIND AGAINST MIND.

Scarecrow felt the powerful madness of the enemy leader. He could feel the reluctance of the children and their leader to fall back. FOR GARVIN! WE HOLD FOR THE WARCHILD! They took up the cry with minds and voices. He repeated the order to the Rose. Scarecrow could feel the almost frantic reluctance to give any ground. I WILL MEET YOU, RUMACK! the Rose broadcast into the dying darkness.

In many of the Warchild Cluster minds was the question, "Why won't the Guardian meet the challenge?" At that moment, tired and aching, with his mind connected to minds linked to Rumack's Hotlanders, Scarecrow wondered the same thing. He had only to reach out and accept to die.

THEY ARE TOO YOUNG TO UNDERSTAND THE LIMITS OF COURAGE. Roger stood beside him. The Talking Suitcase was aware of his thoughts. IT IS A RESOURCE BEST GUARDED CAREFULLY.

Garvin recruited quickly. Stories and rumors of what had happened at the Palace of the Gods went before him. As he crossed a public plaza, a huge man in combat fatigues and an elaborate silver helmet approached him. HAIL, FAVORITE OF THE GODS. I CAN BRING TO YOU A REINFORCED BATTALION AND GUARANTEE EQUIPMENT AND CADRE FOR ANOTHER ONE WHEREVER IN TIME YOU MAY TAKE ME.

'his name is john baltin. he is a hard man and an honest one. that is, he will kill when you tell him to and inform you if he is hired away.'

Garvin waved the man off. He caught the thoughts of the crowd watching him. BROUGHT TO THE PALACE WITH CITY OFFICIALS, RIDERS, AND GOBLINS ALL LOOKING FOR HIS HEAD.

AND HE WALKS FREE. HE IS A FAVORITE OF THE GODS.

OR MUCH MORE.

Garvin turned away some of the most famous mercenaries in Time. He found what he wanted lounging on a corner pretending to be bored, hiding their uneasiness. They were twin brothers, telepaths in their late teens who had traveled years through Time to reach the City. They were a girl who was a telepath and her girl friend who was not. Each had a few followers and nowhere to go. All were uneasy in the City.

He hadn't known that was what he was looking for until he found them. They led him to others. In an enclosed space where a microphone and speakers had been set up, a crowd had gathered, most of them young. They were tough kids dressed like the ones from 1967, huge black eunuch scholars, boy and girl slaves who had slipped off for a few minutes away from Night Town, the huge red-light district of the City.

A Hendrix in chains stood on the stage with his sidemen. He touched his hand to his guitar. Garvin went among the audience. The Oracle had shown him young troops. The Hendrix sang, "There must be some way out of here/Said the joker to the thief."

DIAN IS WHAT I AM CALLED, a short woman with a scar down one side of her face told him. I CAN FIND YOU AUTOMATIC-WEAPONS PEOPLE. IT WILL BE A COMPONENT THAT WILL FIT IN ANYWHERE AND GO ANYWHERE THAT IS FAR AWAY FROM HERE.

I AM MARGAT. This was a young man who looked part pirate and part medic. I HAVE A FIELD HOSPITAL TEAM. WE CAN HEAL ANY WOUND BUT GOBLIN BITES.

YOU ARE HIRED, Garvin told each of them, FOR A SHARE IN THE SPOILS.

"Two riders were approaching," sang the Hendrix. "The wind began to howl."

Darkness passed across the City, but Garvin didn't sleep. He outfitted his expedition quickly. He had a thousand recruits, a lot of them telepaths, most of them young. He left the City by the Silver Gate that faced on summer.

No Riders were in the crowd that saw him off. They withdrew to their own quarters to prevent their Steeds from being near Garvin. Garvin led his little army out the Silver Gate and across the open ground to the portals. People stood on chairs and tables, got on tiptoes, caught at the minds of those in the front rows to see him. Minds tried to touch his.

Garvin looked back at the massive slab of silver. At the window high up, he could see Goblin faces. The hate he felt almost choked him.

'remember your promise to the god.'

YOUR FELLOW RIDERS WERE WILLING TO LET YOU DIE TO KILL ME. THE GOBLINS DID NOT CARE IF YOU DIED ALONG WITH ME. THE GOD DESPISES YOU. I AM YOUR ONLY FRIEND, Garvin told his Rider.

Then he took the first part of his force with him and plunged into Time.

On the veld world the Guvnor galloped before a coming storm and Herself's cavalry. Riding at the very rear of his raiding party, he felt a mind reach for his. GUVNOR, HALT A MOMENT AND LET US PARLEY. It was Herself; he recognized the touch of his enemy. He turned and saw a lone figure on horseback halted about a quarter of a mile away.

YOU HAVE LED US A MERRY CHASE, GUVNOR.

BUT YOUR DEFENSE HAS KEPT ME AWAY FROM THE SUPPLIES FOR THE LAST FEW WEEKS.

YOU HAVE TIED DOWN MUCH PERSONNEL. Dark clouds were swirling behind Herself. The Guvnor wondered where these compliments were leading. LATELY THERE HAVE BEEN NEW REINFORCEMENTS. The Guvnor saw the green skin of Goblins in her mind. THEY HAVE COME FOR YOU. AND YOUR WIND.

Instinctively, he felt above him. The Wind circled in the air. AND YOU WERE AFRAID THAT THEY MIGHT TAKE ME ALIVE.

IT MIGHT PROVE EMBARRASSING. WHY DID YOU GIVE ME THAT ONE CALLED GARVIN TO USE AS A STEED?

YOU WANTED A STRONG, UNFORMED TELE-PATH. . . .

YOU KNEW WHAT HE COULD DO. I WOULD HAVE KILLED YOU MYSELF IF I HAD BEEN ABLE TO DO IT QUIETLY. The Guvnor could feel the Rider's presence behind the telepathy of the woman called Herself. YOU NEVER GAVE ME THE CHANCE. YOUR WIND HAS PLAYED HAVOC WITH MY TELEPATHS. BUT THE GOBLINS BELIEVE THEY WILL TAKE THE WIND CAP-TIVE. THEY THINK YOU WILL BE CAPTURED WITH IT. THEREFORE I OFFER YOU THIS WARNING.

THANKS, BUT YOU ALREADY HAVE ME TRAPPED. NO PLACE MY ARMY CAN GO. YOU BLOCK OUR RETURN TO THE BOSOM OF VICTORIA AT THE START

OF THE APPENDIX AND THERE SEEMS LITTLE SENSE IN GOING TO JOIN OLD SCARECROW.

YOUR ARMY IS DOOMED, BUT YOU ARE NOT. YOU CAN RIDE ON THE WIND SOMEHOW. THAT IS HOW YOU GOT HERE SO MANY WEEKS AHEAD OF ME.

GOTTEN RATHER FOND OF THIS LITTLE FORCE I RAISED, ... the Guvnor began. But the storm had begun around Herself. She turned her horse and galloped off.

BE GONE! That command hung in the air as she disappeared into the early dusk. The Guvnor turned his own horse, called to the Wind, and set off for his camp. It was a dilemma. His army was trained up to a high pitch. They were a credit to him, and he wanted to save them for later use. It was obvious, though, that Garvin wasn't coming back. The boy had done what the Guvnor himself would have done and lost himself in Time.

The Guvnor passed his well-drilled sentry line, irritated that he was going to have to give these people up. It looked to him like another Immortals disaster, in which case it was *suave qui peut* and devil take the hindmost. Rain splattered around him as he approached his tent. There a familiar mind showed him an image of a jeep driving off a cliff. GARVIN! DID YOU SEE THE CITY ON YOUR TRAVELS? he asked.

Garvin had crossed summer like a fury, shuttling back and forth through Time pulling his little army from world to world in Relays. He appointed subcommanders who tried to knit the different units into some kind of fighting force. They slept and ate when they could. Garvin slept and ate when he had to. I AM GOING TO HEAD RIGHT FOR RUMACK, Garvin told his Rider. I WILL COME OUT OF TIME AND KILL HIM WHEREVER HE IS.

'you will be gunned down before you can,' the Rider told him. 'this force is no more than a bodyguard and not one that i would trust very far.'

THE ORACLE SHOWED ME...

'the oracle counted on your having my advice. i will show

you how a few may rout a million.' Garvin was hesitant but he listened.

Later he called the troops together. He had assembled them on the estate of a magnate whose dominion stretched over four North Americas. They had traveled from high summer out to where the evenings got shorter and the rain brought a touch of chill.

The magnate himself cowered in a cottage, overawed by what Garvin had showed him from the City Out Of Time and Palace of the Gods. Bonfires were lighted. Garvin stood on the porch and swept the faces with his eyes. The minds with his mind. He remembered the acid freaks in 1967, New York, French kids by the lake, Cluster Group Two of Weatherhill, and the Mohawks in their cellar.

He showed them all that. Then he showed them something else: the room at the Palace with its mirror and furniture. The little girl floated in air, smiling happily.

'you are a fool to show them that!'

Garvin could feel the minds before him eagerly snatching up any details they could catch. THERE WILL BE HARD STRIDING IN TIME AND THINGS NONE OF YOU WANT TO WITNESS. BUT I PROMISE THOSE WHO LIVE THROUGH THIS WITH ME REWARDS GREATER THAN THE LOOTING OF WHOLE WORLDS.

Later, when the cheering had died down he asked the Rider, WHAT IS YOUR PLAN?

'it involves rolling rumack's army up like a ball of yarn. you will need to use the guvnor. afterward you can do the gods' will with him.'

Garvin would rather have avoided the Guvnor. His promise ate at him whenever he thought of it. But the Rider's plan seemed sound and not likely to cause enormous casualties. So Garvin found himself at the end of summer on the veld world. "I reached the City," he said, and knew the Guvnor understood.

"I daresay the Gods are still looking for my head."

'he knows. kill him now.'

"I had to promise to bring you back ... and your Wind."

"Sticky things, promises."

"The Oracle showed you selling me as a Steed."   .

"Quite right." Rain was coming down heavily now. The Guvnor turned up his collar. "I won't say I was very happy about it, but that's what I did."

"You're as bad as the Gods."

"Probably. But let's go somewhere dry and talk it over. These few months have changed you, old boy."

I COULD CRUSH YOU. Garvin's anger got away from him.

He felt the Rider telling him, 'yes. kill him before his guards come.' He summoned up an image of the elephant with the flag and threw it at the Guvnor's mind like a net. The Wind whipped around Garvin's head.

But the Guvnor just smiled, said "Tantor!" and seized the image at once. Garvin saw the room in bright light with the curtains open. He saw fresh flowers in vases and light patterns on the floor. The view was through the windows. Whoever had seen it was standing on a winter morning in a snow-covered garden.

Suddenly there was a buzzing sound. Garvin gasped at the stupendous explosion as a bomb hit the house. Glass flew everywhere; the French windows buckled. The mirror broke in two and smashed to the floor. The little elephant flew through the air and shattered on the fireplace. The drapes caught fire. The eyes of whoever watched were put out. Garvin recoiled, stunned.

The Guvnor shook his head. "I don't die quite that easily. Not when all you have to show me is Tantor the Elephant. Great-grandfather Lord Tagent brought it back from Burma. I played with it when I was a child in my grandmother Tagent's drawing room in Mayfair. She loved that room. It was the last thing she saw, as I just showed you."

"I'm sorry, I didn't know."

"Decorated in awful taste anyway. You, my boy, are from the other side of the family. The blood of Black Jack Howard runs in your veins. That's what your father claimed." Garvin shivered. "Now why don't we find a dry tent and what passes for food around here and you can tell me your Rider's plan."

Herself's Rider awakened her just before dawn. Her mobile force had returned to the blockhouse line that protected the supply route. RAID! RAID! a young officer telepath was signaling. They were under attack. THE GUVNOR IS SNAPPING UP OUR OUTPOSTS. AND THE WIND . . . His mind was wrenched away.

The Goblins never slept. At the first sign that the Wind was out there, they went after it, commandeering a land rover. They sent a series of sharp, crude images to Herself's Rider.

Herself, half awake, felt her mind giving orders, forming up troops, snapping a Relay into place. She felt like a mad-woman trapped in the tower room of her own mind. She was dressed by servants. Aides awaited her Rider's orders. The raiders were falling back. Pursuit was starting piecemeal. Herself's Rider didn't like that, but it was what the Goblins wanted.

A horse was brought. Herself felt hungry and tired, but she mounted with an easy motion, turned its head, and prepared to lead her cavalry after the Guvnor. A heavy ground fog had formed at night. Sounds of scattered firing came through muffled. In the minds of the telepaths, Herself's Rider caught a confused and blurred series of images. Then one of them shrieked, WIND! WIND! and was caught and devoured.

AFTER HIM, Herself found her Rider ordering. FIVE THOUSAND CREDITS TO THE ONE WHO BRINGS DOWN THE GUVNOR FOR ME. Overhead gray clouds slid by. On the ground the mist was starting to lift. From someone Herself caught an image of the Guvnor on horseback.

IN ANSWER TO OUR CONVERSATION OF YESTER-DAY, he told her, then thumbed his nose and disappeared. I WILL GO DOWN FIGHTING RATHER THAN CUT AND RUN. The pursuit was in the open ground beyond the block-house line. The vehicles, rovers, and armored cars, brought there at enormous expense and labor, began to roll out into the grassland. Patches appeared in the fog. As the gray light came up, Herself could see horsemen running in the distance.

Her Rider's orders came through her mind. CAVALRY CLOSE UP IN SUPPORT OF THE ARMOR. Firing ahead was becoming more intense. THEY HAVE GONE TO EARTH. THEY ARE MAKING A STAND. Herself could see armored cars clustering around a single rover. From this came Goblin images. They were of a vast empty space that was alive with Winds. It was like the inside of a huge container. The Winds rolled in and out among themselves. The Goblins cast their minds toward the Guvnor's position. 'they try to lure the wind,' her Rider told her.

Cavalry galloped up in support of the armor. Herself's Rider remembered there being a portal off on the left somewhere. The possibility of ambush crossed its mind. It was about to order troops to guard the place. Suddenly firing broke out. From minds near the portal, Herself could see figures tumbling out of Time, shooting as they came, trying to deploy. SMASH THEM BEFORE THEY CAN GET ORGANIZED, Herself's Rider ordered through her.

The Rider was reacting quickly. It had seen hundreds of battles. This was not a major threat. It turned Herself's mind to the scene around the portal. The mist was lifting. The new force could be snuffed out quickly. TURN FIRE FROM HALF THE ARMORED CARS. BRING UP AN AUTOMATIC-WEAPONS SECTION. Herself was moving toward the incursion on the horse she rode.

Then a mind had hers. The Rider raised her defenses. But it wasn't able to stop the mind that found her. She caught an image of the tower room and gasped. The door was kicked down. The walls were torn down. Light flooded in. OVERTHROW YOUR RIDER. YOU CAN RIDE IT. She recognized Garvin, the boy who had been turned into a Steed.

Her Rider managed to break the connection. Herself was thrust into darkness. She felt suffocated, a prisoner in her own body. TURN ALL FIRE ON THAT PORTAL. CRUSH THEM! She felt her mind ordering that.

Garvin caught her again. She saw the metal body of the

Armorer of Night. She recognized Sam; their Riders had met. She saw him smashing himself to pieces. HE BROKE FREE BUT HE DIED. BREAK FREE AND LIVE! She saw the globe and peacock screen, the magic image. But it was bathed in bright winter sunlight.

Her Rider started to wrench Herself's mind away. FREEDOM! Instead of resisting the Rider, Herself put all of her concentration on throwing the horse off balance. The animal lurched, stumbled. And Herself was free for a few seconds. CEASE FIRE, she ordered. YIELD TO GARVIN WARCHILD.

Then her shoulder hit the ground and nauseating pain mixed with her awareness of her Rider's terror. 'traitor!' it called Garvin's Rider.

'there is no resisting this one,' was the answer it received as Herself lost consciousness.

There was a long moment when the two forces stood facing each other. Garvin swept Herself's leaderless troops with his mind. He showed them his Rider tamed inside him. Herself's Rider reached out to them. The pain was excruciating. Its terror of dying terrified its followers.

JOIN ME, Garvin urged.

Something was moving. A rover drove toward the portal. The Goblins were heading for safety. Herself's troops started to edge away. At that moment the Guvnor counterattacked. Herself's cavalry began to bolt.

Garvin caught the images from the approaching Goblins. They indicated an open path before them. Troops broke ranks so they could get through. The portal was on a little rise crowned with a few scrawny trees. Garvin stood in front of it and the rover bore down on him. He could see the green heads. There were three of them. "I won't lay a hand on them," Garvin said to himself.

The rifle was in his hands before either he or the Rider were fully aware of it. He shot out the tires. Herself's troops began to run. Garvin's own troops were in shock.

'no! no! no!' His Rider struggled for control.

The Goblins' disdain and disgust turned Garvin's stomach.

They climbed out of the rover and came straight at him, making biting motions with their mouths. His Rider acted on him like a drug. He raised the rifle again and pulled the trigger in slow motion. He shot each of them several times. They fell down but they didn't die. Their minds seemed to withdraw, to hibernate. But they were still alive.

His own Rider had gone dead inside him. His troops stared at him aghast. Garvin grabbed another rifle. The Guvnor rode up. "There's only one way they'll die. And if you've gone this far you might as well finish the work." The Englishman commandeered ropes and horses.

Careful not to touch them, Garvin slipped nooses around the Goblins' necks. The ropes were slung over the branches of the trees and tied to horses. The horses trotted forward. The trees shook but were sturdy enough. And the Goblins seemed very light. They danced at the ends of the ropes. The horses stopped. Gray clouds ran overhead. The Goblins died slowly. "I never laid a hand on them," Garvin thought.

CHAPTER
TWENTY-FOUR

IT HAD RAINED at night and the morning was cool at the Fire Gates. But the bombardment continued and there was no escape from the enemy telepaths. It was all the Select and Companions could do to keep their own sanity and try to shield their people somewhat. SCARECROW, MEET MY CHALLENGE. Rumack's mind led his shamans in a continuous Relay. Defenders reached out listlessly to block.

A TELEPATH-LED ARMY IS ONLY AS STRONG AND AS STABLE AS ITS COMMANDER, Scarecrow told the Talking Suitcase. They were in a camouflaged observation post on the cliffs of the Fire Gates. Scarecrow could feel the tired, hungry troops a short way from collapse; wounded, writhing in pain, children becoming numb to terror.

Roger looked at him impassively. The Talking Suitcase saw Scarecrow's matted and gray hair, felt the pain of his wounds. Only a fever glow kept the man's eyes alive. THERE IS STILL TIME. YOU MUST WAIT UNTIL RUMACK'S ARMY BEGINS TO FALTER AND LOSE FOCUS. THEN YOU MAY ACCEPT THE CHALLENGE.

IF WE FALL, THE REPUBLIC WILL COLLAPSE. THEY

ARE WATCHING US AND WAITING. WHERE IS GAR-VIN? WHAT IS GARVIN?

PERHAPS JUST A WHIM OF THE GODS. I BELIEVE HE MAY BE SOMETHING MUCH MORE.

IF YOU ARE WRONG?

THAT IDEA NO LONGER SHOCKS ME. THE ROSE AND I WILL BE LOST FOR A WHILE. NOTHING WILL SLOW DOWN THE RIDERS AND GOBLINS IN THIS PART OF TIME. THAT WE ARE HERE IS A MEASURE OF MY BELIEF IN GARVIN, JUST AS YOUR BEING HERE IS A MEASURE OF YOURS. I TELL YOU THIS IS NOT YET THE MOMENT TO SACRIFICE YOURSELF.

GREAT RUMACK WILL BOIL YOUR CHILDREN IF YOU PROVOKE HIM ANY FURTHER. There was a crude image of Rumack doing just that. The Hotlander Relay seemed almost as tired and discouraged as the besieged. But not quite. They were miserable, but they were winning. The prize was ready to fall.

The mind pulse of Rumack's army had become such a part of the background of their awareness that it took the defenders a moment to realize when a change took place. Something was rippling through the besiegers. The guns kept firing, but a hint of uncertainty was in their minds.

THOSE WHO WANT TO FOLLOW ME NO FURTHER CAN TURN BACK NOW. FOR THE REST, I PROMISE GLORY AND THE TRIBUTE OF ALL WORLDS AND TIME. Garvin could feel the mind of his little army. They were uneasy about what they had just seen him do to the Goblins. But they were a long way out in Time. Most of them had nowhere else to turn and little to lose.

FOR GARVIN WARCHILD! The Guvnor sitting on horse-back with his cavalry a short distance away made that mind shout, WARCHILD! His people took it up, then started off across the veld after Herself's collapsing army. Mercenary captains grounded their arms, indicating their neutrality. But Hotlanders were pouring away toward the portals in panic rout.

"Keep after them, Guvnor. We can't let them recover."

"Don't worry about that. Most of my troops are as afraid of you as the Hotlanders are." The Guvnor put spurs to his horse and dashed away between the trees where the Goblins hung.

Herself lay in a hospital tent, cared for by Garvin's medics. Her household troops had surrendered and were under guard. She was unconscious still. 'betrayer of our kind,' her Rider ranted at Garvin's Rider.

Garvin had felt how trapped Herself was, how helpless against her Rider. He knew that if he didn't get back to her soon the mind Rider would assert its dominance again. But he had to leave and follow the plan of his own Rider quickly. The enemy must not have a second to recover and think about what was happening.

FORM UP AT THE PORTAL, Garvin ordered. His own Rider lay inside him cold and unresponsive. He tried not to think of it as being coiled and waiting its chance.

Two worlds away at the end of the appendix, Rumack got word of the defeat of Herself shortly after it happened. The Rider let the giant maniac rage. He screamed and stove in the ribs of a pack horse. He chopped the head off a prisoner. SCARECROW, WHERE ARE YOU? RUMACK WANTS TO MAKE YOU DANCE. ARE YOU HIDING BEHIND CHILDREN?

There was no response to his challenge from the Fire Gates. Rumack howled and his Rider ordered, 'maximum fire from the guns. intensify the relay.' It realized it was trapped now. A conclusion would have to be forced that day. Fortunately, the Fire Gates looked about ready to crack. 'close all portals. no one gets through from off-world.'

But by late morning rumors had started in Rumack's army. There were images of disaster, tales of frantic refugees from the veld being shot by guards on the tundra. Just after noon the guards posted on the tundra side of the main supply portal came flooding back. The latest refugees showed something that had shaken their captain badly. GOBLINS HANGED!

He was a mercenary, a hard man. But he knew an eyewitness image when he saw one. GARVIN HAS BROKEN GOBLIN TRUCE! The man was showing everyone what he had seen.

Rumack had ridden partway to the portal which was a couple of miles from his front lines. His Rider let him reach out and grab the minds near the portal. He found riflemen and ordered, SHOOT EVERY TRAITOR WHO HAS RUN HERE. The captain died, but the image he had shown remained. Three green bodies swung in the air.

IT IS A TRICK. GARVIN HAS DONE THIS TO MAKE YOU THINK HE IS MORE TERRIBLE THAN I, Rumack raged. Rumack's Rider understood the game being played. Garvin was trying to break his army through fear. He probably had very few troops. The hanged Goblins were a dangerous trick that would make Garvin an outcast. If the Fire Gates could be taken out quickly enough, Rumack could turn on Garvin and destroy him.

At that moment the Hotland Relay caught an image of Scarecrow, tall and gaunt in his white robes. RUMACK, WHERE ARE YOU? The Guardian's eyes burned. I ACCEPT YOUR CHALLENGE, RUMACK.

A few minutes before, Amre had helped Scarecrow to a blockhouse at the foot of the Fire Gates. He was waiting to die, she realized. There wasn't enough of his world left to keep him alive. His mind strained toward the Hotland position, searching for a sign of some change in the Hotlanders. He found it: uncertainty. The mercenary artillery batteries slackened their fire. Scarecrow sent his challenge and waited.

SCARECROW, YOU HAVE DECIDED AT THIS LAST MOMENT TO COME TO ME! There was an image: Rumack seen by his own shamans standing in a clearing behind his lines alone and unarmed, his huge legs planted on the ground, his arms swinging at his sides.

"He has to do this," Scarecrow told Amre. "His army is barbarians who will stay with him only as long as they fear and respect him. And mercenaries who will be with him only as long as he can fulfill his promises. . . ." Select behind them showed the image of Scarecrow standing alone. Amre came forward and kissed him as the telepaths withdrew their minds.

"Tell them I had enough courage to die," Scarecrow told her. "Even though I didn't have enough to live." Amre stepped back but didn't go into the tunnel that connected to the warren that ran under the Fire Gates. She stood in the darkness with her hand on a gun butt. Scarecrow stood in sunlight just inside the open door of the blockhouse.

WOOD WIZARD, I HAVE YOU NOW! Rumack's mind found his. Both the Relays had pulled back. Scarecrow felt the powerful, raw madness. Rumack the Steed was a psychotic killer whose every fantasy was gratified. The mind that grabbed for him was full of blood and murder. SCARECROW, COME DANCE FOR ME.

And for a moment Scarecrow felt his legs moving him through the door. Then he feinted, blocked with his Umbra, and probed with his Curtain. Rumack knocked that aside. Scarecrow got past the other's defense with his Keep.

He went for Rumack's earliest memories and found a child who had wanted to bathe in blood. He had been a natural telepath from birth. Scarecrow found the day when at the age of three Rumack had made his mother bash her brains out against a rock. He found the time shortly after that when Rumack, drugged and chained, was hoisted in a cage to be sold at market.

Scarecrow felt he almost had Rumack. Then something cold slipped between him and the other mind. 'that is my steed's weak spot, not mine,' the Rider told him. 'he has been a perfect steed in his way. he was tearing at the entrails of a still-living sheep when first i saw him.'

Scarecrow felt his own heart and lungs within Rumack's grasp. He was up and walking toward the door. He was going to walk like a zombie out into the open ground to be gunned down by Rumack's sharpshooters. He used Umbra, Curtain, and Keep to summon up his old observatory at Weatherhill. Rumack tore it apart, burned it, butchered children on the floor.

Scarecrow summoned up a memory of Grim Reaper, made

it leap toward Rumack's mind. 'what a steed you would have made,' the Rider told him. 'powerful and clever but weak enough to be broken and superstitious enough to believe in the oracle. now walk toward me, scarecrow. come into the sunlight and die.'

Scarecrow concentrated on the pain in his leg, let the pain in his leg go out to Rumack. The other mind recoiled like a hand touching something hot. Scarecrow staggered back from the door. The sun shone outside. A stray shot sounded far away. The two armies, tight as fists, watched and waited on that last afternoon.

Distant shots built to a crescendo. Something was happening at the supply portal.

Amre crouching in the darkness watched Scarecrow, unaware of her presence, standing up, shuffling toward the door, breaking free, and staggering back. The firing behind Rumack's lines seemed to be spreading. She could sense his army growing uneasy. She could feel the impatience with which Rumack dragged Scarecrow across the floor again and again.

One final time Rumack summoned him. COME TO ME NOW. I WILL SHOW YOU PEACE AND THE END OF PAIN. I WILL SHOW YOU DEATH. Scarecrow walked to the door, faced the east where Rumack waited across the no-man's land. He lurched through the door, tried to catch himself, failed, and stood in the sunlight.

A commotion started in the Hotland army. They could see him. Then from the east on the other side of the Fire Gates, there were images in the air of hanging Goblins. HE HAS COME! RUMACK, HE HAS BROKEN THROUGH. Distorted by fear, there was an image of Garvin.

Rumack grabbed Scarecrow. DANCE WITH JOY NOW, WOOD WIZARD. YOU WILL NOT LIVE TO SEE ME CUT YOUR HERO UP FOR GOBLIN FOOD. One of Scarecrow's feet lifted off the ground and came down. He was about to do a grotesque dance of death. Amre came to the door of the blockhouse. She cried as she leveled the gun. Scarecrow's white robes and light hair were a blur as she pulled the trigger. His limbs went rigid and he fell with the back of his head smashed. She felt her name in the air as his life went out.

Garvin came through a portal crouching low. A minor shaman and a few riflemen guarded this portal. Garvin had reached through from out in Time and showed them the Goblins. RUN AND TELL RUMACK THAT I AM HERE. They were backing off when he tumbled out of Time. A bullet went over his head. He reached out for the mind that had pulled the trigger. One of his telepaths rumbling out behind him went down with a bullet in his arm.

Rumack's people fell back. Garvin's little force had a bridgehead in the Republic. WHERE IS RUMACK? I CHALLENGE HIM TO COMBAT. Around him his people were deploying. Garvin realized the Hotlanders recognized him from the images thrown out by the defenders.

THE WARCHILD IS BACK! They would spread the word and the panic. Ash gritted under Garvin's feet. The trees around him were blackened and dead. From one of them hung the corpse of a small child with its head bashed in. The air was choked with death. Garvin felt it numb him, making it hard for him to think of what do next. His Rider inside him was gray and cold as metal.

Garvin's little force spread out. He took his bearings and set off in the direction of the Fire Gates. The land was littered with the debris of war: campfires and latrines, burned buildings and garbage. Here something had dug up shallow graves. There a wrecked wagon lay on its side. Ahead of him Garvin could feel resistance beginning to firm up. From far off was the sound of battle. That would be the Guvnor's feint along Rumack's supply line.

Then, nearer at hand from the direction of the Fire Gates on a thousand minds Garvin caught the image. It was him, glorified, triumphant. Scarecrow was still holding on. People were fighting and dying in his name. As Garvin advanced through the burned-out woods, he was aware of Hotlanders, hesitant, frightened, all around him. He was surrounded in enemy territory. There was no more plan from his Rider.

'understand, garvin, that anything will eventually choose death if pushed too far.' It told him then, 'it is better for me to die here than torn to bits by goblins in an arena in the city.' Garvin gritted his teeth, blocked the Rider, and plunged on toward the Fire Gates.

Suddenly, out of the minds that ranged around him in the woods, came one overwhelming mind. It hit him with an image. There was a figure in white robes seen from far away. It moved jerkily toward the viewer, began to dance, fell down on its face, dead. Garvin felt Scarecrow's agony. HE CHALLENGED ME AND HE DIED JUST NOW, WARCHILD. ARE YOU READY TO DO THE SAME?

COME OUT AND DIE, RUMACK. Garvin didn't hesitate for a moment. There was death everywhere around him. How many had died while he had been enjoying himself in Time? How much sooner would he have had to return to save Scarecrow's life? He would end it all now in a single combat.

CLEAR A KILLING GROUND. CARRY NO WEAPONS WITH YOU. Just in front of Garvin's position there was a small rise. He left his troops below the slope in a defensive perimeter. He climbed alone to the top, his hands empty. The rise's top was a flat surface covered with the blackened stumps of trees. But green grass and plants survived. About midway across the area were the skeletons of a horse and a cavalryman, their bones picked clean. A rusty saber lay there.

SHOW YOURSELF TO ME, WARCHILD. The mind of Rumack was coming closer and closer. It showed him the dismemberment of a girl about Garvin's age. She had dressed herself like Garvin. She screamed his name as she was torn apart.

Garvin showed Rumack the death of Sam at the Armory, Herself lying broken on the veld. Rumack screamed aloud. Garvin felt the pain and heard the sound. Then the huge horse and man came into view. Rumack leaped off the animal's back. The wide face was tattooed into a contorted grimace.

The shoulders loomed over the ears. Garvin showed him the Goblins hanging from a tree.

Rumack didn't break stride. From a couple of hundred feet away, he ran right at Garvin. The Warchild went for Rumack's mind. The defense was simple; Rumack let him feel a thousand unarmed prisoners being slaughtered.

Garvin blocked that with his Umbra and went on. He saw Goblins tear at his face. He blocked with his Curtain and grabbed Rumack's motor control. The giant tripped and stumbled. Garvin was ready to seize the heart and lungs of his enemy. Then he felt himself helpless as his own Rider held back his Keep.

Rumack's Rider gleamed like a knife in the maniac's mind. Garvin's Rider reached out for the other.

'you have suffered much,' Rumack's Rider told it.

'all i have done has been in what i thought was the service of the gods.'

Garvin felt his own legs give way. He felt sleepy. He was down on one knee. Rumack was up and running toward him. He threw into the other mind the feeling of Sam as he died, the brief burst of freedom, the terror of the Rider as it died.

Rumack howled. He took the feeling of freedom and showed Garvin corpses and blood up to his knees. He reached out for Garvin, who scrambled past him. He tried to probe the giant and paralyze him. Rumack was stunned for a moment. Garvin stumbled toward the center of the arena. His Rider was like an anchor dragging at him.

'i cannot promise you life,' he could feel Rumack's Rider telling his own.

'i understand.'

Garvin was scrambling on his hands and knees. Rumack was lumbering after him. He reached into the giant's mind. Two Riders dragged at Garvin as he went at Rumack, showed him Herself surrendering her army, the Goblins dying. Rumack barely paused, stamped a foot down on Garvin's leg, reached out for Garvin with huge hands.

He stank of blood and sweat. There was no piece of humanity left in the Steed's mind for Garvin to appeal to, nothing for him to touch. 'he has been most satisfactory for me. i only regret your luck was not as good.'

Garvin tried to squirm away, felt bones under him, realized he was crawling on the skeleton. A huge hand smashed the front of his face. Garvin felt his nose break. He kicked at Rumack and a hand smashed his stomach. The breath went out of Garvin's lungs. Everything turned black. He was lifted up by his ponytail. He saw his own bloody face reflected in Rumack's mind. It was all gone, gone. Everyone who had followed him was going to die. Rumack had something in his hand. It was the rusty saber. He was going to cut off Garvin's head. I WILL DRINK YOUR BLOOD.

Garvin exerted all his power against Rumack's right arm. The sword cut through the air with great effort.

'can you hold him more firmly?' asked Rumack's Rider. 'make him hold his head up straighter. the pain will be less. the death will be quicker.'

'i understand,' his Rider told the other. September sun shone on the blade. 'understand now, garvin, what it is to be helpless in the hands of another. do not forget this for the rest of your life.'

Rumack screamed, tightened his grip on the sword. Blood ran into Garvin's throat, and his heart ached with each beat. 'i think you understand how much you need me,' his Rider told him.

Suddenly Garvin's hands were free. His Rider was not blocking him. It turned on the other Rider. 'we fought and schemed and conquered together, and you would end my life as easily as that!' it raged. Rumack's face turned black with effort. But his sword arm was caught and held.

Garvin tore the blade from his neck. It cut his fingers as he yanked and broke the chain. He slashed the arm of Rumack that held him up. He cut it from elbow to wrist. The giant howled. The hand let go of him.

Without Rumack holding him, Garvin staggered. But he brought the blade up. He felt the giant trying to smash him with the sword. He slashed the blade along Rumack's stomach, once, twice, three times. Their blood mingled. Rumack screamed long and loud. Rumack's Rider wailed in Garvin's mind.

Garvin staggered aside as Rumack crashed to the ground. 'it is done, garvin, it is done,' his Rider told him.

His own troops rushing forward found Garvin holding himself upright on the rusty sword. "We need to rest," he told them.

For several days that's what he and his Rider did. The Fire Gates stank of death to Garvin. He asked to be taken to Weatherhill. The shell of the observatory remained. Amre went with him and Miche. Warchild Cluster guarded him. Darrel and Maji had survived, scarred and hardened. At Garvin's orders Herself was brought there as soon as she could be moved. While he rested, those were the only ones Garvin wished to see.

"If I hadn't delayed," he told Amre, "if I had understood sooner..."

"He didn't want to live, Garvin, in the world he saw coming." She shook her head. "He felt he had lived as long as he could."

It was the next day, on a fine fall morning, that his Rider told him, 'rumack's captains await your pleasure. it is necessary now that we begin to consolidate our position.' Garvin called an assembly of all the Companions, the Warchild Cluster, the telepaths who had followed him from the City Out Of Time, Scarecrow's Select.

Before they came together, the Guvnor appeared. "Come to collect my mercenary fees," he told Garvin. "There are those who have decided they want to follow me. Mostly, they're the ones I had on the veld. But there are others who feel more comfortable with the mercenary life. They think you may be mounting a crusade."

"Who are you, Guvnor? Was any of what you told me true?"

"All of it, more or less, old man. I had a run-in with your father once. He claimed me as a half brother, filled me in on some family business, tried to claim my loyalty. My reaction was about the same as yours."

"You lied about not being able to Time Stride, though. You went in a few days from November to June."

"In the mouth of the Wind, Garvin. Not a way I like to travel."

"But you did it so you could sell me."

"At the suggestion of the Talking Suitcase. A beastly way to have treated a nephew, but just think of me as your wicked uncle and try to be forgiving."

"He made me promise to bring you and the Wind back." Garvin was smiling despite everything.

"We will come back in ways he never imagined. Perhaps we will see each other again, Garvin." The Guvnor smiled, gave a little bow, and left.

Garvin summoned the Talking Suitcase and the Rose. Her child's head sat alone on an adult body. She ran over and held his hand. He turned his mind to the Suitcase. Roger stood at ease, holding it in one hand. MY FATHER SAYS THERE IS NO ORACLE.

IF HE IS ALL KNOWING, THEN HE IS CORRECT. IF HE IS ALL POWERFUL, THEN WE ARE JUST DOING HIS WILL. IF HE IS ANGRY AT WHAT HAS BEEN DONE, HE SHOULD BE ABLE TO STOP US. IF THE ORACLE IS SOMEHOW HIS CONSCIENCE, HE MAY HAVE FORGOTTEN ABOUT IT.

The Rose smiled, bright eyed, and patted Garvin's arm. BECAUSE OF YOU, WE WILL WIN, she told him.

Then Garvin walked out to the common with the Immortals behind him. The telepaths were standing waiting for him. Some wore tattered Select robes, some Companion's black, some mercenary fighting gear. Behind them the troops were ranged in the blackened woods. Darrel and Maji and others from Warchild Cluster stood around him.

Garvin caught up the minds in front of him. I WANT YOU TO GO AND SHOW THE WORLDS OF TIME WHAT YOU HAVE SEEN. AND TELL THEM THIS. Garvin caught his image in their eyes and showed them what he saw: the army assembled in sunshine. YOU WHO SIT IN WORLDS YOU THINK ARE SAFE, KNOW THAT THE GOBLINS AND RIDERS ARE NOT FAR BEHIND MY MESSENGERS. GARVIN WARCHILD CALLS ON YOU TO RISE UP AND STRIKE DOWN THE CITY AND THE GODS.

Then he saw it in the air, a V of geese. Everyone looked where he did and saw the birds fly like an arrow over the ruined forest. They went from blue water and green grass to green grass and blue water. For a few moments Garvin and the Relay followed them as they flew over the world from summer to summer.